PAST TENSE

PAST TENSE

A NOVEL

BOB LEVY

My best always,
Bob Levy

SUNSTONE PRESS

This book is a work of fiction.

Names, characters, places, and incidents are either the product

of the author's imagination or are used fictitiously.

Sunstone books may be purchased for educational, business, or sales promotional use. For information please write: Special Markets Department, Sunstone Press, P.O. Box 2321, Santa Fe, New Mexico 87504-2321.

FIRST EDITION

10 9 8 7 6 5 4 3 2 1

Library of Congress Cataloging-in-Publication Data:

Levy, Bob, 1953–
    Past tense : a novel / Bob Levy.—1st ed.
       p. cm.
    Sequel to : Broken hearts.
    ISBN: 0-86534-341-1
       1. Ex-police officers—Fiction. 2. Memphis (Tenn.)—Fiction. I. Title.

PS3562. E9249 P37 2002
813' .54—dc21   2002070790

Published in SUNSTONE PRESS
Post Office Box 2321
Santa Fe, NM 87504-2321 / USA
(505) 988-4418 / *orders only* (800) 243-5644
FAX (505) 988-1025
www.sunstonepress.com

For my mother, Evy Halle Levy,
my late father, J. Lawrence "Dooley" Levy,
my brother, Bill Levy,
and my sister, Sue Jacobs—
with love always

Acknowledgment

A novel, contrary to what many people believe, is the result of more than just the author's hard work. It is a collaboration between not only individuals the author must rely on for research purposes and technical expertise, but also those who have left their imprint on the author's own life. The special people mentioned below have had a hand in helping this book become a reality. I now thank them for their guidance and their friendship.

To Dr. O.C. Smith, Shelby County Chief Medical Examiner, Dr. Steven A. Symes, forensic anthropologist and assistant professor of pathology at the University of Tennessee Medical School, and Dr. Hugh Berryman, forensic anthropology consultant to the Central Identification Laboratory in Hawaii, who continue to amaze with their knowledge of bringing the nuances of death to life.

To former Memphis Police Director Melvin Burgess, Sr., and Inspector T.C. Hasty and Lieutenant Dave Martello of the Memphis Police Department, for their help and encouragement along the way.

To Bunny Cohn, Jack Kenner, Dr. Jerry Engelberg, David Clark, Mike Cody, Nick Nixon, Lonnie Easterling, Susan Malone, Bill Thompson, Debbie Sherman Pitts, and Hampton Pitts for their respective contributions.

To J. Clay Tidwell, whose love of all things Irish proved to be an inspiration, just as he continues to be every day of his life.

To Stanley Thompson, my "typing hands," who is a wizard at transferring my handwritten words into their present form.

To my publisher and editor, James Clois Smith, Jr., whose confidence in my ability has been constant, and to Brenda Meeks and Vicki Ahl, the wonderful support team at Sunstone Press, for their hard work on my behalf.

To anyone whom I have left out, please accept my apology and know that I will always be appreciative of your particular contribution.

To my family, especially my sons, Jim and Chris, of whom I will always be so very proud, for their encouragement as they saw that dreams can indeed come true.

And, finally, to those who hold a special place in my heart, and you know who you are, my thanks and love for being there when I needed you most.

"To be ignorant of what occurred before you were born is to remain always a child.

For what is the worth of human life, unless it is woven into the lives of those who have come before us."

The Roman orator, Cicero
106–43 B.C.

1

1947

"Gimme that money you owe me, you sonuvabitch," mumbled the elderly drunk standing on Beale Street in downtown Memphis. A green street-car rumbled behind him, heading down Main Street past the flashing yellow lights of the Malco Theater marquee.

"Forget that shit, you old codger," slurred the equally drunk, middle-aged man in a foul-smelling trenchcoat. "You *gave* me that five dollars."

"You're nuts, you slimy bastard. Do I look like Harry Truman handin' out cash?" He shivered, then rubbed the arms of his red flannel shirt. His warm, bourbon-laced breath steamed in the cool night air. "I need that money to buy whiskey."

"You're the crazy one, Pops, if you think I'm *ever* gonna owe you shit." He grabbed the old man by the neck and bellowed above the sounds of the passing traffic, "Now git the hell away."

"Wait a minute, wait a minute," said a muscular policeman with a thick Irish accent. His six-pointed badge shone in the light of the corner street lamp as he walked over to the quarreling pair. "What seems to be the problem, boys?"

"He owes me money," shouted the old man, tucking long wisps of grey hair behind his ears.

"I don't owe him a goddam penny," said the man in the stained trenchcoat.

"From the looks of it, I'd say you both been on a fine tear."

The old man closed his left eye to focus better. "You're O'Riley, aren't you? I lent him five dollars yesterday to buy some booze, officer."

"I don't remember him giving me no five dollars," said the other drunk, scratching the top of his balding head.

"You know," said the policeman, "that doesn't surprise me. Let me tell you boys a couple of things. First, it's illegal to be drunk in public, which even you two geniuses can figure out. Secondly, I'm fillin' in tonight because we're short three good men. I haven't had *any* problems, and I know you don't want to be my first."

Both drunks shook their heads.

"Here's what we're gonna do. I'm hauling you both down to the slammer." O'Riley stood directly in front of the heavy-set drunk. "Or you're going to pay this man the five dollars you owe him."

"All right, all right," the drunk replied, frowning. "Calm down and I'll get it for him."

O'Riley turned to the older man who was rubbing the stubble of grey beard on cheekbones gaunt from a preference of drink over food. "After you get your money, you go home. No liquor. Understand?"

The man in the trenchcoat reached into his pocket and pulled out a gun just as O'Riley turned around. "Here's something you'll both understand," he snarled.

Two sharp pops echoed in O'Riley's ears. A burning pain seared his abdomen and he collapsed to the pavement.

"No, no," pleaded the old man, his face sober with fear. "Keep the money."

"I will," replied the stocky drunk as he pressed the muzzle against the old man's forehead and calmly pulled the trigger. A fine mist of warm blood rained down on the chilly sidewalk.

The killer ran east down Beale, trenchcoat flapping behind, just as the audience poured onto the street from the nearby theater.

"Call an ambulance," yelled a man who noticed the dark blue color of the fallen officer's uniform. "A policeman's been shot!"

O'Riley struggled to speak, his face chalky white. A single word, faintly whispered, drifted from his lips. "Joey."

2

The three had been inseparable. For as long as they could remember, they had shadowed one another. Playmates, classmates, friends. Joey O'Riley, Jenny Adair, Will Harrison.

But as they grew up, their feelings toward each other changed. Jenny and Will found the type of love everyone searches for but few find—love unconditional and everlasting. Joey felt that kind of love for Jenny as well, even though he knew he must be content with only her friendship. He could never jeopardize his relationship with Will by revealing his feelings to either of them.

Now, on the way to his father's funeral, Joey sat in the back seat of the Lincoln limousine with Jenny and Will, knowing he would have to rely on his two best friends to help him make it through the worst day of his life.

The procession stretched down Second Street. Grey, billowy clouds hung over downtown Memphis, darkening the damp, mid-March morning as the motorcade turned east on Union Avenue toward its destination, Elmwood Cemetery.

Four police motorcycles led the way, followed by the slain officer's black police sedan, the first post-war model Ford. Next came the hearse, the funeral home's limousine carrying the family, and three more police squad cars bearing the commissioners of the police and fire departments, the chief of police, and the inspectors of police and detectives. Mayor Franklin Hart, driven by his grandson, Adam Baldwin, in the mayor's Cadillac sedan, was followed by over thirty squad cars and twice that number of other vehicles from Chevrolets, Fords, and Hudsons to Buicks, Packards, Lincolns, and Cadillacs. It was one of the largest funerals Memphis had ever seen.

Police Lieutenant Patrick O'Riley, known by all as Paddy, had been the father all boys dreamed of having. The stern but lovable son of Irish immigrants who had settled in Memphis's Pinch district had the temperament of a teddy bear. Paddy loved the Pinch, named after the pinch-gut appearance of the Irish who settled there in the mid-1800s after fleeing the great potato famine in their homeland. He requested the Pinch beat when he first became a policeman in 1912. As his seniority increased, he could have moved into a comfortable desk job, but opted to remain in the Pinch, protecting and watching over the Jewish merchant community that had gradually replaced the old Irish neighborhood.

Married late in life, Paddy O'Riley's pride and joy had been his only child, Joey, born when Paddy was almost forty years old. The early death of his wife, Louise, from appendicitis at the age of thirty-one, had left Paddy to care for his five-year-old son on his own. Young Joey became a mascot of sorts to the other policemen, and official eyes were averted when the youngster occasionally accompanied his father on his beat. Now, Paddy's senseless murder left his son bereft and cast a heavy pall over the entire city as well.

"This is quite some car, isn't it?" said Police Captain Mike Kelly from the jump seat across from Joey, Jenny, and Will. His full-dress uniform fit snugly around his expansive mid-section. With drooping eyelids, ridged nose, and thick accent, there was no denying his Irish descent.

The three sixteen-year-olds nodded slightly, barely noticing the luxurious car. Jenny and Will glanced at Joey.

Joey fidgeted on the tan leather seat, running a finger through his rusty brown mop of hair. After adjusting the bulky knot of his black print necktie, he tugged at the collar button of the heavily starched white shirt that squeezed his neck. Finally he relaxed, leaning back as his gaze and thoughts drifted to the three sitting in silence with him.

Will stared out the window, running slender fingers through his own ash-blond hair, just as Joey had done moments before. An orphan, he had been adopted at two by Vivian Harrison, a childless widow whose husband had died in World War I. She devoted herself to him, never remarrying, supplementing her income with a second job whenever possible to make ends meet. She always made Joey feel welcome in their home on North Angelus, one street over from his. Joey shook his head. He was now an orphan—just as Will had been.

He next glanced at Jenny, her wavy brown hair perfect for her blue-green eyes. With a banker father and housewife mother, she had a stable, loving home life that was lost to him forever, except in his dreams.

And, finally, Mike Kelly—Uncle Mike—although he wasn't really an uncle. His father's best friend. Drinking buddies. The man who held his father's hand at the hospital when death came. The man who confided to Joey his promise to Paddy that he would not allow his son to go through life alone.

"Uncle Mike?" said Joey, breaking the silence. "Are you all right?"

"Aye, lad, I am," replied Kelly as he wiped his glistening hazel eyes. "I just got lost in a memory there for a wee bit." A shallow grin crept across his rugged face. "Irish cops do that every now and again. 'Specially when they partake of a little Bushmills, which, I'm sorry to say, I failed to bring."

For the first time that day, Joey, Jenny, and Will all smiled.

The river of cars flowed down Bellevue, passing the four-story, red-brick Central High School where Joey was the perennial clown in their tenth-grade class.

Joey's left hand clutched Jenny's right, resting in her lap. Will held her other hand. The link felt strong and warm.

"We're almost there," said Kelly.

The stark, unsightly warehouses and lumberyards that lined Dudley Street came into view as they approached the historic cemetery at the end of the road. The jet-black limousine shone under the darkening sky as the procession snaked across the single-lane bridge that marked the entrance. A black wrought-iron sign spanned the bridge: "ELMWOOD CEMETERY. Founded 1852."

A long row of police sedans passed the gray-stone, gothic cottage that served as gatehouse and office. The cars lumbered down one of the many little roads, some paved, others gravel, that formed a maze through the sprawling hills of the tree-filled cemetery. Joey gripped Jenny's hand more tightly as the limousine rocked down a bumpy, narrow path past mausoleums and massive stone monuments, many carved with statues of angels and human faces preserved for eternity. Each road had a name. Addresses for the dead.

A light rain began to fall as they slowed to a stop. Joey, Jenny, Will, and Captain Kelly got out of the limousine and stood under black umbrellas as the crowd of mourners closed around the burial site. Paddy's rosewood casket was pulled from the hearse by the chief of police and eleven officers.

Joey looked away from his father's freshly dug grave and stared at his mother's white marble tombstone:

Louise O'Riley—An Angel On Earth
February 4, 1905—April 5, 1936

I won't cry, he thought, throat aching. With Will on his left and Jenny on his right, he repeated his promise as the tears welled up in his brown eyes.

Father Terence Mulligan, dressed in a long black robe covered by a purple surplice, presided over the service. He opened his Bible, its leather binding chipped and frayed. The New Testament readings and recitation of the Lord's Prayer were punctuated by the faint *woooo, woooo* of distant train whistles, which sounded like the souls of those departed welcoming a new arrival.

The ceremony seemed endless. Finally, Franklin Hart, the city's portly old mayor, took his place near the coffin. "It is with a heavy heart," he said, eyeing Joey, "that I join you all here today. For you see, we have all been robbed. Memphis has been robbed of a dedicated servant. Every one of you has been robbed of a kind and decent friend. A boy has been robbed of his loving, hard-working father."

The mayor's ruddy face turned crimson as his voice filled with anger. "Acts of lawlessness and violence, such as the one that has taken Police Lieutenant Patrick O'Riley from us, shall *not* be tolerated on the streets of our fair city while I remain your mayor. The perpetrator of this crime against us all has been apprehended and will pay for it with his own life. I am personally going to guarantee that."

The assembled mass of mourners stared at the mayor, spellbound. His voice then took a more sympathetic tone. "Nothing will bring young Joey O'Riley's father back to us. But, with God on our side, we will prevent other senseless tragedies. May the soul of Patrick O'Riley reside here in eternal peace."

Father Mulligan then brought the service to a close. "May the soul of Patrick Joseph O'Riley and all the souls of the faithfully departed, through the mercy of God, rest in peace. Amen."

The throng, including Hart and his strapping young grandson, then passed by Joey, offering their sympathies. After it was over, Joey, Jenny, and Will got back into the limousine, Will with his arm around Joey's shoulder, Jenny clasping both of his hands firmly in her lap. Joey glanced back for an instant as the car drove off, leaving the dispersing crowd behind.

Joey and Officer Kelly stood alone in the cool night air outside a white stucco bungalow on North Avalon, its grey fieldstone chimney twinkling in the light of the street lamps.

"I remember when your father built this house way back in 1919," said Kelly as he gazed at the front steps. "He was real proud o' that sleeping porch upstairs." He stared into Joey's eyes. "This is your house now. That's the way your father wanted it."

Joey pointed to the two massive, bare-branched oak trees in the yard. "It's funny, I remember when those trees didn't seem half that tall. Daddy hated to mow the yard. As those trees grew, they killed off some of the grass. Daddy began planting ivy three years ago, hoping it would cover the yard someday. Then he'd never have to mow again. Now we've got patches of grass *and* ivy."

Kelly smiled as the two started inside. The screen door slammed behind them. "It's late," said Kelly. "We've had a tough day. Do you want me to stay here tonight?"

"You don't have to. I'll be all right. Will's gonna sleep over again. He's just walking Jenny home. He'll be back in a minute."

Kelly smiled again and put his beefy hand on the boy's shoulder. "I know you'll be fine, Joey. The thing is, I think it would make *me* feel better."

Joey bit his lower lip. Tears began to trickle down his cheeks. Kelly pulled him closer and, as his own eyes glistened, the two embraced.

"I miss him, Uncle Mike, so much," Joey said, his voice muffled against Kelly's coarse wool uniform.

Kelly took a deep, calming breath. "Everyone who knew him misses him. It's tough right now, but just wait. We'll make it. We'll make it, you'll see."

Joey slowly pulled away from the burly policeman, then quickly wiped the tears from his face as Will's feet skipped up the concrete steps to the front porch.

"Why don't you go wash up," said Kelly. "I'll keep Will entertained for a bit."

"Thanks," Joey said, opening the hallway door to the second floor. "I think I'll sleep upstairs for a few nights. As Daddy used to say, it's a little bit closer to heaven."

"That it is, me boy," replied Kelly with a nod. The stairs creaked under Joey's weight and that of his German shepherd, Bullet, who followed his master.

When Will entered the living room, Kelly was standing in front of the white marble fireplace, his gaze fixed on a picture of Paddy O'Riley in full dress uniform. The officer's chest heaved with a sigh. "It's a little bit closer to heaven," he whispered.

3

The mayor climbed out of the passenger side of his yellow Cadillac, followed by his grandson on the driver's side. "Maybe we'll go to a movie after dinner again one night next week. Sorry you had to go to that funeral earlier. I'll make it up to you tomorrow," he said with a wink. "Not the way you'd like to spend the day before your sixteenth birthday."

"Not the way to spend any day," Adam Baldwin replied, slamming the car door in the dark garage of the mayor's mansion. "Especially not for *him*." He waved a hand above his head in the shadows, grasped a string hanging in the air, and tugged. A light bulb flicked on. "At least it got me out of school."

"You still mad about that fight last fall? Sometimes you have to do what's right for appearance's sake. It's called being diplomatic."

Baldwin's thoughts drifted back to that October day and the collision outside the restroom at Central High that left Joey O'Riley sprawled on the hallway floor beneath three of Baldwin's snickering football teammates. "Sorry, O'Riley, I didn't see you there, pal." He grabbed Joey by the arm and helped him roughly to his feet. "By the way, the girl's room is over there," he added with the flip of a thumb.

Joey's cheeks burned. He jerked his arm from Baldwin's grip. "Just stay away from me, you Little Lord Fauntleroy." He reached for the books Jenny and Will had gathered off the floor. "You think everybody should bow down to you because you're the mayor's grandson. Somebody's gonna put you in your place one day."

Baldwin's face tightened with anger. "You think you could do it, O'Riley?"

Joey's eyes narrowed. "*You* don't scare me. I don't care how big you are."

"Let me tell you something, pip-squeak. You're gonna get into real trouble if you don't watch out. You may be the class clown, but you don't make me laugh. People only laugh because they feel sorry for you. I don't feel sorry for you, even if your mother is dead. My mother's been dead for years and my father died before I was born—"

"So they say."

"What's *that* supposed to mean?" snapped Baldwin as students gathered around, sensing a fight.

"It means I think your father was alive when you were born. But when he saw your ugly yap, he had a cardiac and died right on the spot. Go ahead and take a swing at me, you gorilla. I ain't afraid of you."

"You bastard," Baldwin yelled, grabbing Joey by the collar. His right fist glanced off the shorter boy's cheek. Joey fought back, swinging wildly, and landed a direct hit to his nose. Bright blood spurted onto Baldwin's green letter sweater and Joey's white shirt. The crowd began to chant: "Fight, fight, fight, fight."

The clanging of a bell pierced the din. Students fell silent as Principal Charles Jester, bell in hand, his pale face impassive, walked up and surveyed the bloody combatants.

"Mr. O'Riley," the wiry principal said with a slight smile, "I would have thought you'd have learned to pick on someone your own size by now. Normally, Mr. Baldwin, this would be grounds for expulsion but, given my penchant for a winning football team and your prowess as quarterback, especially the way you helped to defeat Tech this past season, I find I must slightly alter my rules. Therefore, I shall pretend this incident never occurred. However, should you two *ever* come to fisticuffs again, I shall have no choice but to expel you. Do I make myself clear, gentlemen?"

They nodded.

"Are you both bleeding?" asked Jester.

"I'm not, sir," Joey replied. "It's his blood on my shirt."

"In that case, Mr. O'Riley, I suggest you go home for the remainder of the day and wash up. Mr. Baldwin, you go to the school infirmary and then home. Let me assure you that your grandfather, whom I know very well, will hear of this incident. You might want to tell him about it yourself, first."

"Adam? You hear what I'm saying?" repeated the mayor.

Jolted back to the present, Baldwin nodded. "Sure, Grampa. Diplomatic."

"Speaking of which, how'd I do?" Hart patted his grandson's muscular shoulder twice, ushering him toward the back door.

"The newspapermen ate it up. That speech will be all over the front page tomorrow. I'm sure it'll get you a few more votes. That is, if any stiffs are left in town who don't already support you."

"That's the idea," the mayor said with a laugh. "God, I love politics."

*

"Umph," grunted Hart the next day as he whacked a forehand shot down the left side of court number one at the exclusive University Club. He squinted in the bright, late-afternoon sunlight.

The mayor's grandson raced to his right and smashed the ball back across the net. Hart swung vainly as the ball kicked up a tiny cloud of grey dust when it hit the clay court.

"Just because it's your sixteenth birthday doesn't give you the right to run your decrepit old grandfather ragged," said the mayor. His round face was flushed from exertion, his thick white hair a tangled mass. With bushy eyebrows protruding above tiny spectacles, he looked like an oversized pixie.

"You don't fool me, Grampa. You're about as decrepit as a viper." Baldwin took his place behind the baseline. "Five to three, my favor. Your serve."

Hart took his service stance, bounced the ball twice, and lofted it upward. Unfazed by the glare of the sun, he slammed a serve toward the other side of the court, acing his grandson.

"Maybe you meant a rattlesnake," yelled Hart. "They can be deadly, too."

"No," replied Baldwin. "I had it right the first time. Rattlesnakes make noise before they strike; vipers don't. You're a viper, no doubt about that."

Although being clever, Baldwin knew just how right he was. He'd done his homework, thanks in large part to his grandfather's massive scrapbook of newspaper clippings on display atop a coffee table in the living room.

Franklin Hart, born on a farm in rural Mississippi in 1885, inherited the estate of a rich uncle in 1914 and decided to move to Memphis. Through a series of canny investments, he parlayed his inheritance into more than two million dollars and set himself up financially for life. But the life of the idle rich was not for Franklin Hart.

Hart delved into the world of politics and found it to his liking. By 1920, elected first a councilman and then police commissioner, he felt the time was right for a run at the mayor's office.

Memphis at the time turned a blind eye to gamblers, prostitutes, and thugs. Hart was a tough, street-smart politician. He labeled himself a reformer whose platform of law and order and fiscal responsibility would transform the city into a place where all honest citizens could feel proud.

The election was not an easy one. Hart won by only two hundred three votes, but he loomed as the new political leader of the entire region.

Memphians soon learned that their new mayor was true to his promises. His revamped police department cleaned up the most blatant gambling, prostitution, and street crime. Hart saw to it that existing streets were widened and new ones constructed. He expanded city services and built schools, parks, playgrounds, and hospitals. And by portraying himself as a hero to the common man, he forged a powerful coalition of supporters. Through the repeal of the city law that limited the mayor to only two terms, Hart became an institution.

For over three decades, Franklin Hart and his political machine won elections with monotonous regularity. With each victory, he became more powerful, not only in the eyes of the people but in his own as well.

To the people of Memphis, Hart seemed elegant yet down-to-earth, and they treated him with fondness and respect. Any man who needed a job could expect help from Hart's office. Any firm wishing to do business with the city got a friendly hearing, often receiving more than had been requested.

Hart also became known as a ruthless tactician. Those who crossed him found Memphis a decidedly unpleasant place to live. All high-ranking officials who owed their posts to Hart knew that anyone who strayed from his basic beliefs would be defeated in the next election by a more "devoted" believer. Hart men learned to obey his every whim with fervor and dispatch.

In trying to maintain his image of propriety, Hart never smoked and seldom drank spirits, even after the repeal of prohibition in 1933. And he was devoted to his grandson, Adam, one of those children apparently born with a silver spoon in his mouth. At least, that's how his grandfather tried to make it seem.

In truth, courtesy of the loose lips of Hart's long-time cook and live-in maid, Tessie, Baldwin knew his background was shady. His mother, Darlene, Hart's only child, had been so promiscuous even she didn't know who Adam's father was. The mayor sent the twice-divorced Darlene away to have her baby. Then he started a rumor that she was with her third husband, an Army officer named Baldwin. Baldwin was supposedly killed in an accidental explosion while stationed in Europe, according to Hart. The shock of her husband's death sent Darlene into labor, delivering a son prematurely. According to the public record, Darlene then fell into a deep depression and had to be institutionalized. Actually, she had fled to Hollywood, leaving Adam in the care of her father, who became the child's legal guardian.

Newspaper reports arranged by the mayor said that she died in the

institution in 1938. Her actual death from a drug overdose was never discovered by the media, an especially impressive feat that could only have
been orchestrated by someone as powerful as Franklin Hart. The mayor even
gained the public's sympathy and admiration for taking in his grandson and
raising him as his own son.

"Out," yelled Baldwin, as the ball bounced just inches behind the dusty
baseline tape. "Game and set."

Hart approached the net to shake hands, grinning. Adam knew his
grandfather planned an illustrious future for him, foremost the scaling one
day of political heights he himself had lusted after but abandoned as being
unattainable. Adam would be successful. Hart would do all in his power to
bring that end about.

"You played good, boy," Hart said.

"You played pretty good yourself," replied Baldwin, wiping perspiration from his handsome face with a white towel.

Hart reached into his racket bag. "I've got a little something here for
you." The mayor handed over a small, black velvet-covered box that fit
squarely in the palm of his grandson's hand. "Happy birthday."

Baldwin flipped the box open, exposing a gold, bell-shaped Saint
Christopher's locket. The front appeared to be a stage with curtains on each
side. In the center was Saint Christopher with the baby Jesus on his shoulder. Baldwin picked up the locket by its gold chain and twirled it around,
exposing the back. He read the inscription aloud. "To Adam Hart Baldwin. I
will always be with you. Lovingly, Grampa."

"There's a latch on the side, Adam. Go ahead, open it up."

Baldwin opened the locket to reveal two small photographs. On the
left was his grandfather's round face, white hair, bushy eyebrows, and shining spectacles, all in miniature. On the right was a tiny copy of one of
Baldwin's Central High annual pictures.

"Let me help you with that." Hart placed the locket around Baldwin's
neck and locked the chain. "As long as you wear it, I *will* always be with
you."

28

"Grampa, you'll be in my thoughts with or without this locket." He dropped the shiny pendant down his shirt.

"You know, Adam, this is just the beginning. You study hard at school and you'll get to the top one day at Harvard. After you get your law degree, we'll pull a few strings. Once you get elected to office, the sky's the limit. Believe me," he said, his piercing brown eyes burning into his grandson's face, "the country is changing. We city leaders don't have to be so isolated from the politics of the whole country like we were when I was younger. You have a chance to be more than I ever was—a member of the House of Representatives, possibly a United States Senator. Perhaps even more. It's up to you. You can go as far as you'll let your talent take you."

Baldwin toyed with his new chain. "Grampa, tell me. What's the best thing about politics? Why do you like it so much?"

A grin crept onto Hart's face. "Well, son, you want people to think you're helping them get what they want. People like to believe you're in it for love. Or maybe honor. But only one thing matters. One thing. Men will lie, steal, and cheat for it." His dark eyes flashed. "It's the one thing in this life worth fightin' for. *Power*. You say that for me, Adam."

"Power," replied Baldwin, eyes aglow.

"Power," repeated Hart. "The higher up the ladder you go, the more power you'll have. Power to get what *you* want. Power to make those around you obey without question. Power over people—the common people, maybe even the higher-ups." He paused for a moment, staring into his grandson's blue eyes. "And do you know the best way to hold on to power? Fear. Once you've attained enough power, people will fear you. Combine your power with their fear, and you can get just about anything—and anyone—you want."

Hart relaxed and smiled again as a petite brunette walked by. She waved at Baldwin, who winked at her.

"You must know her," Hart said. "Classmate?"

"One of the many young ladies on my date list waiting for that special phone call. Name's Allison Tucker."

Hart's eyes narrowed. His face grew taut. "Is she the daughter of Robert Tucker, the banker?"

"I believe so," answered Baldwin. "Isn't she a looker?"

The mayor's face again flushed, this time from anger, not exertion. "You listen to me, Adam, and you listen good. I'm only going to say this once. You are not, under *any* circumstances, *ever* to be around that girl. Not for a date, not even for so much as a dance at a party. That father of hers crossed me once, and I won't tolerate my own flesh and blood in any way associated with him. Do you understand?"

"Yes sir," replied Baldwin crisply, concealing his disappointment. Allison Tucker was the one girl in his class he wanted most to conquer.

"Good." Hart broke into a smile once again. "Where do you want to go for your birthday tonight?" he asked as they strolled along the winding, red-brick walkway that led to the club's front drive.

"Can I drive your Cadillac?"

"What difference does that make?" responded the mayor.

"If I'm driving, I want to go as far away as I can."

"And that would be where?"

"The Davis White Spot, way out on Poplar. I can hear a big, juicy T-bone calling my name."

"You're sixteen. As far as I'm concerned, you can drive any car you get your hands on as far as it'll take you."

They walked beneath the columned portico at the clubhouse entrance past beds of brightly colored pansies and daffodils.

"Look over there, Grampa." Baldwin pointed at an older model car parked at the edge of the club parking lot. "It's a Cord. Let's take a look."

"It's liable to make you jealous you don't have one of your own."

"Just a couple of minutes. Please."

"As I said before," Hart said, "it's your birthday, so you can damn well do as you like."

They approached the sleek car with its coffin-shaped hood and chrome trim. The glossy, maroon vehicle shimmered in the sunlight like a giant ruby.

"It's a '37," said Baldwin, his tone high-pitched. "And it's super-charged. Look at those coils coming out of the hood. I think this one's an 812 Supercharged Beverly."

"How do you know so much about Cords?"

"They're the car to have, Grampa. Jean Harlow had one and so did Tom Mix out in Hollywood. You've heard me talking about them at home, haven't you?"

"I'm not sure," the mayor said, the corners of his thin mouth rising in a smirk. "Maybe once or twice."

Baldwin pressed his face against the driver's-side window and peered in at the maroon leather upholstery, fascinated by the black-and-chrome dashboard. "I think it's got more gauges than an airplane. Who do you think it belongs to?"

"I only know of one other one in town, the one the Snowden boy had. But that was years ago."

Baldwin sighed. "I'd give anything to have one of these."

"Anything?" Hart extended his right forefinger toward his grandson, dangling a shiny new set of car keys. Baldwin's jaw dropped. "The locket was an appetizer. Happy sixteenth birthday. This *was* Jean Harlow's. I bought it from her estate."

Baldwin wrapped his arms around his grandfather. "Thank you, Grampa, thank you. I'm the luckiest kid in the world." He let go his embrace, pulled open the door, and slid into the driver's seat, the sweet smell of leather filling his nostrils.

Franklin Hart's face filled with pride. He placed a thumb and forefinger under his grandson's chin, turned the boy's head toward him, and looked directly into his eyes.

"I've done this for one reason, Adam. It's because you're a very special young man. You deserve this. You will find as you grow older that you have a gift. Just like me, you have a gift to be a leader. That is your destiny and I don't want you to ever forget it. Do you understand me?"

"I only want what you think's best for me, Grampa. I'll never forget the things you tell me. I promise."

"Do you remember the trip we took to Hyannis when you were eight? Spending time with Joe Kennedy and his boys?"

Baldwin nodded.

"He and I talked long and hard while you kids played on the beach. We both wanted success for our boys. Main difference is, he had four chances. All I have is one. You."

"I'll never let you down. That's another promise."

"Good," said Hart, mussing his grandson's thick brown hair with a wave of his hand. "I guess this means we'll be going to the White Spot for sure?"

Baldwin winked. "But I won't be driving your Cadillac."

"I should hope not," said the mayor. "Maybe, if I'm lucky, you'll let me drive your car on the way back."

"As long as you get us home by eight-thirty," said Baldwin, grinning.

"What's the rush?"

"I got a date. She thought it'd be fun to go out on my birthday. I lined her up weeks ago."

"This is a school night, you know."

"And it is my birthday."

"Trading me in on a newer model, eh?"

"I prefer to think of it as enjoying all ages, both male and female," Baldwin replied.

The mayor beamed. "Spoken like a true politician."

4

Joey paced anxiously on the platform at Central Station, awaiting the arrival of the Panama Limited from Louisiana. Everything was brightly decorated with garlands and red ribbon, ready for Christmas just four days away. He slid his hands into his pockets, grateful that the heavy wool of his uniform helped ward off the growing chill as daylight faded.

Two years had passed and Joey was now a policeman. Will was at Tulane University in New Orleans, with Jenny at nearby Sophie Newcomb College for Women. The time apart had strengthened their friendship.

The muted sound of a train whistle in the distance preceded a faint, then increasingly brighter light as the diesel locomotive approached the station. Within minutes the train was within the yard limit and then, with brakes whining and screeching, it slowly came to rest.

Joey spotted Jenny and Will coming down the steps of car number six. "Hey you two," he yelled, "over here."

They ran to each other, and to Joey's surprise, Jenny grabbed his face in her hands and kissed him squarely on his mouth. A wide smile spread across his face. He then clasped Will's hand in a vigorous handshake that turned into a tight, back-slapping hug.

"Gosh, Jenny," said Joey, taking a step back, "you look like a . . . woman."

She laughed, blue-green eyes sparkling. "I'm scared to ask. What did I look like before?"

"I mean, you know, you looked like a high school girl. Now . . ." He could detect the shapely figure beneath her lace-collared tan blouse and green wool jacket. "Now you look like a grown-up. You too, Will."

"I guess that's what college does to you," Will said, lips pinched, shaking his head. "Look at this." He pointed to his blond hairline starting to recede. "But it's not just us. You look older, too. Not to mention you've grown about two inches. You six feet yet?"

"Close. The uniform makes me look taller."

"Any plans for us tonight?" asked Jenny as they joined the flow of passengers toward the terminal.

"You better believe it," replied Joey with a nod, one hand in his pants pocket, jingling his key chain. "I'm gonna take you two to the Davis White Spot."

"Boy, I've missed my old car. You haven't wrecked it, have you?" Will asked.

"Not a scratch," Joey replied.

"You look so good in that uniform," Jenny said. "I know your father would be proud."

"I'm sure he is," Joey replied, holding the terminal door for Jenny as he glanced skyward.

Will drove, squinting as the headlights of an oncoming car reflected off the glossy, black front fender of his Model A. "You must really have gone to town with the wax," he said to Joey, who sat in the back seat for the first time in almost four months.

"It wasn't any big deal. Least I could do," Joey replied, grateful Will had left his treasured car in his care while he was away.

Later that night the three friends pulled into the gravel parking lot of the Davis White Spot restaurant.

Inside, a portly, black-haired woman was wiping her hands on her apron. The doughy aroma of fresh biscuits hung in the air.

"Table for three?"

"Right on the money, Mrs. Davis," replied Will. "We're home from college and have a reason to celebrate, so we came out here to enjoy your fine food, if you know what I mean." Liquor sales were illegal in Memphis, but Will knew Mrs. Davis wasn't much on that.

"Follow me," she said with a sly grin, leading them to a table at the back of the room.

Jenny sat between the two men. "Tell us, Joey, are you a full-fledged policeman now? You looked like it at the station."

"Well, the answer is yes and no. I am a policeman but I'm in a rookie probationary period for nine months. Then there's a three-week course. I have to average at least seventy in that. But that shouldn't be too hard. It's only a little lower than what I averaged at Central." All three laughed. "Then I become a permanent police officer."

As they were ordering, Joey leaned over to the red-haired waitress. "Three Bushmills Irish whiskey," he whispered. "Make the lady's two parts water. The gentleman and I want ours straight up."

The waitress winked. "Be back in a few minutes."

"Good thing I'm not a real policeman yet," Joey whispered.

Will and Jenny grinned. Then their eyes met and Jenny nodded.

"Joey, we've got something to tell you. We wanted you to be the first to know," said Will. "Jenny and I are going to be married."

Joey stared at them, brow furrowed, running a finger along the scar on his left temple.

"Aren't you happy for us?" said Jenny, frowning.

"Sure, sure I am," Joey said. "You just took me by surprise. I mean, I knew you'd be getting married someday. I just didn't expect it this soon. Congratulations, Will," he said, reaching over the white tablecloth and firmly grasping his best friend's hand.

"Congratulations to you too, doll," he said as a bittersweet pang scratched his heart. Of course he was happy for his closest friends. Sure he was. But hearing once and for all that Jenny would never be his still hurt, even though he had long ago convinced himself that he could never pursue that dream.

"Does this mean I'm going to be an uncle?" Joey asked with a quick smile.

"Maybe someday," replied Jenny, "but not anytime soon."

"What it does mean," said Will, "is that you're going to be a best man."

"I wouldn't want it any other way, pal."

At that moment their drinks arrived and they hoisted their glasses, the pinging sounds of glass on glass returning Joey's spirits.

"To happiness in marriage for the two best friends a guy could ever have."

"And," added Will, "to our special friendship, our special tie that binds. May we feel it not only now but in the decades to come."

5

That holiday season was the happiest Joey could remember since his father died. A Christmas Eve policeman's party at his home, Christmas morning present-opening at Will's, and a sumptuous meal at the Adairs'.

Joey had pulled the late-evening shift for the Friday night after Christmas, the last weekend before Jenny and Will would return to college. But his friends promised to pick him up at the police station at midnight so they could squeeze in a little late-night dancing at the Peabody Hotel.

Meanwhile, Will and Jenny had four hours to kill.

"Come on, it'll be fun," Will said, steering his car onto Southern Avenue.

"Oh, Will, it's been ages since we went parking on Goodwyn," replied Jenny.

"It's only eight o'clock. For old times sake, okay?"

Jenny nodded and squeezed his arm with a smile.

Will drove the Model A along Southern past the fairgrounds and the huge Southern Railroad yards. Just before reaching the small Buntyn Station, he turned onto Goodwyn Avenue and pulled off on the grassy shoulder of the gravel-topped street. The chain-link fence of the Memphis Country Club golf course lined the right side of the road. To the left sat the mansions and manicured yards of some of Memphis's high society.

A few minutes after the couple had climbed into the back seat, Jenny jolted upright, staring across the street. "Will, there's someone there."

The dim light from a nearby street lamp reflected off a man's slick scalp.

"You worry too much," Will said as the man turned and vanished into the darkness beyond the blue stucco mansion.

Jenny's slender shoulders relaxed.

Will slipped an arm around her in the darkness. "We've never done it in Memphis," he whispered.

"We shouldn't," she said as she lightly kissed his neck.

He ran a hand under her pink angora sweater. Easing back on the car seat, arms encircled, they kissed deeply, their passion rising as they shared the intimate warmth of their bodies.

Afterward they lay back, heads resting on the worn, brown mohair upholstery, gazing into each other's eyes. Will gently stroked Jenny's flushed face with the back of his hand, then outlined her lips with a soft touch.

For a split second her thoughts drifted to the words of Paddy O'Riley, spoken in his thick Irish accent when she was only ten years old. "Jenny, me little lass, if you ever wish a man to forever fall in love with you, say this verse three times to yourself:

> Thee for me,
> Me for thee
> And for none else."

She silently repeated the words once, twice, a third time, just as she had done hundreds of times before. She couldn't remember a time in her life when she hadn't loved Will. Did he feel the same? Would their love last?

*

"Did anybody see you?" Adam Baldwin asked, pushing open the front passenger door of his Cord.

"Not a soul," replied the petite brunette, smoothing the skirt of her floral print dress. Its maroon background almost matched the color of the automobile. She hopped into the car and slammed the door. "My parents went downtown to a movie. I told them I was going out with Lisa Mitchell."

"Good," said Baldwin as he slipped the car into gear. Then he grinned. "If your father knew, he'd probably kill you."

"Oh, I don't think he'd go that far." Allison Tucker giggled. "Although he might pull me out of college and lock me up in the basement for a year or two."

"How's Southwestern? What's it like going to school here at home?" Baldwin asked, surprised at how nervous he felt. He didn't usually have to make small talk to break the ice.

"It's good and bad," she replied, running a manicured finger along the car's shiny, lacquered dashboard. "The occasional meal at home's pretty nice. So is having my laundry done. But I love dorm life. Unfortunately, being so close, my parents can check up on me anytime. How's life up at Harvard?"

"It's okay," Baldwin said as the car sped by the fairgrounds.

"Did I ask the wrong thing?"

"No, not at all," Baldwin replied. "It's just that Harvard's pretty tough and my grades haven't been law school caliber so far. My grandfather's riding me hard. I'll do better, though. Just need to buckle down."

Allison crossed her arms, rubbing her hands on her sleeves. "Goodness, it's chilly out tonight, isn't it?"

Baldwin glanced at her, then grinned. She, too, was feeling self-conscious. "If you're cold, I got just the thing." He handed her a small empty glass, unscrewed the top of a bourbon bottle, and poured almost two jiggers. "Just sip it. It'll warm you up for sure."

"Gosh, Adam," she said sheepishly, toying with her gold necklace. "I hardly ever drink. My father's pretty strict and—"

"Aw, go ahead. He'll never know." Baldwin put the bottle to his mouth and took two quick gulps.

Allison's green eyes widened. She put the glass to her lips and took a sip, wincing as she swallowed.

"That wasn't so bad, was it?" he said with a sideways glance.

"It really does warm you up, doesn't it?" She smiled and took another sip.

"Makes for a real good mood. You want to get a bite to eat?"

"It's up to you."

"Well, since it's taken so long for us to finally get together," he said, taking another swallow of bourbon, "I'd like to take you to a special spot first. It's quiet and secluded. We can take a little walk, or just sit in the car and talk. How's that sound?"

She took another sip and nodded. "Do you go there often?"

"Hardly ever," Baldwin replied with a politician's smile, thinking of the number of girls who had lost their virginity at his special Goodwyn Avenue spot. "But you're different, Allison. You know, special. I really want to get to know you, whether your father likes it or not."

Allison blushed, twirling a lock of her shoulder-length brown hair.

"We'll be there in a minute," said Baldwin, turning onto Goodwyn. He parked beside the wrought-iron fence that surrounded a blue stucco mansion and its huge manicured lawn, paying no attention to the Model A Ford down the street on the other side of the road.

Jenny and Will had been oblivious to the sounds of passing traffic. But when the super-charged engine rumbled by, they took notice.

"Sounds like a tank," Jenny whispered.

"Gotta be Adam Baldwin."

They peered over the Ford's front seat.

Will nodded. "See? I knew that sounded like a Cord."

"Can you tell who the girl is?"

"I'm not sure. I'll tell you one thing, though. If she's not planning on some serious necking, she better be wearing boxing gloves. The guys at Central used to say things about him and his dates that I wouldn't think of repeating."

Jenny frowned. "Look, they're getting out of the car. Is that—"

"Allison Tucker. Her father would kill her."

Jenny frowned again. "What for?"

"You kidding? I thought you knew. From what I hear, Allison's father can't stand Mayor Hart. Seems Hart tried to close Tucker down during the Depression by spreading rumors that his bank was in trouble. Caused a run. But Tucker managed to survive. He was pretty burned though, and he told Allison he'd disown her if she ever went out with Baldwin. There's just bad blood between the families. No telling what Hart would do to Baldwin if he found out. Probably kick his golden butt down to the Mississippi River."

"Look," Jenny said, "they're walking off into the shadows."

"The only thing I can see is a liquor bottle in his hand."

Baldwin downed another mouthful of bourbon and grasped Allison's hand as they walked down the street in the cool night air. She glanced at him, then swiftly looked away.

"What's the matter?" Baldwin asked.

"Just a little nervous, I guess."

"What for? I'm not gonna bite you," Baldwin said, his tone gentle.

"It's not that," she said. "It's just that," she paused for a moment, "you act like you really like me."

"Allison, I *do* like you," replied Baldwin as he stopped on the side of the street. Slowly he put his arms around her and drew her mouth to his as his heart raced. Then he smiled and put his hands in his pockets. "Let's go back to the car," he said.

Back inside, Allison took a last sip of bourbon. Baldwin turned the pint bottle up, finishing it in three gulps. He placed his arm around her and they leaned into one another, kissing passionately.

Baldwin groped Allison's breasts. "No, please don't," she whispered.

He reached under her dress and stroked between her legs.

"I said *no!*" she yelled, pushing him away.

Baldwin gritted his teeth. "Don't get sanctimonious with me. You want it bad as I do. You know it."

"That's not true!" she said as Baldwin pulled her dress up over her thighs. "Take me home right now! You're just as bad as my father said."

Baldwin glared at her, blue eyes narrowed. He lashed out, slapping her twice across the face. "You dirty little bitch. I get whatever I want."

Allison swung, hitting Baldwin squarely on the cheek. She opened the car door and lunged out. He yanked her back and slammed the door shut as her fists beat against his face and chest. Baldwin grabbed her head firmly in his hands. Allison ripped the Saint Christopher's locket from his neck, trying to choke him just as he smashed her head against the car window.

The glass cracked, sending tiny fragments to the pavement outside. The girl's body stiffened, her hands clenched tight. She slumped against the door.

Panic flashed in Baldwin's glazed eyes. "Allison?" He felt her head. No blood. He felt for a pulse in her neck. It seemed fine. He looked around. Nobody in sight. Just an old Ford parked down the road. Then Allison's body began convulsing violently.

"Jesus," yelled Baldwin, pushing away as the unconscious woman thrashed about wildly, her head jerking backward. The convulsions stopped and she slumped back against the door, wisps of disheveled brown hair hanging over her ashen face like strands of a wet mop. A faint sound, a cross between a cry and a gasp, eased from her quivering lips. Then silence. Again, he felt for a pulse. None.

Stunned, he closed his eyes, heart pounding. It was an accident. He didn't mean to. But they wouldn't care. He saw his grandfather, head shaking, bowed in disappointment. Hopes for law school and a career in politics. Dashed.

His stomach churned. A fullness snaked up his throat. He flung open the door and, shuddering, spewed onto the darkened grass. A moment's silence preceded three dry heaves, sounding like a wild animal in pain. He leaned back in his seat, sweat chilling his forehead, and wiped tiny specks of vomit from his chin with a sleeve.

His grandfather's image again flashed in his mind, the old man's voice forceful and exorting. "Power. Power over others is like a ladder. As a politician, you climb it daily. Over time, with each rung you scale, you get more powerful. Cardinal rule number one—you slip, you're lost. You'll never make it to the top. You remember that, boy."

Baldwin turned and stared at Allison's lifeless body. Indecision and thoughts of hollow apologies vanished in a veil of hardened resolve. This was *her* fault. He'd be damned if he'd pay for it the rest of *his* life. The solution was simple. In fact, it was better this way. Criminal charges by an injured woman would have definitely derailed his law career. If he could just dispose of her body, no one would be the wiser. After all, no one knew he and Allison had been together. He had never taken her out in his life.

Baldwin looked around, started his car, and drove away.

Within minutes he was peering into the den window of his grandfather's mansion on Central Avenue. The mayor had fallen asleep listening to the Bob Hope radio show, as was his habit. He lay nestled in his favorite flame-orange chair with slippered feet propped up on the matching footstool. No chance the mayor would hear him. Baldwin breathed a sigh of relief.

He stepped around the back of the house to the tool shed and spotted a red-plaid wool blanket. Perfect. Grabbing a flashlight and shovel, he walked down the driveway and cut across a neighbor's yard to the corner of Central and Haynes where his car, with the body of Allison Tucker on the floorboard of the front seat, stood parked in the shadows. He cranked the engine and turned west toward Overton Park, only ten minutes away.

*

Jenny and Will kept Baldwin in sight as they followed the Cord's tail lights from a safe distance down Central Avenue.

"I swear he's killed her," said Will, hands tight on the vibrating steering wheel as the car strained to keep up. "You saw everything, just like I did."

"We've got to tell Joey," replied Jenny, voice quivering.

"Sure," said Will, "just not yet. We need to see where he goes."

When the Cord veered into Overton Park, Will followed, turning off his headlights as they entered the pitch-black woods.

"Don't lose him," Jenny said.

"Not a chance."

The tail lights of the Cord brightened as Baldwin slowed to a stop.

Will cut his engine. He and Jenny quietly slid from the car and tiptoed down the shadowy roadside. They huddled together behind a fallen tree with Baldwin in sight, thirty yards away.

Baldwin attacked the ground with a shovel, using all the strength his athletic, muscular frame could muster. After thirty minutes of digging, he slumped down on an old tree stump. With each strained breath, vapor puffed from his mouth and hung in the cold night air. He stared at the deep, freshly dug hole he had carved in the dark soil.

In the light of Baldwin's flashlight, Jenny and Will watched dry-mouthed as he spread a red plaid blanket on the ground, took the girl's body from his car, and wrapped it tightly in the blanket. He then dropped the corpse into the shallow grave and quickly began to shovel dirt on top of it.

44

The Cord's coffin-shaped hood reflected the dim light of the moon through the barren trees, taking on the identity of the deathmobile it had become.

Jenny hugged her chest. "I'm scared," she whispered. "We've got to tell the police."

"Soon," Will replied, his eyes fixed on the burial site. "I just want to lead Joey to the exact spot. Help me remember that crooked little tree." He scanned for other landmarks.

Baldwin was now packing the soil tightly, followed with a coating of brush, leaves, and branches.

Will finally whispered, "Let's get out of here."

They found the edge of the road and ran for the safety of Will's car. But just then Jenny tripped in the darkness, a muffled whine escaping her lips as her knee scraped the pavement.

Baldwin's head jerked around. He aimed his flashlight in their direction. The beam blazed in Jenny's and Will's eyes. "Son of a bitch," Baldwin yelled, piercing the silence.

"Hurry, start it up," Jenny screamed as they slammed the door shut.

The old engine turned over and over, unable to start.

"Come on, dammit, come on," urged Will, striking the dashboard with his right fist.

The smell of gasoline filled the car and, abruptly, the engine cranked. Will yanked down on the hand throttle and roared off as Baldwin's motor revved.

The Ford turned out of the park. The Cord followed, racing past Southwestern College. At East Parkway, Will turned back into the park with the Cord only a few car lengths behind, hoping the dark, winding roads would slow Baldwin down. But the Cord's heavy chrome bumper rammed into the Model A, knocking it off balance.

"That bastard's trying to run us off the road," Will yelled.

"What are we gonna do?" Jenny cried.

"Don't worry," Will replied, gripping the steering wheel tightly as he squinted to make out the darkened road. Baldwin's high-beam headlights glared in his rear-view mirror. "I'll get us near the Parkview Hotel. He'd be nuts to try something there."

The Cord rammed the Ford again, knocking Jenny against the dashboard. She sobbed as pain shot through her left arm.

"Brace yourself, Jenny. I'll get us out of this. Hold on tight." Will fought to control the speeding car on the bumpy, narrow road. "Look out! He's gonna hit us again!"

This time the Cord rammed the Model A with such force that the lightweight sedan fish-tailed out of control off the road.

"Will, watch out—"

The car smashed into a massive oak, the gas tank exploding, engulfing the car in a ball of flame.

6

Joey stared at the smoldering mass of metal for a long time. The reporters had already rushed off to make their deadline. A sickening charred odor permeated the air. Tears ran down his face as a hole widened in his heart. He had tried to be strong, a true policeman in uniform. But the fact that he would never see Jenny and Will again hit hard. He began to sob.

Captain Mike Kelly broke away from the other officers and walked over. He put his arm around Joey, the only comfort for the young man who now had no one else. Kelly's Irish accent sounded just like Paddy O'Riley's. "It's sad to lose loved ones, Joey. You and me, we been through this before. It's okay to cry, 'specially if you're an Irishman. It shows you got compassion in your heart."

Joey embraced Kelly, something he hadn't done since the death of his father. The musty scent of wool was the same Joey remembered as a boy when Paddy would hug him goodnight in bed after coming in from walking his beat in the Pinch.

"You need me," Kelly went on, "you know where to find me, lad, just two doors down any time o' day."

Joey eased away from Kelly, wiping his eyes with a sleeve. "Thanks, Uncle Mike."

"C'mon, let me give you a lift home. I'll find somebody to take your squad car in," Kelly said as Joey fought back the tears. "You know, there's a case of a missin' girl I want you to help with. These old guys could use some young blood on this one. What d' you say?"

Joey nodded.

"She's a banker's daughter. A goody two-shoes. Never missed a curfew in her life. Her parents have been ringing the phone off the wall down at headquarters. If she hasn't turned up by morning, then we definitely got a problem. The newspaper guys sniffed it out and jumped on it like a pack of Irishmen set loose in a field o' four-leaf clovers. It may just be a problem o' raging youth." Kelly smoothed the ends of his grey moustache and smiled. "Don't forget, I was young once meself. I know what's on a young person's mind."

Joey returned the smile. "How old is she?"

"Your age. Graduated from Central in your class. Name's Tucker. Allison Tucker."

Joey's stomach, already churning, clenched. His thoughts swept back to the graduation night dance on the rooftop of the Peabody Hotel, the Clyde McCoy Orchestra belting out the big-band sounds of Tommy Dorsey, Benny Goodman, and Glenn Miller. Allison Tucker, dancing in his arms as the band played its finale, *Moonlight Serenade*. The sweet scent of her hair. The warmth of her body against him. The bittersweet notes of the soprano saxophone wafting upward into the darkness at song's end. The gold script necklace that spelled *Allison*. And the kiss.

"Maybe now you'll always remember me," he had whispered.

Allison had locked the clasp behind her neck, her brunette hair draping her shoulders. "It's the prettiest necklace I've ever seen. Friends, Joey. Always."

With eyes closed, he had felt her lips, soft and wet, on his.

"Joey?" said Kelly. "You all right?"

Joey's eyes blinked open. "Yeah. Just caught me by surprise. I knew her pretty well."

"You never told me about her."

He shrugged. "Nothing to tell. Kinda lost track at the end of the summer when she started college. Guess she got busy."

48

Kelly frowned. "Maybe I should assign someone else."

Joey shook his head. "No, I want to."

Within minutes they were turning onto North Avalon.

"Are you sure you don't want to stay over tonight?" Kelly asked, bringing his car to a stop in front of Joey's house.

Joey opened the squad car door. Jenny and Will would want him to be strong. "I'll be fine. I'll see you in the morning and get right on that case, if she hasn't turned up. Thanks for everything, Uncle Mike."

The older officer waved as Joey slammed the door and started up the steep steps.

As the car pulled away, Joey turned and sat down on the top step. He couldn't bring himself to go in. The first thing he'd see would be the silver-framed picture on the coffee table of Jenny, Will, and himself, smiling and embracing on graduation night.

He stared at the dim, deserted street below. A montage of images flashed through his mind.

He saw Jenny, Will, and himself as four-year-olds, tricycling to Green's Drug Store, their first unchaperoned trip in the neighborhood. Clutching shiny new Buffalo nickels, they gave their orders to Mister Green at the fountain. Jenny and Will wanted Black Cows. As Mr. Green dropped a scoop of chocolate ice cream into each of their Cokes, Joey, with an ever-present miniature policeman's cap on his head, decided on a strawberry soda.

Then he remembered three ten-year-olds making their Saturday afternoon pilgrimage to the Ritz Theater and Henry's Lunch counter.

He visualized them again, this time at twelve, hopping onto a streetcar in downtown Memphis, where they stocked up on sugary perfume balls at Lipford's Candy Store.

The smile on Joey's face faded as he focused on the dark street once more. He stood and went inside, taking the graduation picture from the coffee table and placing it on the nightstand in his upstairs room.

"I'll never forget you," he murmured as he gently touched the corner of the frame. He crawled into bed and, with his dog at his feet, flicked off the small bedside lamp. For the first time in his life, Joey O'Riley cried himself to sleep.

*

Franklin Hart's face was buried in the Saturday morning sports section as he read it a second time. He tapped his foot impatiently against the hardwood floor in the breakfast room. His eight a.m. departure for the mayor's office, to which he steadfastly adhered six days a week, had been delayed for over an hour.

"You sure there ain't nothing else I can get you, Mister Franklin?" the old cook asked as she cleared the mayor's breakfast dishes.

"No, Tessie, I'm fine."

"How come you ain't gone to work yet? I ain't never seen you this late."

"I have to have a little discussion with my grandson this morning, if you know what I mean."

"If it's about that busted-up car of his, then I sure do." She squeezed her massive body sideways through the swinging door to the kitchen.

A few minutes later Adam Baldwin, wearing a navy silk paisley robe, sauntered in and sat down across from his grandfather. "Morning, Grampa," he said, flashing a smile.

Hart slowly lowered the newspaper, his face full of anger. "Do you mind telling me what on God's green earth happened to your car last night?" His bushy white eyebrows arched as he noticed his grandson's reddened, bruised cheek. "And your face. My God, boy, what is going on?"

"Some toughs from Tech followed me after I left the Pig 'N Whistle," replied Baldwin, poker-faced. "They forced me to pull over on Belvedere, then they yanked me out of the Cord. They knew who I was from the car."

"Then what happened?"

"They started calling you names. Said you were crooked, too old to know what you were doing. So I swung at one of them. Then they punched me in the face and held me while they went after the car with a baseball bat and tire iron. They whacked the front bumper and knocked out a window."

Hart's ruddy complexion turned even darker. "The bastards. I'm going to call up that Tech principal. He'll heed what I say. That is, if he wants to keep his job."

Baldwin smiled inwardly.

"Don't you worry, Adam, they won't be bothering you anymore. I'll have it all taken care of by the time you get back to Harvard."

"Thanks, Grampa," he said, touching a finger to his bruised cheek. He winced slightly.

"You hungry, boy? I know you are. Bring some of those pancakes over here to Adam, Tessie."

"And some bacon, too," added Baldwin.

As Tessie served, Hart picked up the paper again. "This will be of interest to you, Adam," he said. "Two Teens Die In Fiery Overton Park Car Crash."

Baldwin took a slow bite of pancake. "How did it happen?"

"Doesn't say. That's the problem with the youth of today. They're not responsible like my generation was. Those two were probably drinking and speeding through the park. Serves 'em right, if that's the case. They got what they deserved."

"You're right, Grampa. You play with fire and you get burned. Can I see that?"

Hart handed it to his grandson, who studied the rest of the front page. A corner of his mouth made a crooked grin when he found a smaller headline in the lower right-hand corner:

"Police Baffled By Disappearance
of Prominent Banker's Daughter."

7

Present Day

Adam Baldwin's steel-blue eyes scanned the Washington treetops from his perch in the Dirksen Senate Office Building, coming to rest on the enormous white Capitol dome. The tall, tanned Senator was as fit and vigorous as a much younger man, exercising daily to keep his athletic body from yielding to his rich tastes. His once-balding head sported a generous growth of grey hair, the successful result of a hair transplant aimed at maximizing his marketability for a planned foray into the national limelight.

With handsome looks, a captivating personality, and excellent legislating skills, he had amassed a growing popularity, not only among Democrats of all ages but with women from both political parties. When he flashed his trademark smile, cameras clicked in unison, especially any held by females. Young, old, any age. They flocked to him as if he were an aging movie star who still dripped testosterone like sap from a maple. Remarking on his striking blue eyes, a *Time* magazine cover story had recently proclaimed him "the Paul Newman of American Politics."

Baldwin's public image efforts, honed in recent years with the skill of a diamond cutter, downplayed his star quality by representing the candidate as a friendly grandfather, always willing to pitch in and help, whether serving in a homeless soup line or hammering away on a Habitat for Humanity house. Campaigning tirelessly, his charisma and a sense of presence preceded every step. He enthralled crowds with his seeming sincerity and keen sense of humor.

He was a chameleon, able to turn on the charm or display the appropriate emotion in an instant. Subdued resentment, glazed-eyed sentimentality, and immeasurable outrage were the classics in his repertoire. As for mistakes, simple slips of the tongue—he rarely made them. When he did, eloquence immediately provided cover.

Baldwin's eyes followed the capital's skyline. He'd moved into the Rayburn Building, there in the distance, in 1958, after winning his first election to the House of Representatives. The years had left an illustrious trail of political achievements in their wake. After two terms in the House from Tennessee's seventh district, he had figured in one of the most controversial decisions to ever take place in the Senate. In an unprecedented example of political favoritism, the President, acknowledging his own childhood friendship, had used his clout to maneuver newly elected Senator Adam Baldwin into the chairmanship of the Senate Budget Committee. Baldwin took to his duties with the stamina of a marathon runner, amassing power on Capitol Hill to an extent that surprised even the most seasoned political veterans. Six more successful senatorial elections followed.

During those years, Baldwin had served as chairman of the powerful Senate Judiciary Committee, as Democratic whip of the Senate during the Carter Administration, and as Senate minority leader during the Reagan years. He finally attained the honor of Senate majority leader when the Democrats regained control of the Senate during George Bush's term as president. When fellow Democrat Albert Jefferson ran for president, Baldwin had expected to be his running mate. After all, he had been the public's favorite. But he was passed over at the party convention for the more youthful Thomas Benson. Baldwin resigned as Senate majority leader when they won.

The relative youthfulness of president and vice president nearly brought down the highest office in the land. They had surrounded themselves with career academicians their age or younger—inexperienced idealists who had never met a corporate payroll, were unschooled in foreign diplomacy, and refused to adhere to the accepted norms for political and social behavior. When an investigation uncovered a sexual indiscretion on the part of the chief executive with a prostitute, Jefferson was forced to resign midway through his second term, elevating Benson to the presidency. As the election year primary season approached, an examination of Benson's campaign finances revealed numerous fund-raising violations, many tied to oil interests in the Middle East. Washington insiders and the country itself clamored for a change.

Hoping to capitalize on this feeling was the Republican Party's nominee, John Titus—as well as Democrat Adam Baldwin. His party had rallied behind him, turning the age factor into Baldwin's greatest asset. Party leaders now championed him as the possessor of an immense wealth of political experience who could keep The White House in Democratic hands. President Benson, realizing he had no chance at re-election, gracefully bowed out and threw his support to his vice president, William S. Taylor, for the party nomination. Baldwin's landslide victories in the ensuing Democratic primaries virtually annihilated the opposition, forcing the sitting president to accept a secondary role in his own party.

Now, looking out his window on this hot mid-summer morning, Adam Baldwin could see nothing but green trees, blue skies, and a political future as bright as the light shining into his office. He had certainly devoted his life to building that future. He turned from the window, and his gaze came to rest on a group of family pictures: his son, Adam, Jr., with his son's wife, Beth; daughter Amy with her husband, Bob Burgess; and Baldwin's wife of over forty years, Doris.

Baldwin had married the much younger Doris when he was thirty-two, a year after his election to the Senate in 1962. At first a philanderer, he had kept his indiscretions from his wife. When media scrutiny into politicians' private lives became an issue, however, he had altered his lifestyle to include marital fidelity. Power, after all, as his grandfather always said, was the strongest aphrodisiac.

Baldwin's gaze settled on the largest picture in the room, a sixteen-by-twenty-inch aerial photograph of The White House. His sights were firmly set on the biggest prize of all. His time had come.

He remembered that day when he was five years old, standing wide-eyed in the foyer of The White House, hiding behind his grandfather's trousers, tightly clenching the older man's hand. President Roosevelt rolled toward them, nodding, cigarette holder jutting from the corner of his mouth. That was it. The moment he decided to be president when he grew up. Then he could have a wheelchair all his own.

He smiled at the memory and glanced over at the faded photograph of his grandfather, Franklin Hart, on his desk. The mountain of destiny Hart had expected his grandson to climb was sheer glass, but, little by little, Baldwin had scaled that peak, often invoking his grandfather's name. He now stood near the top, ready to claim his place.

"That's going to be my next house, Grampa, just as you had hoped," he said out loud. Turning back to the window, he looked out again over the city. "No one will stand in my way," he vowed. "No one."

8

Joe O'Riley, the long-retired Memphis Chief of Police, sat on the top step of his tiered front walkway, brown eyes staring down North Avalon Street. A box of glazed doughnuts for the police department's Homicide Division sat at his side. He barely noticed the hot, damp air of early-morning August as he took a breath. How little North Avalon had changed.

Some things had, however. His white stucco house had turned a dirty grey and his once-dark crop of auburn hair had become handsomely laced with streaks of silver. But O'Riley loved his old house. It was part of him, an old friend who had endured times of happiness and sorrow.

He scanned the front yard, a large, sloping bed of dark-green ivy so thick only an occasional weed took root. The shade of the two red oaks, huge with age, would allow little grass to grow even if there were no ivy. O'Riley grinned. That fact would surely make his father, Paddy, smile in heaven.

Inside, the house had remained nearly untouched over the years. The same furniture, the same Oriental rugs stood where they had for decades. Interior decorating had not been a priority for his wife, Evelyn, much to O'Riley's delight. Being from a modest family, Evelyn had brought few material possessions but much love to their marriage in 1951. Her mild-mannered sweetness balanced the stress of police work, constantly lifting O'Riley's spirit. Her inability to have children was never a source of conflict between them. They had each other, and that was enough.

But all this was shattered with Evelyn's brutal murder in 1957 at the

56

hands of the so-called Hollywood killer who had terrorized Memphis in the late 1950s. The grieving policeman began sleeping upstairs, seeking refuge from the loneliness of their downstairs bedroom which still seemed to belong to the two of them. Nights spent in the starlight of the upstairs sleeping porch made him feel closer to Evelyn, comforting him as in 1947 after the death of his father. Sleep came easily there, especially after a couple of stiff shots of Bushmills, his nightly habit.

After Evelyn's death, O'Riley threw himself into his police work. He personally took on the case of the Hollywood killer and managed to catch the criminal, Jimmy Seabold, responsible for the murder of his wife and nine other women. His efforts were rewarded when he was named chief of police in the early 1970s. Then, after twenty years of service as chief, he retired.

For someone used to twelve-hour workdays, this became a burden. O'Riley's neglect of hobbies in favor of police work left him sitting in a recliner staring at television. Boredom quickly set in, and he soon was visiting his old friends in Homicide. Once a week at first, then twice, sometimes three times. But trips to police headquarters tapered off to once a week when Nancy Summerfield dropped into his life like an unexpected Southern spring shower—cooling, calming, leaving vibrancy in its wake. O'Riley was in love. His faded memories of what it was like to touch and be touched, physically and mentally, rushed through him, renewed. She had saved his life.

And he ended up saving hers when another serial killer surfaced, mimicking the case in the late 1950s that had claimed his wife. Nancy had been the final target. But Joe had saved her and caught the killer.

Now Nancy was teaching in France as part of a Memphis University School faculty exchange program, an opportunity that couldn't be passed up. But for O'Riley, four months in France were too many. His one-week stay in Paris convinced him of that.

The saucy food clashed with his meat-and-potatoes tastes. Gruff people. Uppity. Not like Americans, especially not like Southerners. And the language. He couldn't understand a damn thing.

Their love would endure. They knew it and accepted their fate, along with the prospect of monstrous phone bills. When Nancy returned, they would settle down together. The shiny diamond he had slipped on her finger that last night in Paris made sure of that. She wasn't going to let him slip away either, ring or no ring.

Thinking of her, O'Riley sighed and eased his nearly six-foot frame up when he heard his German shepherd barking inside. "I'm coming, I'm coming," he bellowed as he opened the front door and walked into the living room where the black and tan dog rocked back and forth, tail wagging furiously. The shepherd lunged upward, planting his front paws on the softness that hugged his master's waist.

"You're nothing but a big baby, Bullet," O'Riley said with a smile, scratching the dog behind the ears. He had had many dogs over the years, all German shepherds named Bullet. "Get down now, boy. I've got to go to the station. I'll be back," he promised, tossing a large dog biscuit into the dining room to mask his escape.

Twenty minutes later, O'Riley crunched across the loose gravel on the freshly repaved street in front of Memphis police headquarters. Behind him, cars whooshed down Second Street amid an occasional honk and the squeal of brakes. Waves of heat shimmered up from the sidewalk as he paused at the curb, wiping small beads of perspiration from his upper lip with the cuff of his white dress shirt.

Suddenly, a familiar voice pierced the sounds of morning traffic.

"Hot out here, ain't it?"

O'Riley nodded. "So damn dry I saw two trees fightin' over a dog."

The aged, black shoeshine man grinned. "How's it going, Chief Joe?"

"Top of the morning to you, E.," replied O'Riley, moving quickly toward the man like an athlete, shoulders broad, back arched.

"And the rest of the day to you," said E., finishing off the Irish greeting he had shared countless times with O'Riley over the years. "Want a shine?"

58

"You know I do." O'Riley climbed onto the rickety, portable red-cushioned chair and placed his feet on the worn, grey metal stirrups. "Where you been lately? The guys said you were here one day, gone the next. I figured you packed it up and finally called it quits."

The old man shook his bald head. "I ain't never quit nothin'. Had a problem with my ticker. Been laid up for close to a year."

"Heart attack?"

"Almost. Had to do one of them highway procedures on me."

O'Riley tilted his head, squinting into the bright sunlight. "Bypass?"

"Yep, that's it. Bypass."

"Double? Triple? Quadruple?"

E. pulled his lower lip through his dentures and shook his head again. "Never could understand what they was tellin' me. But think of a four-way stop and I'm smack dab in the middle of it. They worked on my heart from every direction."

"Quadruple," O'Riley said with a slight smile. "But why the hell are you out here in this heat and not inside at the shine stand?" He glanced toward the 100 North Main building across the street.

"I feel cooped up inside," E. replied, soaping down the dull finish of O'Riley's black leather shoes. "The heat don't bother me none. Cold don't neither. Only thing drive me inside with them softies is the rain. I like it out here. I'm free as a bird." He looked up, eyeing O'Riley's blazer and grey slacks, and scratched the top of his head. "How come you all dressed up in your Sunday go-to-meeting clothes? I ain't seen these shoes in years."

"Today's special. The chief wants to see me. Says he's got a big surprise. Thought I'd dress up for the occasion. You don't suppose he wants to give me a case of Irish whiskey for my years of dedication, do you?"

"I doubt that, but you can dreams all you want. Me, I'd settle for a bottle of Jack Daniel's black label," E. said, as he dabbed a piece of cloth in a small round tin and began spreading a layer of polish on O'Riley's shoes. "You minds if I asks you somethin' else?"

"Name it."

"You been coming down here, what? Once, maybe more a week since you done took retirement, right?"

"Yeah, I guess so."

"And every single time you done come down to the station, you get your shoes done 'the E. way,' am I right again?"

O'Riley grinned and nodded. "What's your point?"

"Well, all these years I been meaning to tell you. Your shoes don't never need shinin' or saddle soapin'. 'Cepting these old ones today. They usually in good shape from the last shine. I bet you don't wear but three pair of shoes anyways. How comes you keep getting 'em shined?"

"It's like this," said O'Riley, as the old man buffed his wing-tips with a fraying rag. "I guess I just enjoy sitting down and talking to you. Make sense?"

"Makes damn good sense," he replied. "I talk to myself all the time. I can be plenty amusing, if I do say so myself." He paused again, his cloudy brown eyes focused on O'Riley. "But you don't have to pay me to talk to you, Chief Joe."

"I know that, E., but did you ever stop to think that paying you for a shine I might not need makes me happy?"

"Well then, by golly, you keep right on paying, if it makes you happy. I ain't one to keep a man from parting with his money." He made a popping sound with the buffing rag across the toe of each shoe. "There you go," he said, drying off the edges.

O'Riley handed him a crisp five-dollar bill, but his old friend shook his head vigorously.

"Just this once, I'm afraid I gotta make you unhappy. The shine's on me."

"I can't let you do that."

"You got no choice."

O'Riley smiled and opened the box in his lap. "Doughnut?"

"You got enough for all the boys?" E. asked, arching his grey eyebrows.

"If there's not, I'd rather you have one than Driscoll."

"Oh, if it might be Driscoll's, I'll take one. He don't never stop for a shine," E. said with a laugh.

O'Riley eased from the chair. "Thanks for the freebie." He winked. "And the conversation."

E. patted his sweaty forehead with an old, yellowed handkerchief. "You remember me if they gives you some booze. Hear?"

"I will," replied O'Riley, walking quickly toward the front steps of the building. "Promise."

The former chief shifted the doughnuts from his right hand to his left as he grasped the heavy metal door handle. "Jeez, you'd think that door wouldn't be so hard to open after all these years," he muttered, stepping into the grey marble entryway.

"What's the matter, old man?" echoed a voice from the second floor balcony overlooking the atrium lobby. "Getting a little hard at your age?" Sergeant Ken Driscoll, the youngest detective in the Homicide Department, looked down at the former chief with a barely concealed sneer. "Looks like you forgot to eat your Wheaties this morning. Or was it the Geritol?"

"You're a perfect example why brothers don't marry sisters, Driscoll," shouted O'Riley.

Driscoll scowled, then vanished through the swinging glass doors into Homicide.

O'Riley turned to his left and continued down the hallway past the wide marble staircase that led to the second floor.

Within minutes he was sitting in a brown leather swivel chair facing the cluttered desk of Memphis Police Chief Charlie Perry, awaiting the chief's arrival. The walls were lined with pictures and clippings chronicling Perry's rise as the first black Memphis officer to attain the highest rank on the force. A large bookcase filled with volumes pertaining to the law and its enforcement stretched across the wall behind the desk. Photographs of the chief's wife and two grown sons were interspersed between the books. An autographed picture of famed Grambling football coach Eddie Robinson was the only reminder of Perry's alma mater.

O'Riley heard voices outside. Sounded like men. Two, maybe three voices. One was Perry's.

He picked up the previous day's *USA Today* sports section from the chief's desk and glanced at the headlines. Yankees win. Braves win. Detroit loses. Some things never changed.

"Hello, Joe," boomed the chief as he burst into the room, his round eyes smiling behind thin-framed tortoise-shell glasses.

"It's nice to see somebody around this place getting some work done," said O'Riley, shaking Perry's strong outstretched hand.

"I see retirement still hasn't softened the edge on your humor," Perry said, laughing. "Of course, not too many police chiefs come out of retirement to catch a serial killer." He shook his close-cropped head, wide mouth arched in a grin. "You sure you won't come back to help us in Homicide a couple of days a week? I still have you classified as an inspector."

O'Riley shook his head. "Not just yet. But I won't rule it out. Whatever it takes to get Sergeant Driscoll's blood pressure up to dangerous levels."

"Off the record, I hear that's the game plan of every detective down there," said Perry, running a knuckle along his salt-and-pepper moustache.

"What's the reason for the dress blues?" O'Riley asked, eyes fixed on the gold trim on the chief's uniform.

"The reason's you. You know that new training center going up under the Poplar Avenue viaduct?"

"Sure. Costing eight million bucks, right?"

Perry nodded. "Plus change. Anyway, its official name is going to be the Chief Joe O'Riley Police Training Center."

"You're kidding," O'Riley said.

"Bring him on in, John," yelled Perry to his administrative assistant, who quickly ushered *The Commercial Appeal* photographer into the room. "Come back here behind my desk, Joe."

The two shook hands and smiled as the camera flashed. Black spots danced in O'Riley's eyes.

"Thanks, guys," said the photographer as he left. "You'll be in the funnypapers tomorrow."

"I don't know what . . . what to say, Charlie," O'Riley stammered. "I'm honored, I'm embarrassed. I thought you had to be dead to have something named after you."

"You deserve it, Joe. This department wouldn't be what it is if it weren't for you, and you know it." He planted a firm hand on O'Riley's shoulder.

"I better let you get back to work," said O'Riley, trying to hide his pleasure. He held out his hand. "Thank you, Charlie, from the bottom of my heart. I'll never forget this."

Perry gripped O'Riley's hand. "Not so fast. You're not gettin' off the hook that easy. The boys down in Homicide have a cake for you. I'm the escort. You might as well dump the doughnuts."

"Cake for breakfast," O'Riley said. "I've had worse."

"Maybe not," added Perry. "Harris made it."

O'Riley stopped dead in his tracks, clutching the box to his chest. "Dump 'em, hell! You eat cake. I'm eating doughnuts."

9

"I'm not selling my house," Jim Hale said from the back seat of his son-in-law's Toyota Avalon. His handsome, square-jawed face flushed red as he gritted his teeth. "Don't forget. I'm still the parent and you're the child. You remember that." He ran a hand through his blond hair, thick for a man of fifty.

"We're not saying you have to move, Dad. Just think about it. The doctor said it might be best. Our house is plenty big for all three of us. Isn't it, David?" said Jim's daughter, Sarah, sitting beside her husband, David Dern, in the front seat.

"There's more than enough room for you, Jim," replied David, "as long as you don't take over my favorite recliner." He winked in the rear-view mirror at his father-in-law. Two against one in an attempt to humor Sarah. He turned the car west onto Southern Avenue and cracked the driver's side window, sending a breeze throughout the sedan. The balmy air hinted an approach of rain.

Sarah flinched as the sudden burst of air mussed her curly brown hair. With her slender form, olive complexion, and hazel eyes, she looked just like her mother who had died three years earlier.

"How are the treatments going, Jim?" David asked.

"Not bad. Two down, two to go."

"Can you tell any change?"

Jim's blue eyes lit up, eyebrows arching. "Actually, I don't seem to be forgetting things anymore. Or, at least, not so much. I think this Dr. Morgan's on to something."

"That's great." David turned to his wife. "Honey, why didn't you tell me?"

"There's still a ways to go," she replied softly as her husband eased through a green light past the Memphis Country Club. "I don't want anybody to get up any false hopes. David," she shouted, "turn here!"

"Damn," he said, thumping his chest as he jerked the car north onto Goodwyn, "you trying to give me a heart attack?"

"Don't be silly. Sometimes you act like some of my second-graders at P.D.S. I wanted Dad to see some of these beautiful old homes."

"Sarah," Jim said from the back seat, pointing a finger, "you're not going to buy a new house just so I can have my own little private home out back where you can care for me. I'm gonna lick this Alzheimer's thing. You hear me?"

Sarah stared up through the sun roof, ignoring her father's remark. "I had hoped after those morning showers we'd have some clear skies," she said. "I guess I was wrong."

A bank of puffy, grey thunderheads loomed above, turning the daylight into dusk. The huge old trees along Goodwyn swayed to and fro, dancing in the stiff breezes.

"Pull over," Sarah said. "I want to look at that house for a minute." The car plowed to a stop on the right side of the two-lane road. "I love not having sidewalks along here. Wouldn't it be nice to live in that house?" She pointed to an ornate, blue stucco just ahead. "Dad, your antique would feel right at home parked along here."

He figured the two-story mansion with its guest house was of 1920s vintage. A wrought-iron fence circled the property. The second floor opened onto a covered balcony that afforded an unobstructed view of the manicured Memphis Country Club golf course across the street.

"How would you like to call that guest house home, Dad?" said Sarah, staring at the mansion. "Enough room for you?"

Jim sat in the back seat, cross-legged, one shoe tapping the floorboard, gaze fixed on an old street lamp near the driveway entrance to the property.

"I'm sure your father would love it here, Sarah, but there's one little problem. Other than it not being for sale, it would cost about $800,000 more than we could afford. Upkeep on the yard alone would probably put me in bankruptcy," said David, his voice edgy as he flicked on the windshield wipers to erase droplets of rain.

Jim kept staring at the street light, listening to the swoosh-swoosh of the wipers. Suddenly the street light blinked on, responding to the darkening skies. A blinding white light flashed through his mind.

Before him, parked on the left side of the road, was a maroon 1937 Cord sedan. Its passenger door flew open and a young dark-haired woman fell halfway out. An athletic young man grabbed her and yanked her back in, slamming the door shut. Jim heard a thud and the almost musical chiming of glass fragments bouncing onto the pavement.

"Dad . . . Dad. What's the matter?"

The vision turned hazy, like scenes from a half-forgotten movie, a movie where the actors, the ending, even the title could hardly be remembered. Then it vanished, no match for Sarah's high-pitched voice. "I'm okay," Jim replied, his forehead a mass of wrinkles.

"You looked like you were in a trance or something."

He shook his head, puzzled. "It's just that . . . I've been here before."

"Of course you have," said Sarah, "we've driven down this street loads of times."

"No, I don't mean like that. A long, long time ago."

Sarah and David shot a concerned glance at one another.

Heavy raindrops spattered the windshield and tree branches rocked back and forth in a frenzy, losing leaves that swirled into the whipping wind.

"We better head home," said David, as rain pounded the sedan's grey metal body. "The bottom's about to drop out."

As they drove home, Jim sat silently. In the middle of rumbling thunder and flashing bolts of lightning, he realized one thing—he had not imagined his vision. He had actually seen it. A part of a past unknown to him had joined with the present.

*

Six days later, Jim lay on his bed in Dr. Peter Morgan's experimental treatment recovery room at St. Jude Children's Hospital after undergoing the third of his four treatments. The row of six rollaway beds, normally used for children receiving chemotherapy, had been designated on Wednesdays for Dr. Morgan's patients. Each bed had a wall-mounted television to entertain participants during the three-hour recovery period following treatment, as well as stacks of magazines on bedside tables. Pink curtains could be pulled between the beds for privacy, but none of the patients chose to use them, preferring instead conversation with fellow volunteers in the experiment.

Jim lay on the fourth of the six beds. Today he noticed for the first time a woman to his far right who had changed from her blue surgical gown into street clothes. Trim and attractive, shapely, she was about forty, he guessed, with oval eyes accentuated by a light dusting of make-up, as was her mouth, its corners slightly lined with smile wrinkles. Blond hair, gently curled, barely touched her slender shoulders.

She passed down the row of beds on her way out, saying goodbye to the old man next to Jim. Then she glanced at him, smiling politely.

A shiver ran up his spine as he looked into her soft, blue-green eyes.

"Cute girl, ain't she?" said the short, lean old man, scratching his two-day-old stubble.

"She sure is," Jim replied. "But . . . I feel like I've seen her somewhere. It's the eyes. There's just something about her."

"I'm seventy-eight," the old man said with a grin and a shake of his head, "and, at my age, there's something about nearly every woman. Especially blonds. I just can't do anything about it."

Jim chuckled, eyes burning with curiosity. "Do you know anything about her?"

"A little. I talked to her for a good hour after the first treatment a couple of weeks back. Our recovery room time overlapped and her bed was next to mine. Like me and you. I got so excited talking to her I'd a gotten a hard-on, that is, if I could still get a hard-on." He sighed, his concave chest heaving. "Time passes, and everything goes with it."

"What happened to her? She's not old enough to have Alzheimer's."

"Accident. Car wreck about twenty years ago, right after college. Name's Jean King. Graduated from a school with a V in it. Virginia, Vermont, one of 'em. I forget. Ha! Guess I need another treatment, don't I? Wreck wiped out her memory of school. All of it, all gone."

"I've never been one to be attracted to younger women. I must be at least ten years older," Jim said, shaking his head. "She married?"

"Nope. Lives with her parents. Said she's a photographer. How 'bout that? Guess I remember more than I think. You married?"

"My wife died three years ago. Cancer."

"Well, by golly, if you ain't married, age don't mean nothing. I'd hop on the chance to meet her if I was you. I can't hop on nothing 'cept the toilet."

Jim grinned. "I think I just might have to meet her next week."

"Last chance," snapped the old man, turning back to the television.

Jim reached over to the magazine table by his bed and picked up a three-week-old *Time* with Adam Baldwin's picture on the cover. *The Paul Newman of American Politics—Adam Baldwin Grasps For The Presidential Brass Ring*, read the caption. He glanced nonchalantly at the article's photos until he focused on a high school picture of Baldwin. His eyes widened. It was the face of the man in his vision.

"My God!"

"What's the matter?" the old man asked, turning from the television.

"It's a long story," replied Jim, "and you'd probably think I was nuts."

"I might think you're nuts, but hell, who ain't?"

"You know something?" said Jim. "We don't even know each other's names."

"Hank, Hank Kearny," said the old man. "Nice to know you, son."

Jim reached for Kearny's gnarled hand and grasped it firmly. "I'm Jim Hale."

"Now, you were saying?"

"Hank, do you think these treatments are having any effect?"

"To be honest, Jim, I'm doing *damn* good. I hadn't woken up once in the middle of the night and not been able to find the bathroom. I swore my son's house didn't have one. I could never find it when I needed it. Since we started these treatments, I found three of 'em! And that stuff I told you about Jean King. Before, I wouldn't a remembered her name two minutes after I heard it." The old man took a labored breath and continued, "Tell me, Jim, you're a youngster compared to me. What kind of problems were you having before these treatments?"

"Well, I started to forget the names of customers and procedures at work. I'm a clothing salesman so that put me in a pretty bad light. And when I drove around town—sometimes I'd forget where I was going and how to get home."

"That *is* a problem. I'm glad you're not driving me to these sessions!" Both men smiled nervously, haunted by the shadow of the disease. "Let me ask you," Hank said. "Are these treatments doing you any good?"

"On one hand, my mind seems as clear now as it ever was," Jim replied. "I don't seem to forget anything. But . . ." He inhaled deeply. "Do you promise you won't think I'm crazy?"

Kearny tilted his chin to peer over wire-framed glasses. "Go on, shoot."

Jim let out his breath. "I've seen something that wasn't there. Not something that I imagined. I mean, I felt like I had lived what I saw. Like before I was born. Maybe in another life. Tell me now, does that sound crazy?"

Hank Kearny's dark-brown eyes brightened. "To be honest, Jim, ever since we started these treatments, I been having this same dream, or what I thought was a dream. I'm looking all around me and all I see is devastation. Except for this big building on top of a hill. There's fires and smoke and people wandering all around. Looks like a hundred years ago. The women have on long dresses . . ."

"I've seen pictures of a scene like that when I visited San Francisco. During the Great Earthquake of 1906, all that was left on Nob Hill was the Fairmont Hotel. Everything else was rubble."

Kearny's gaunt cheeks wrinkled as he winced. "I don't know about that. I never paid much attention to history. All I know is I just keep flashing back to this vision. Sometimes I'm asleep, other times I'm just sitting in my chair at home. I've even seen it while I was being driven down here to the hospital. Most of the time it has sounds, but sometimes it's like I'm watching a silent movie. It's weird—like I'm right there. I can feel the heat and smell the smoke and let me tell you, I feel the fear, too. Then a middle-aged man with a handlebar moustache and a derby takes me by the hand. And sometimes a lady in a long pink dress with white trim holding a pink parasol comes up and tells me not to cry. She says they'll find my parents. She hugs me, but I can't stop crying. Then I wake up or snap out of it."

"Incredible," Jim said, dark blond eyebrows raised. "You think this is happening to all of us?"

Kearny ran a hand through the remnants of his grey hair and shook his head. "I know it ain't, 'cause I already told three others here about it, and they looked at me like I was on furlough from the funny farm. What do you think's going on?"

"I don't know, Hank. I just don't know. Something *real* strange, that's for sure." He paused.

Kearny looked over, motioning for Jim to continue.

"As crazy as this may sound, I think these treatments are somehow affecting our brains, some of us, anyway. I think we're seeing things that happened to us in previous lives."

"You sure you ain't been nipping the sauce before you came down here today?" Kearny asked with a half-smile.

Jim shook his head. "Course not. How else can you explain what's going on?"

Kearny cackled. "Hell, maybe before this is over I'll be on *Oprah* with them sons who found out their sisters were really their mothers!"

Jim muffled a laugh as an attractive young nurse walked up to the old man's bed. "You can put on your regular clothes now, Mr. Kearny," she said, pulling her short black hair behind her ear.

"Show me where," he said, sitting up. The nurse pointed to a door. "Can you come in and help me get my pants on?" he asked with a sly smile.

"Mr. Kearny!" the nurse said. "You had your fun with that last time."

"See you next week, Jim," Kearny whispered as he shuffled off. "We'll each do some investigating and then compare notes." He took one last look at the nurse who was bending over another patient. "You know what they say," he called out with a grin, "if you ain't thinking about it ninety-five percent of the time, your mind's wandering."

The next afternoon Jim sat in his navy Oldsmobile, parked on Goodwyn near the wrought-iron fence surrounding the blue stucco mansion his daughter had liked so much.

Hoping his vision would reappear, he waited. The sun crept in and out from behind clouds high in the sky. The air conditioner droned on monotonously, warding off the ninety-degree heat. He stared at the street lamp and at the patch of road where the Cord had appeared, his gaze steady for three full hours.

By sunset, he decided to go home. Tired, his stomach growling with hunger pangs, he looked to his gear shift before glancing one last time at the street lamp.

His field of vision suddenly burst into a flash of white light. As it slowly faded, he spotted the 1937 maroon Cord parked by the street lamp, exactly as before. Only this time, the boy and girl got out of the car and walked slowly down the street. He swigged from a liquor bottle and took the girl's hand. They stopped, kissed one time, then walked back to the car. Adam Baldwin looked just like the magazine picture, only slightly older. The college-age girl was wearing a maroon floral-print dress. They got back in the Cord.

The couple soon appeared to be fighting. The door flung open and the girl fell halfway out. Then she was snatched back and the passenger door silently slammed shut. Suddenly the girl's head shattered the window.

The man looked about anxiously for a few minutes and abruptly opened his door, vomiting. He then started the car and drove off.

Jim felt a tug at his arm. Sitting next to him was an unfamiliar girl. He gazed, astonished, at her blue-green eyes.

He blinked, and she was gone. But the image of her eyes was seared into his memory. The eyes of Jean King.

10

"How's it going, Chief Joe?" said E., squinting into the bright, late afternoon sunlight.

"Pretty good, E., pretty good," replied O'Riley as he walked down the front steps of the police headquarters building and took a seat on the shoeshine man's weathered chair.

A city bus pulled to a stop at the corner, brakes whining. Its hydraulic door whooshed open to take on a passenger before rumbling off, belching diesel fumes into the sticky air.

"Be glad when those things go electric," E. said, wrinkling his nose.

"Don't hold your breath," O'Riley replied. "We'll both be long gone by then."

"Speak for yourself," E. said, white eyebrows bobbing.

"If you don't mind me asking, how old are you?"

"I'm old as the Buffalo nickel. You knows anything about coins?"

"I used to collect nickels when I was a kid. Jeffersons came out in 1938. *That* was a good year. I remember when I got my first one. After school one day at Fortune's on Belvedere. You remember Fortune's, E.?"

"Yessir. Us old folks remember places like that. Sometimes I'd chauffeur the family I worked for into town for ice cream. They had a big ol' Cadillac I sho' did love to drive."

"The day I got that new nickel, I was with my two best friends, Will Harrison and Jenny Adair. They were killed in a car accident not long after we graduated from high school," O'Riley said, surprised by the melancholy in his voice.

"How'd it happen?" asked E., flicking a knuckle across the tip of his nose as if it were running.

"Couldn't ever tell for sure. It was in Overton Park. They just seemed to run off the road into a tree. Car exploded on impact. Wasn't much left by the time I got there. Just a smoldering shell of a Model A sedan. I was a rookie cop back then. Don't think I've ever gotten over losing those two." O'Riley leaned back in the chair and closed his eyes.

E. buffed the soft tan leather of O'Riley's Rockports and hummed a few bars of *Swing Low, Sweet Chariot.* Then he glanced up at O'Riley. "Back to how old I am, Chief. Buffalo nickels."

O'Riley's eyes opened wide, locking onto E.'s. "1913 . . . damn. I can't believe it. Almost ninety. No way I'm making it that far. I'll be taking a dirt nap by then." He checked his watch.

"Go on—I ain't stopping you." E. grinned. "I'm done. Your shoes can't get nicer than they is now."

"Thanks, as always, for the shine. See you next time." O'Riley stuffed a five-dollar bill into the old man's hand and walked down the sidewalk past the Fire Museum to his black Continental.

He drove across the Auction Street bridge to Mud Island and soon stood in a heavily wooded area at the island's northern tip, the waters of the Mississippi River lapping at his feet.

The afternoon heat was stifling. Sweat dripped down his barrel chest, staining his light blue knit shirt. He felt as if he were wearing a down jacket. He swept a hand through his silver-streaked hair and then planted it, balled in a fist, on the waist of his khaki slacks.

A warm breeze, like one late in the summer after his high school graduation, kissed his face, transporting him.

"I . . . love you," he had whispered, surprised he had finally summoned the courage.

"Oh, Joey, this is really hard," Allison Tucker had replied, her forehead wrinkling as if gazing at an injured pet, her green eyes soft and empathetic. "I love you, too, but . . ." She fingered the gold script necklace bearing her name. "As a friend. Remember? I don't mean to hurt you. I wouldn't do that for the world." She had taken his hand in hers and squeezed.

Joey had nodded, squeezing back, staring at the ground as an emptiness gripped his heart.

O'Riley sighed, remembering. Long lost pangs of love, diminished by the years, still struggled within him.

Grass along the bank, tan from the oppressive heat, contrasted with the verdant green at river's edge that benefited from the constant rush of brown water against the shore. Small eddies and whirlpools danced on the surface of the treacherous waters, threatening to devour any object at a moment's notice, sucking it under, later loosening its hold down river in Tunica, Vicksburg, or New Orleans. If at all.

Had that been what happened to Allison Tucker? Could it have been a kidnapping? Raped, beaten, and left for dead in a field across the river in Arkansas? Murdered and the remains set afire? Run away from home? Not her.

For over fifty years her fate had vexed him. He could accept what happened to Jenny and Will. Heard about a car wreck. Model A. Two fatalities. Went to the scene. The shock. The pain. How it happened, he didn't know. Resigned himself to the fact he never would. But the case of Allison Tucker was different.

He lost count of the number of times he looked for clues. His first case. Unsolved. The trail always led to a dead end. He backed off physically for years, but mentally he couldn't shake it. It stuck to him like a tattoo, even in retirement.

Retirement had given him plenty of time to think. To renew his search.

O'Riley turned and walked back to his car, parked at the end of the island access road. He paused a moment and bent to pick up a smooth flat rock imbedded in the dusty trail. He grunted, heaving it side-armed in frustration at the rushing water. It skipped twice, then vanished. Just like Allison Tucker.

11

"Mr. Hale," a buxom, red-haired nurse repeated, "you really better change. Your daughter is here to pick you up. We've got others who'll need the dressing room in a few minutes."

"Just one more second," Jim replied as he sat on the end of Jean King's bed. "Saturday night at seven?" he asked, his tone soft, face reddening slightly.

Jean pursed her lips. "I'll look forward to it." Dimples framed the corners of her mouth.

"I'm usually not this bashful," Jim confessed. "It's just that I haven't done this in about twenty-five years."

"That's sweet," she said, displaying flawlessly straight white teeth. "I'm honored, really, I am."

"I'll see you then." Jim stood and walked toward the dressing area.

After slipping on his black slacks and cream silk shirt, he headed back to the recovery room. "Saturday," he said with a smile as he passed Jean's bed.

"We'll celebrate our treatments being over," she replied, tucking a blond curl behind her ear.

A familiar voice called from the last bed. "Way to go, Romeo."

"Hank. When did they wheel you in?"

"A couple of minutes ago. Looks like you took my advice," the old man said with a wink.

"I sure did." Jim paused by Kearny's bed.

"Well, I checked up on what we talked about."

"You looked up the San Francisco earthquake?"

Kearny's craggy face wrinkled. "Hell no. I ain't no candy-ass. I flew out there on my own."

Jim frowned. "Your son didn't go with you?"

"He didn't even know where I was until I called him up from the Fairmont Hotel. Scared shit out of the whole family. They thought I was lost somewhere on the streets of Memphis, but I showed 'em. Came back the next day. The only problem was the thousand-dollar airfare I put on my son's Visa. But he can take it. He's a lawyer. I gigged him, so now he'll have to gig one of his clients a little more to make up for it." The old man laughed.

Jim grinned and shook his head. "Did you find out anything?"

"You bet your ass I did," Kearny replied, slapping his mattress. "I'll be damned if you weren't right, you S.O.B. They got a hallway in the old section of the hotel with these huge, blown-up pictures of the area around the Fairmont after the big quake in 1906. Would you believe it was just like in my vision? I was there in another life, no doubt about it. I just sat down in a chair in that hallway, stared at them photographs, and started flashing back like I put a five-cent piece in a nickelodeon. I still can't believe it. How 'bout you?"

"My story's about like yours. I went back to the place I saw in my vision. It took a while, but it finally appeared. There weren't any sounds or noises like in the first one, but it lasted longer this time. Seems to be from the late 1940s." He paused. "I saw a girl get killed."

Kearny smacked a loose fist into his open palm. "How'd she get knocked off? Shot? Stabbed?"

"Blow to the head."

"A hammer? Tire iron? Shovel?" Kearny's droopy eyes lit up as if taking part in a crime program on television.

"She was in an old Cord with a guy who smashed her head against the window."

"That'll do it every time," said the old man. "Did you see who did it?"

78

"I could pick him out," Jim cautiously replied, "if I saw a picture of him."

"Have you thought of telling the police?"

"Nah. They'd just label me some looney tune."

"Aw, c'mon, Jim," Kearny said. "You know that old saying, 'You only go around once in life.' What if that's a crock? We may go around two, three, four, hell, I don't know, maybe ten times. Think about it."

"You have a unique way of putting things into perspective," Jim said, patting Kearny on a bony shoulder.

"Seriously, you should go to the cops," Kearny said, pointing a crooked finger. "Murder is murder."

"And if they take me straight to the nuthouse and lock me up," Jim said, smiling, "are you gonna come see me on visitors' day?"

"No problem," Kearny replied, laughing. "I'll be the one carrying the cake with the file and hacksaw inside."

"Here's my phone number." Jim handed a slip of paper to Kearny. "You call me if you get a chance."

12

The next day at noon, Jean King and her mother sat inside the Buntyn Restaurant on Southern Avenue, just east of the Memphis Country Club. The old, white-painted storefront with large plate-glass windows, originally a dry-goods store, had been converted during the late 1940s into a cafe serving home-style plate lunches and dinners. At the peak of lunch hour, the restaurant was packed.

"Tell me about this date you have on Saturday night," Dot King said.

"He is so good-looking, Mother," Jean replied. "Dark blond hair, piercing blue eyes, nice build. Just tall enough. About six feet, I guess. Kinda reminds me of Robert Redford."

"A younger Robert Redford? Like, your age?"

"No, he's . . . older."

Mrs. King paused in mid-bite. "How old is he?"

"About fifty or so," Jean replied.

"Land sakes, Jean, he's not married is he?"

She shook her head. "Widowed. I found that out from an old man in my treatment group at St. Jude."

"And you don't think he's too old for you?"

"Mother, if you haven't noticed, men aren't beating the door down to ask me out."

"It's not because of your looks. You just don't make yourself available."

Jean let out a sigh. "There's something about him. I can't put my finger on it. He's just real attractive to me for some reason," she said, staring out the window at a slow-moving freight train.

"I'm not a big believer in love at first sight, but you sure seem to have fallen under this man's spell."

"Oh, Mother, don't be silly." Jean poked at a side order of black-eyed peas. She put down her fork and reached for one of Buntyn's famous rolls. "Calories be damned," she said. Suddenly her eyes widened.

"Grillswith!" she said.

"Grillswhat?" her mother asked, eyes wide as Jean's.

"Grillswith," Jean repeated, placing the roll on her plate. "From the University Diner in Charlottesville. We ate them all the time when I was at UVA. The cook would drop a doughnut on the grill, flip it over, and plop a big scoop of vanilla ice cream on top. They called it a grillswith. Must've had about four thousand calories."

Mrs. King put her fork down. "Jean," she said carefully, "do you remember anything else?"

"Poe's," she replied. "I used to drink beer there." Memories began to pour back through the disintegrating barriers in her mind like water rushing through cracks in an old earthen dam.

"Is that all?"

"No, there's more. The Corner. That's where Poe's and a bunch of stores were. Eljo's. Mincer's Pipe Shop. The Virginian. Unicaf—that's what we called the University Cafeteria for short. The Mousetrap. University Hall. That's where the basketball team played." She spoke with a gleam in her eyes.

"Anything else?"

"The best resort was The Boar's Head Inn. And Miss Ida's dumpy little restaurant out Route 250 West. It was in an old gas station. Just a cut above dog food."

"I'd say those treatments at St. Jude are helping you quite a bit."

Jean blotted her mouth with a napkin and placed it on the green-and-white checkerboard tablecloth. "I'm so excited I can't eat."

"Me, too," her mother said, a smile on her puffy face. "I can't wait to tell your father."

They got up and Mrs. King handed the woman at the register a twenty-dollar bill.

"How was everything today?" the elderly cashier with a beehive hairdo asked.

"Better than you'll ever know," Mrs. King replied, quickly stuffing the change into her brown leather purse.

Jean and her mother left the restaurant elated, each lost in thought. Mrs. King drove her blue Cadillac down Southern past the red-brick wall of the Memphis Country Club before turning north on Goodwyn.

"Drat," Mrs. King said, catching her glasses as they fell from her nose. "It's that little screw that holds the left arm on, I just know it." She eased the car to the side of the road. "Do you mind driving home, honey? I'm blind as a bat without these things."

Jean nodded. "I've put more miles on your car than you have."

Mrs. King got out. "Just scoot on over. I'll go around."

Jean slid across the seat to the monotonous dinging that signaled an open door with keys still in the ignition and focused on a street lamp across the road near the iron fence of an Italian-style blue stucco mansion.

Mrs. King quickly slammed the door and walked around behind the car.

The slamming sound suddenly created a blinding flash in Jean's mind, followed by darkness. The street lamp now illuminated an antique maroon car that shone in the darkness. The passenger door flew open and a young girl struggled with a handsome young man, who yanked her back into the car and slammed the door. The struggle continued until the girl's head smashed against the car window, shattering it. Glass danced in slow motion as it bounced off the pavement, ringing in high-pitched musical notes before settling into a silent mass on the deserted street.

Jean looked on in horror as the girl thrashed about wildly, then slumped against the car door.

Hands quivering, Jean looked away. Beside her was the face of an ash-blond, blue-eyed young man she had never seen before.

"Jean," Mrs. King said from the passenger seat. "What's wrong?"

Jean was staring out the driver's side window into the bright sunlight that streamed through the trees, left hand pressed against the glass as if holding on to someone. She turned toward her mother. "Nothing," she said, "I . . . was just remembering something. I must've been daydreaming."

"About Virginia?" her mother asked, frowning.

"How'd you know?" Jean replied, not wanting to reveal what she'd just experienced. "It was something else from college." She rubbed her eyes for a moment.

Mrs. King tilted her head, still frowning. "Dear, are you positive you're all right?"

"It's so strange," Jean mumbled. "I've been here before. A long time ago." She slipped the car into gear and drove down Goodwyn toward Central Avenue.

"Of course you have. We go down this street whenever we leave Buntyn's. You know, maybe your father and I should postpone our trip for a few weeks. Until you're feeling better."

Jean shot a disapproving glance. "Don't be silly, Mother, I'm fine. You and Dad always go to Captiva Island this time of year. You'll be home by Thanksgiving. I can take care of myself. Don't take this wrong, but I seem to come up with my best photographs in the fall, when I can be alone with my thoughts."

"No offense taken," Mrs. King said. "I know how you creative people are."

As they turned west onto Central, Jean was sure she had witnessed a murder. But from the looks of the car, it had to have happened years before she was born. How could that be? And who was the boy she had turned to?

13

O'Riley leaned forward in the swivel chair near the Homicide Department's entrance, nursing a cup of coffee, lost in the sports section spread out on the desk before him. Just then the clear glass double doors swung open. O'Riley looked up as a man entered.

"What can I do for you?" the young officer manning the old wooden entry counter asked.

"My name is Jim Hale," the man said. "I have information about a murder."

O'Riley put down his coffee cup and leaned back, measuring the man with a stare. Maybe fifty. Attractive. Well-groomed. No wedding ring. Stylish taupe slacks and a black blazer. Appeared normal enough.

"When did this murder occur, sir?" the entry officer asked.

"I'm not exactly sure but I think in the late forties, like 1948 or 1949."

"Excuse me?" the officer said.

"I think 1948 or 1949," Jim repeated.

A smile spread across the officer's face. "Hey," he yelled, turning to the detectives' desks behind him. "Who's taking care of murders from the forties this week?"

The six detectives and O'Riley looked at one another, eyebrows raised, waiting for the punch line.

"Hey, Harris," the officer called out. "How about you?"

"Nah," replied the sergeant, running his thumbs down his maroon suspenders. "I solved all those cases from the twenties last week by myself. Give it to Mills."

Sergeant Trevor Mills stood and adjusted the knot in his tie. "Sorry, I can't stay and play," he said, slipping a Zegna sportcoat over his broad shoulders. "Gotta question a guy downstairs who found his brother shot and stabbed. Said it looked like suicide." Mills grinned. "Shouldn't take long." He hooked a thumb in O'Riley's direction. "Give it to him. At least he was alive back then."

O'Riley pushed the newspaper aside. "So I'm the lucky one, eh? Like the leper with the most fingers." He motioned to Jim. "C'mon over here."

Jim sat down on a small, wooden chair next to the desk, and for five minutes provided all the personal information required on the police report. The next five minutes were spent recalling the pertinent details of his seemingly farfetched story.

"So let me get this straight," O'Riley said, putting his pencil down and exhaling deeply. "What you saw, or better yet, what you think you saw was Adam Baldwin and a girl walking hand in hand. They get back in the car after kissing or whatever, and the guy smashes the girl's head against the car window, which breaks. Her body partially flops out of the car door, which opens from the force of the blow. The guy pulls the girl back in, shuts the door, and splits."

"No," Jim said, head shaking emphatically. "The girl fell out first, trying to escape. He yanks her back in, slams the door, smashes her head against the window, then drives off. I snapped out of it then."

"Snapped out of it?"

"The vision."

O'Riley crooked his neck. "Vision? So this just appeared out of thin air?"

"That's right."

"Where were you?" O'Riley asked.

"Sitting in a car on Goodwyn, over near the Memphis Country Cl—"

"Yeah, yeah, I know where Goodwyn is. In this vision, what kind of car was the guy in?"

"Have you ever seen a Cord?"

"Seen a Cord? Hell, yes," replied O'Riley. He rubbed a finger along the fading scar on the left side of his forehead. Adam Baldwin had a maroon Cord in high school, he thought to himself. "Tell me, what color was this Cord?"

"Maroon."

O'Riley's brow wrinkled for a moment. Just long enough for him to discount the answer as coincidence. "Now was the guy you saw about seventy? You know, did he look like the guy who's running for president?"

"Look, officer—"

"Do me a favor. I hate to be called officer. I used to be an officer. I'm retired now. So I'm not an officer anymore. I used to be six feet in my prime. I got older. I shrank to five-eleven. I'm not six feet anymore. Get it?"

"I'm not sure," Jim replied, propping an ankle on his knee. "What do I call you? Mr. Inch Shorter?"

O'Riley smiled for the first time during their conversation. "Most people call me Joe, just plain Joe, or an assortment of names behind my back. Why don't you just call me Joe?"

"Well, to answer your question, *Joe*, the guy I saw was Adam Baldwin, but not as he is today. In his late teens."

"How do you know it was Baldwin?"

"I saw a picture of him in a *Time* magazine article—a high school picture. Looked just like the guy in my vision."

"Looked like?"

Jim tilted his head, frowning. "Okay, it *was* the guy in my vision."

O'Riley rubbed the scar on his forehead again. "You know a lot about old cars?"

"More than most people."

"You sure the car was a Cord?"

Jim rolled his eyes. "Officer, er—Joe. I'm positive. I know about antique cars. Packards, Lincolns, Cadillacs, Auburns. You name it. I'm driving one right now."

"No shit?"

"No shit."

"What is it?"

"A Model A Ford."

"Tudor sedan?"

"No, Fordor."

"Deluxe?"

"Nope. Standard model."

O'Riley's eyes were wide, a grin from ear to ear. "What color is it?" He folded his hands on a legal pad.

"The fenders and top are black, like the trim around the windows. The body is navy blue."

"What about the body striping? And the spoked wheels?"

"Cream."

"Son of a bitch," O'Riley said, pounding his fist on the desk. The detectives looked up at the sudden noise. "That's just like the car my best friend had back in the late forties. Mind if I go out and take a look?"

"Are we finished with my report?"

"I got all the info. If I have any other questions, I'll give you a call. I got your number. Let's go see that car." Prodding Jim toward the door emblazoned with black block letters three inches high that spelled HOMICIDE, O'Riley looked back with a quizzical glance at the detectives who had been straining to hear Jim's revelations.

Four of them grinned and tapped their temples meaningfully.

Jim and O'Riley quickly walked down the white marble staircase to the first floor lobby and emerged from the building, both squinting in the bright sunlight.

"There it is." Jim smiled, pointing to the gleaming Model A parked near E.'s shoeshine stand.

"What do you think of that, E.?" O'Riley asked as they passed.

"Brings back memories," E. said, taking refuge from the heat under a big, rainbow-paneled umbrella.

"I'll be damned." O'Riley shook his head slowly as Jim opened the front passenger door. "This is just like Will Harrison's old car." He rubbed his hand across the brown wool ceiling fabric. "Floating gas gauge, right?" he asked, staring at the nickel-plated dashboard.

Jim nodded.

Awash with memories, O'Riley examined the levers on the steering column. "Spark on the left, hand throttle on the right?"

"You got it," replied Jim. He sat in the driver's seat, switched on the ignition key, and pressed the starter button on the floor with his right foot.

Urrrr, urrrrr, urrrr. The engine strained, then turned over.

"After all these years," O'Riley said, "that noise still sounds familiar."

"You know where to find me, Joe, if anything comes up," Jim said, slipping the stick shift into gear.

"Sure," the former chief replied. "If something comes up, I'll call you." He slammed the car door shut and waved as the relic from the past pulled away.

Jim hit the horn button and waved into the rear-view mirror. *Ah-ooh-gah, ah-ooh-gah*, echoed down the street, scaring pigeons into flight.

O'Riley's mouth dropped open. "Holy Mary, mother of God." He suddenly remembered seeing Will Harrison drive away in his Model A after dropping him off at home after school. Always honking twice. Always waving in the rear-view mirror.

O'Riley turned and sat in the shoeshine chair. He placed his feet on the stirrups and leaned back, stretching.

"I know you don't need no shine," said E., "cause these is still shining."

O'Riley took a deep breath. "You ever heard or seen or felt something that you never told anybody about, that just eats you up inside?"

"Everybody's got something held back like that, Chief. What you thinkin'?"

"Remember those friends of mine I told you about?"

"You mean the ones killed in the car?"

"Yeah, that's them. Will's Model A was exactly like the one that just pulled off. To this day, I feel bad because I never got to tell them how much they meant to me." The two men sat in uncharacteristic silence until O'Riley asked, "How 'bout you, E.? Anything bother you like that?"

E. raised his white eyebrows, thinking. "We all gots regrets. Things we'd a done different. I'm a truthful man. I always tell the truth. People who lies always get tripped up sooner or later cause they can't remember who they told what to. But this one time, I . . ." He paused, looking down at the sidewalk.

"Didn't tell the truth," said O'Riley.

E. stroked his bony chin with a thumb and forefinger. "Well, you might say I wasn't as truthful as I shoulda been."

"Tell me about it sometime. I promise you'll feel better afterwards."

"We'll see," E. replied.

Within minutes, the former chief was back in Homicide.

"What was that about?" Harris asked as O'Riley sat down.

"The guy claims he knows something about a murder from over fifty years ago."

"How old was he? Looked about fifty himself. My age."

O'Riley nodded.

Harris's eyes lit up. "What an idea for a TV series—Real Life Baby Detective Stories. We'll make a fortune."

"What the hell did you have for breakfast? Prozac and coffee?"

"Just the usual," Harris replied, patting his curved stomach, "bourbon and doughnuts. What about this murder?"

"He said it was some girl, about college age. Dark hair. There's a Cord automobile involved. They were only made in the thirties. At least, the one he's describing. Pegs the time frame, maybe a little later. Says he knows who did it."

Mills, back from his interrogation, looked up from his desk. "Who'd he say?"

"Get this. He fingered the guy who's gonna be the Democratic nominee for president."

Mills half-swallowed. "He thinks Adam Baldwin killed somebody?"

"You got it, Einstein."

"C'mon, gimme a break." Mills rolled his blue eyes. "I know politicians are cutthroat, but not literally."

Harris's bushy black eyebrows joined over his deep-set brown eyes. "That accusation pinpoints him as a possible threat to a presidential candidate. You'll have to notify the Secret Service on this one, Joe, no matter how crazy it seems."

O'Riley shot a look at Mills. "Damn," he muttered, "more paperwork. Do me a favor, will you, Harris?"

"Sure. Name it."

"Run a quick check on the guy in the computer for me." He handed over his notes. "Computers and I don't speak the same language. I'm gonna hit the can."

Minutes later, O'Riley returned to find Sergeant Driscoll sitting at the desk next to Harris. The young Driscoll thought of irritation as an art form, raising it to a level no one else could achieve. No one except O'Riley.

O'Riley typified the old guard police force. Find clues. Make observations. Track leads. Utilize informants. Collar the suspect. Kick his ass. Take his confession. Lock him up.

Driscoll's methods spelled new breed. Today's police. Round up information at the crime scene. Question witnesses. Enter the information into his computer. Pick up the suspect. Scare the hell out of him with computer-ese threats until he confesses.

It wasn't really that easy, but it seemed that way to O'Riley. He didn't like change. But the times and technology had left him by the wayside. He had no one to vent his frustration on. Then he met the new kid on the block. Fresh to Homicide. He decided to blame him. It was a good choice.

Ken Driscoll received a degree in computer technology from the University of Memphis with a 3.96 G.P.A. His proficiency in computer skills mirrored a deficiency in people skills. Crass and disdainful of older individuals, he felt anyone over sixty should be locked up in an old folks' home. Especially retired chiefs with nothing better to do than hang around police headquarters and get in the way.

"Whatcha got for me, Harris?" O'Riley asked.

"Guy's clean, Joe. No arrests, wants, or warrants."

"Look, O'Riley," Driscoll said wearily, "why don't you go home and do whatever it is you retired people do."

"Tell me, smart-ass," O'Riley snapped, face turning red, "just what is it that we retired people do?"

"You know, catch a game show, maybe a little *Oprah*. Take out the garbage. Walk the dog."

"If you don't mind, I happen to be working on a murder case."

Driscoll's jaw dropped. "A murder case? I hoped you were swearing off the force after that last one almost got you killed. From when?"

O'Riley cleared his throat. "Around 1948 or '49."

"Wait a minute," said Driscoll, tugging at his right ear, "I must have punctured an eardrum this morning when I cleaned my ears. I could have sworn you just said 1948 or '49."

"I hope you did puncture an eardrum. And I did say 1948 or '49."

Driscoll's pale face flushed. "You gotta be kidding me. Look, O'Riley, I'm on the streets busting my balls day and night, trying to solve murders, get a little justice. We need all our resources for cases that still mean something. Even if you did solve your . . . case, or whatever the hell you call your wild-goose chase, it won't have any impact on anybody."

If Harris or Mills had said something similar, O'Riley would have agreed. He might even have said it himself. But not coming from Driscoll.

"Look here, Mister Shit-For-Brains," O'Riley said, "this case'll probably have more impact than any case you'll ever solve."

"Right," Driscoll replied, his thin mouth turned down at the corners. "Maybe I should just retire now so I can become productive." He lit a cigarette and blew a smoke ring upward.

"If I wasn't such a nice guy," O'Riley said, "I'd be tempted to stick a red-hot poker up your ass."

"Wouldn't try it," cautioned Mills with a shake of his head. "You'd probably burn his thumb."

Driscoll sneered amid the muffled laughter from the other detectives and took another drag on his cigarette.

"Those things'll kill you," O'Riley warned. "Do us all a favor and keep it up."

The balding detective flipped his portable desktop shut, grabbed his wrinkled sport coat, and eased over to O'Riley, poking a skinny finger in his face. "Listen, butt-wipe, I ain't arguing with a guy who got a full refund on his brain tax."

O'Riley wrinkled his nose. "Better brush, honey. You smell like an ashtray."

Driscoll turned and stalked out, the Homicide doors swinging behind him.

O'Riley leaned into the window overlooking Adams and braced his hands against the sill, looking down at the street where the Model A had been. His right shoe swung back and forth, its rubber sole squeaking as it skimmed across the concrete floor. "I got a strange feeling about that Hale guy."

14

In St. Louis the next morning, a light drizzle fell as Tom Stafford slammed the door of his black Lincoln stretch limousine and entered the ornate lobby of the Hyatt Regency in Union Station. Tall and muscular, he walked quickly through the lobby, tan raincoat flapping behind him, passing business people, tourists, and a fanned-out army of Secret Service agents.

Noticing the Dierdorf and Hart's restaurant sign in the shopping mall below, his mouth began to salivate.

"A big steak with scrambled eggs would make one helluva breakfast," he mumbled, regretting his bowl of raisin bran, hardly enough to take the edge off the appetite of the former Secret Service agent, now trusted top aide and campaign co-ordinator for Adam Baldwin. Damn shame they don't open until lunch, he thought. We'll be in Chicago by then.

Stafford hurried inside a waiting elevator that whisked him up to Baldwin's fourth-floor suite where three Secret Service agents stood guard. "I'm here to see Topper," he said, using Baldwin's Secret Service code name, derived from the old movie in which a ghost returned to the real world, just as Baldwin had come back from a failed presidential bid to challenge for the presidency.

He knocked on the door three times, paused for a moment, then knocked once more.

"Be right there, Tom," came the relaxed reply from inside. The lock clicked, and the door to the suite opened. "Come on in," said Adam Baldwin with a smile, tying the knot of his bright red Hermès tie.

The elegant suite stank of cigar smoke. Stafford's nose burned at the smell. It was the one thing about Baldwin that Stafford couldn't stand. "Put that damn thing out, will ya?"

Baldwin arched his grey eyebrows, deep grooves forming across his well-tanned forehead. "It relaxes me."

"It also makes your breath stink to everyone you shake hands with."

"That's what Listerine's for."

Stafford followed him into the sitting room. "We've got a big day, Adam. Fifteen hours of speeches, interviews, glad-handing, and backslapping in four cities. Breakfast speech here in St. Louis, lunch in Chicago, afternoon rally in Detroit, and a late dinner speech in Milwaukee. I won't bother you with the cities we hit next week out West. Of course," he continued, taking off his raincoat and placing it on the turquoise sofa, "the week after that we've got your coronation at the convention in New York. You up for the grind?"

"Tom," Baldwin replied, smiling, "I've been waiting my whole life for this particular grind. I'm loving it. I'm *reveling* in it."

"If you're this happy now, I can't wait to see what you're like after you get nominated."

"You can put this in the bank with interest. Whatever I'm like after the nomination, you can triple it after I'm elected." Baldwin slipped on his charcoal suit coat. "Anything I need to know going on in the real world?"

"Oh, the usual assortment of minor problems passed on to us by the Secret Service. Two in particular. The first was a complaint by a young woman in D.C. saying you're the father of her child."

Baldwin threw his head back and laughed. "Great, that makes sixty-eight crank calls this month." He sat down at the large mahogany writing desk. "Let's see, I'm losing count—is that sixteen or seventeen paternity allegations? I only wish I were that virile. On the bright side, paternities are beating the death threats, seventeen to ten. What's the second problem?"

"It came from the Memphis police yesterday morning. Involves a supposed murder from years ago. Some guy named Hale says you were involved. Another wacko."

"Goddammit," Baldwin yelled, his calm political demeanor evaporating like raindrops on a hot summer sidewalk.

Stafford flinched. He knew when Baldwin's radar was on, it was unfailing. The wily politician could spot a ruse to discredit him blindfolded. This was different. Baldwin looked like a trapped animal. Desperate.

"Handle this one right away," Baldwin said, his tone bitter, blue eyes wild with anger. "Personally. Do you hear me?"

"Sure, Adam. No problem," Stafford calmly replied, trying to ease Baldwin's tension. "I'll find out all about it."

Baldwin shot him a look to kill. "You do more than find out about it. You nip it in the bud. Understand? I don't need bullshit allegations. Even false allegations lose votes."

"Adam, relax. You got a speech in thirty minutes. Take a deep breath, will you?" Stafford picked up his raincoat and walked to the door. "I'll make sure this guy won't cause any more problems."

He left Baldwin's room and winked at the three Secret Service agents as he went by. "I'll be back in a few minutes. Don't you guys go anywhere."

"Not a chance," said a red-haired agent. "Even if we wanted to."

Stafford walked to a secluded area of the hallway that offered a good view of the hotel swimming pool below. It was deserted. He pulled a flip-top cellular phone from his raincoat pocket and punched the numbers.

"Hello?" a man's voice answered, deep and deliberate.

"Is that you?"

"Who the hell else do you think's gonna answer my phone?"

"Sorry," whispered Stafford. "Habit. I've got a job. Can you fit it in?"

"Depends."

"Depends on what, the job or the money?"

"You know the answer. I can do any job."

"The money won't disappoint. Take my word for it," Stafford said.

"What do you have?"

"I need surveillance on a guy. Also a situation report and an intelligence report. Tack on a psychological profile for background and personality. I've got to have photo reconstructions of an average day in his life. Where he goes, what he does, how long he's gone, what he buys at the grocery, when he eats. Even when he goes to the goddam bathroom."

"That it?" the voice said with a cigarette rasp.

"Depends," replied Stafford.

"Depends on what?"

"The money."

"If you need to add on to the job?"

"You got it," Stafford replied. "If we're so impressed with your initial work that we want you to add one final touch."

"Same as usual."

15

"Are you always this punctual?" Jean asked as Jim slid into the driver's seat of his navy Oldsmobile.

"I try to be," he replied, starting the car. "Jim's Place sound good?"

"You don't take all your first dates there, do you?"

"That was no joke at the hospital the other day. You really are the first woman I've asked out in more years than I care to remember," Jim said.

"Are you divorced?" she asked, although she already knew the answer.

Jim shook his head. "Widowed. My wife died three years ago. Cancer."

Jean's face tightened, her blue-green eyes turning soft. "I'm so sorry," she said, wishing she had taken Hank Kearny at his word. "Do you have any other family?"

"A daughter," he replied with a nod. "Sarah. She's been a real trooper. Everything happens for a reason. Some good comes out of any situation, no matter how bad. Sometimes you just have to look a little bit harder to find it."

"That's an optimistic way to approach life," Jean said. "I guess all of us from the hospital have to think that way, don't we?" She paused, running a hand through her blond hair, gently patting a few strands into place. "Why were you in the group?"

"Alzheimer's. Early onset. You?"

"An accident. It's a long story."

"We've got all night," Jim said with a grin.

"Do you want the abbreviated version or the long one?"

"Abbreviated's fine for now."

"I was born on January 11, 1962," she began. "An only child. I was spoiled rotten but I didn't know it until I got to college. Before that, I went to St. Mary's. Are you from Memphis originally?"

"All my life," replied Jim.

"Then you know about St. Mary's. Okay, let's see," Jean said, assuming the matter-of-fact tone of someone checking items off a list. "I went to the University of Virginia where I double-majored. Got a B.A. in psychology and sociology in 1984, and was romantically involved for two years with a guy in the UVA Med School. We planned on getting married. Thought we'd wait until he graduated. But the accident happened first."

"Car wreck?"

"Bad one." Jean closed her eyes and shook her head, lowering her voice. "Just a month after I graduated and moved back home. A drunk driver hit me head-on. He died instantly. My seat belt malfunctioned and I went through the windshield."

Jim winced.

"I was in a coma for a month. When I finally came to, the doctors thought I'd have permanent brain damage, but after two years of rehab, the only thing missing was my memory of the years just before the accident. It wiped out every memory of college. The doctors called it retrograde amnesia. Oh yes, one other thing was missing. My fiancé. Couldn't handle the idea of damaged goods," she said, offering a glimpse inside her scarred heart. "I've been pretty wary of men ever since."

Jim smiled. "Until tonight."

Jean returned his smile. "Until tonight."

"What do you do for a living?"

"I'm a photographer. Mainly landscapes. I haven't been real successful. Enough to keep afloat. Doesn't take much. I live with my parents, which isn't too bad. They're in Florida six months out of the year. How about you?"

"I used to work at Oak Hall. Suit salesman." His cheeks puffed as he let out a deep breath. "I'm on leave. A forced medical leave."

She adjusted one of her small silver earrings. "It's like you said. Some good comes out of every situation. If all these things hadn't happened, you and I wouldn't be together tonight."

Jim smiled and nodded as he turned into the restaurant's driveway.

Four large magnolia trees, white-petaled flowers in full bloom, stood in the front yard of the stately old house. The early evening sun lit the terracotta-painted restaurant and its grounds, meticulously landscaped with shrubbery trimmed in animal shapes. Beds of pink and red roses lined the brick walkways.

"This place is gorgeous," Jean said.

They parked and Jim led the way through the carved wooden doors and into the foyer. The maître d' greeted them and took them to a table in the casually elegant Garden Room with its dark green walls, rose-tiled ceiling, and marble columns. Paintings on one wall balanced the windows overlooking a shady back patio on the other.

"How's this?" Jim asked.

"Nice," she replied, easing up to the table, just as he reached to help. Her cheeks blushed slightly. "Sorry. Been doing things for myself too long, I guess."

A waiter brought menus and placed a basket of toasted bread strips next to a flickering candle in the center of the table.

As they made small talk after ordering, Jean thought how handsome Jim looked. Blue eyes. Neatly layered blond hair. Not too long, not too short. And she felt his gaze, penetrating, noticing every detail of her appearance, from the champagne linen pantsuit to the white cotton blouse with ivory lace V-neck and small ivory rose at the point of the V.

Jim's eyes moved from her hands to her lips, then to her eyes. "I know this is going to sound really strange," he said. "I feel like I've known you my whole life."

"That *would* sound strange," Jean replied, "if I didn't have the same feeling about you." The flickering candle cast a gentle light on her face. "I've had it ever since I first saw you at the hospital."

Jim leaned forward. "Tell me. Have the treatments helped you?"

"Help's not the word for it. Try miraculous. The day after the last treatment, all of a sudden, my college days came back. Like a flash bulb popped in my head. I remembered everything—people, places, things I'd done. I couldn't believe it."

Jim sat back in his chair. "So only things came back that you could actually remember?"

"How do you mean?"

"Like, were there any things that . . . well, that you never remembered happening?"

Jean touched a finger to her chin. "Did you?"

Jim glanced sideways. "Twice."

"What things?"

Jean sat spellbound as he told her about the visions of a murder.

"The thing that struck me most," Jim said, "was toward the end of the second time, when I felt a tug on my arm. There was a young woman on my right. Maybe eighteen, nineteen years old. But her eyes," he said, staring directly at Jean, "her eyes looked exactly like yours."

Jean glanced down at her water glass and took a deep breath. Looking up, she said, "I thought I was the only one."

"You had a vision, too?"

"Not just a vision," Jean replied, shaking her head. "I saw exactly what you just described."

In a whisper, she told him how it had happened.

Jim's jaw dropped. "An old man in our group, Hank Kearny, had a vision we figured out was during the San Francisco earthquake of 1906."

Jean smiled. "I remember him. The geriatric Don Juan."

"And now you have a vision that matches mine."

"There's more," Jean said. "When it was over, I was afraid. I reached to my left—"

"As if tugging at someone's arm."

"Yes. And I saw a blond-haired young man looking at me." She looked down. "Then it all vanished. But I had the strangest sensation. I felt as though someone had been with me." She paused and looked at Jim. "You."

Jim took a deep breath. "The way I look at it, either the drug treatment is making us see the same thing or, a side effect is creating visions of past lives. Which would mean that you and I are reliving a shared experience."

"It seems unbelievable. First meeting you, then the vision . . . if you really were the person in my vision, and if I was in yours." They sat in silence as the waiter brought their entrees. Then Jean said, "You and I, we were friends, weren't we? We were the young woman and the young man."

Jim shrugged his shoulders, eyes round. "I don't know any other way to explain it. Let me ask you something else. Do you know who the murderer was?"

"No," Jean replied. "But I can picture him. He had dark hair."

"Would you know him if you saw him?"

"I think so."

Jim reached into his back pocket for his wallet. He took out a small photograph.

Jean's hand flew to her mouth. "That's him!"

"Do you know who he is?"

She shook her head.

"Does the name Adam Baldwin ring a bell?"

"The presidential candidate?"

Jim nodded. "What do you think we should do?" he asked.

"We should notify the police. But they'd think you were crazy if you made an accusation and couldn't back it up. Especially if you tell them why you know Baldwin is a murderer."

"I've already gone to the police," Jim said.

Jean's thin eyebrows arched. "And?"

"A former police chief took down a report. He was more interested in my antique car than he was in my accusation."

"What kind of car?" Jean asked, a smile returning to her face.

"A 1930 Model A Ford sedan."

"What fun," she said.

"I'll take you for a spin sometime. Anyway, the police. They acted like I was nuts. They tried to be polite, but I could sense it. It all sounded so bizarre. Even to me."

"What next?"

"That retired chief—O'Riley's his name—said he'd get back to me if anything comes up. I kind of think he's blowing me off. Can't really blame him. I'd probably act the same way. But I still wish . . ." He pursed his lips.

"I've always heard it's better to keep one's mouth shut and be thought crazy than to open one's mouth and prove it," Jean said, smiling.

Jim laughed. "That's supposed to make me feel better?"

Later, as Jim walked Jean to her front door, she paused and said, "I would ask you in, but my parents are leaving for Florida in the morning and the house is a wreck."

"I'll give you a second chance. You have any plans for next Friday night?"

"If I did, I'd break them," she said, unlocking the door and turning to face him. "I've had a wonderful time."

Jim reached out and slowly pulled her to him. Their mouths met in a long kiss as his hands rose, gently caressing the back of her neck.

"I'll pick you up about six-thirty," Jim whispered. He turned and walked down the porch steps, smiling like an eighth-grader on a first date.

"I'll look forward to it," Jean replied as she went inside. She closed the door, then leaned against it, eyelids shut tight, reliving the kiss.

Suddenly the voice of a kindly man with a deep Irish accent echoed in her mind. "If you ever wish a man to forever fall in love with you," said the voice, "say this verse three times to yourself."

Jean began to recite the words aloud,

> "Thee for me,
> Me for thee
> And for none else."

She repeated it a second time, then a third. A moment later, she opened her eyes, chest rising and falling with each breath. Where had the words and voice come from? And what if Jim was right? What if he was a love from a past life?

16

Jim expertly maneuvered his car along the winding streets of his daughter's neighborhood, turning onto Devon Way. Most Fridays he had dinner with her and his son-in-law. Tonight he would have to take a rain check.

He pulled into the sloping driveway at 6:15 P.M. on the dot, just as Sarah and David were getting out of their grey Avalon. Each carried a brown paper bag.

A lawn sprinkler clackety-clacked in the front yard, shooting a hard spray over the thick, green zoysia under three white birches in the front yard.

"Hi, Dad," Sarah said, walking over as he opened the door.

"How's it going, Jim?" David said.

"If I felt any better, I couldn't stand it," Jim replied, grasping David's hand firmly as Sarah kissed him on the cheek.

"We've been to a matinee and stopped for some take-out at Formosa. Is that okay?" Sarah asked.

"That would have been fine, honey, but I've got to pass tonight. I tried to call to let you know, but your answering machine wasn't on."

"Got a hot date?" David said with a laugh, scratching his balding head.

"Well," Jim replied, "it won't be hot but I *do* have a date."

"Where'd you meet her?" Sarah asked, a smile on her face.

"At the hospital. She took the same treatments I got."

"You dog, you!" David blurted out as he pulled a new pack of Marlboro cigarettes from his shirt pocket.

"I better get going," said Jim. "I'll give you a little more notice next time."

"Have fun," Sarah said, hugging her father tightly. "I love you."

"I love you, too, Baby Doll," Jim replied, calling his daughter by her childhood nickname for the first time in years. "I'll call you two tomorrow."

He got into his car, turned the key in the Oldsmobile's ignition, and waved to the couple as he backed down the driveway and drove up the street.

A few moments later, as Jim was thinking about Jean, the ground shuddered from a massive explosion that rocked the neighborhood. He slammed on the brakes. The sedan fishtailed, skidding to a screeching halt. He looked in the rear-view mirror. A bright yellow-and-orange fireball was soaring skyward, followed by a billowy plume of dark smoke.

Jim U-turned, knocking over a mailbox as he floored the accelerator, tire tracks burning into the pavement.

He covered the two hundred yards in seconds and slammed on his brakes in front of his daughter's house. The street was littered with fragments of brick, wood, metal, and glass. He rammed the gearshift into park and flung open the car door, horror etched on his face as he raced into the debris-strewn yard amid a blanket of lingering smoke.

"Sarah!" he screamed, his heart pounding. "Help! Somebody, help!"

*

Joe O'Riley settled into his dark-green tweed recliner, waiting for the local news.

"It's about that time, Mr. Bushmill," he said, picking up the half-full bottle of Bushmills on the small table next to him. He unscrewed the cap and inhaled deeply. The slight scent of charcoal, combined with a soft, sweet floral aroma, was like a breath of fresh air invigorating his lungs. "Ain't nothing like Irish whiskey to bring on the sandman."

A few bars of music signaled not only the ten o'clock hour but the beginning of the former chief's nightly two-shot ritual. He took a sip of ice water, then gently lifted the shot glass to his lips. The slight bitterness was offset by a warm, soothing sensation that spread slowly downward.

"Good evening, everyone," the handsome television anchorman said. "This is Jerry Birch with the Action News 3 Ten O'Clock Report. Police and fire officials are on the scene tonight of a deadly house blast that has apparently claimed two lives. Val Calhoun is live at the site of the explosion. Val, what are the details?"

The screen faded to a mound of fragmented debris bathed in high-intensity floodlights. "Jerry, as you can see behind me, all that is left of this once beautiful home at 131 Devon Way in East Memphis is a mass of broken bricks, twisted metal, and shattered glass. The entire Hedgemoor neighborhood was rocked by the explosion which took place a little bit after 6:15 tonight."

O'Riley focused intently on the twenty-five-inch television screen, just as he always did whenever the police or fire departments were involved, hoping he might recognize some of his old friends. Turning away for a moment, he threw down his second shot of whiskey.

"Evidently," the reporter continued, "the couple who lived in the house, Mr. and Mrs. David Dern, were home at the time. That's according to Mrs. Dern's father, James Hale, who had been visiting his daughter and son-in-law only minutes before the explosion."

Hale was standing in the background with a group of fire department officials, pointing to the wreckage as the reporter spoke.

"That's him," O'Riley said, beginning to feel a slight buzz from the alcohol. "You got to be kidding me." He poured another shot and gulped it down, one more than usual.

"Mr. Hale, who is behind me on the left," the reporter said, "had just driven to the top of Devon Way when he heard what he described as 'a bomb explosion from a war movie.' He said the whole ground seemed to shake. When he returned seconds later, there was just this mass of smoldering rubble."

"Any idea on the cause of the blast?" Birch asked, tugging at his barely-visible earpiece.

"Police and fire officials have talked to Mr. Hale to see if he remembers anything unusual, like the smell of gas, but he says he didn't actually enter the residence. The Federal Bureau of Alcohol, Tobacco, and Firearms has been called in to assist. Viewers can probably see the white truck behind my shoulder marked 'ATF Explosive Investigation.' It arrived on the scene about 8 and was manned by two agents from Memphis. I have with me Mr. J.N. Pritchard, assistant special agent in charge of the ATF Nashville office."

The reporter turned to the stoic-faced middle-aged agent who had shed his coat in the humid nighttime heat. "Mr. Pritchard," she asked, "can you comment on the personnel who have been brought in for this investigation?"

"Of our eight agents at the scene, six are members of the agency's National Response Team. The team members include a chemist and an explosives technician. The other two are local field agents."

"Any possible cause for the blast?"

"It would be premature to speculate on that," he answered. "We suspect no foul play, but our investigators are searching for clues and we'll go from there. If a cause can be determined, rest assured we will find it."

"There you have it, Jerry. Back to you in the studio. This is Val Calhoun for Action News 3."

"Val Calhoun will keep us updated on that story as it unfolds," the anchorman said with a smile, looking directly into the camera. "In national news, the president continues taking care of his lame-duck presidency from The White House as the race to succeed him heats up. The Democratic National Convention, which starts on Monday, will determine who faces Republican Party nominee John Titus in the November presidential election. By all accounts, Tennessee Senator Adam Baldwin is a virtual shoo-in for the party nomination. When asked to comment on Baldwin as an opponent, Titus said . . ."

O'Riley was oblivious to the rest of the broadcast. How could all these coincidences be springing up? Jim Hale and his strange murder story with its accusation of a presidential candidate and this explosion that had almost killed him. The antique car like Will Harrison's. Even the same honk of the horn. He swallowed another shot.

"This seems like more than just some hurricane in the open ocean," O'Riley mumbled.

But what was it? A prickling sensation moved up his spine. Just the slightest hint of discomfort, but he knew the sensation well. During his years on the force, he'd felt it every time a deeper truth lay under the guise of accidental death.

Retirement be damned. He could feel it. The thrill of the hunt. Rushing through his veins. Just like the old days.

17

The sudden ring of a telephone broke the nighttime silence in the luxurious home in the Washington suburb of Great Falls in northern Virginia. The two-story colonial-style house, situated on four acres of gently rolling countryside, was much too expensive for a former Secret Service agent's salary. It had been a gift to Tom Stafford from a grateful Adam Baldwin following an assassination attempt on the senator's life in Nashville during his unsuccessful campaign for the 1984 Democratic presidential nomination.

Stafford's heroic leap into the path of a bullet, fired by a disgruntled government employee as Baldwin waded into a throng of supporters after a speech, had resulted in a serious wound to Stafford's abdomen—a move that solidified a powerful lifelong friendship between the agent and the politician.

Stafford pawed sleepily for his alarm clock in the darkness and then realized the phone was ringing. He picked up the receiver.

"Hello?"

"Tom, you asleep?"

"Yeah, but it's all right. What's up?"

"What's up?" Adam Baldwin snapped in anger. "I'll tell you what's up. My goddam blood pressure is up. I want you in my office in twenty minutes, you got it?"

"For crissakes, what's going on?"

"In my office. Put your ass in gear."

Stafford put down the phone, sat up in his king-size bed, and massaged his eyebrows.

"I'll be dipped in shit," he said, glancing over at the glowing green numerals on his bedside clock radio. 1:32 A.M. He quickly pulled on a pair of tobacco-colored microfiber slacks and a black polo-collar silk knit, accidentally kicking his English bull terrier, Victory. The dog nipped at his leg.

"Son of a bitch, Vic! I got enough people snapping at me." The snow-white dog's ears pinned back at the harsh tone. Stafford reached down and gave the pup a pat on the head.

In a few minutes, Stafford was downstairs in his silver Lexus hardtop convertible sport coupe. The tranquility of the early Saturday morning in the country was broken as tires screamed on asphalt heading north to D.C.

A breathless eighteen minutes later, he reached the Dirksen and Hart Senate Office Buildings. Stafford flashed his credentials at the guard stationed in the underground garage and wheeled the Lexus into the deserted parking area. Soon he was opening Baldwin's office door.

The Tennessee senator sat behind a large mahogany desk, its legs hand-carved in deep relief. Quarter-inch plate glass protected the glossy top covered with mementos from his forty-plus years of public service.

"Shut the door, will you?" Baldwin said sternly. Even at 2 A.M., his Zegna suit coat was buttoned as he nursed a Scotch-and-water. He let a moment pass in silence, his blue eyes staring through narrow slits. He possessed the gift of timing, a gift inherent in most politicians from birth.

Stafford had seen that look just one week before, in St. Louis.

"Before you sit down, Tom, do me one more favor," Baldwin continued calmly.

"Sure, Adam, anything."

"Tell me something, if you don't mind." Baldwin's face turned crimson as he jumped from his chair and pounded a fist on the desk, veins the size of pencils popping out on his forehead. "What the hell happened in Memphis tonight?"

"You mean the explo—"

"You're goddam right I mean the explosion!" Baldwin's voice dropped to a whisper. "I told you to take care of the situation. I said handle it. I thought you'd discredit him somehow. Hell, the guy we're concerned with didn't even get nailed—two innocent people died."

Stafford shrugged. "I thought it was the best way to handle the problem. Don't worry," he said, divining Baldwin's true concern, "nothing can be traced, no matter who they bring in."

"No matter who they bring in, huh? You better be right. They've already got the ATF there. The Memphis fire chief's brother is some ATF bigwig in Nashville. He was down there almost before the smoke cleared. For all I know, they'll call out the National Guard and bring in the goddam Cub Scouts to boot. I don't need this shit. Not now." He held a hand to his forehead and winced.

"I'm owed a few favors over at ATF from my Secret Service days. I'll call in a big one," Stafford said with the coolness of a chess grand master positioning himself for checkmate.

Baldwin's anger subsided as quickly as it had erupted. "How big?"

Stafford walked to one of the club chairs facing the senator's desk and rested his elbows on its back. He leaned his muscular frame forward, a gleam in his dark eyes. "Put it this way. What if you were photographed with a really, I mean really, voluptuous young blond—in a compromising position?"

Baldwin leaned closer, craning his neck to the right. "How compromising?"

"Let's say totally naked. And what if you were still married to the middle-aged woman who was your wife when this little snapshot was taken?" He dropped into the club chair and stretched.

"Hmmmm." Baldwin's eyes gleamed. "That could get quite uncomfortable."

"You don't know the half of it. What if the man in the picture was the newly appointed director of Alcohol, Tobacco, and Firearms?"

Baldwin relaxed with a soft chuckle. A smile spread across his face. Fears dashed, he walked over and placed a hand on Stafford's shoulder. "You're a work of art, Tom. A sonuvabitchin' Rembrandt. You head on back home and get some sleep. I think my worries were a little ill-founded. You seem to have the situation under control."

18

O'Riley parked his black Lincoln in the front lot of the Memphis Funeral Home on Poplar Avenue and ambled toward the tan brick building, pulling at the waist of his grey suit pants, still a comfortable fit. The only thing worse than having to put on a suit was having to put on a suit and go to a funeral home.

As he entered, he noticed the sweet aroma of carnations in the reception area, an attempt to conceal the air of death that hung over the building. A smiling receptionist approached.

"May I help you?" the small middle-aged woman asked.

"I'm here for the Dern visitation," O'Riley replied.

"That's in the Williamsburg Room," she said, still smiling. "The last door down the hall to your left."

O'Riley paused to sign the registry at the doorway and then walked in. Two shiny grey metal caskets sat on pedestals toward the back, surrounded by brightly colored floral sprays. Dressed in a navy windowpane suit, Jim was standing near the caskets with sunglasses concealing his eyes. A slight smile of recognition passed over his pale face at the sight of O'Riley.

"Joe," Jim said, clasping his hand firmly, "you didn't need to come. This is real thoughtful of you." He took off his sunglasses, revealing dark circles under his eyes.

"I saw you on television. It's the least I can do. As my father used to say, 'A man's only half a man if he doesn't have friends.'"

Jim pursed his thin lips. "I feel lost," he said, looking down. "I have no family left. Hardly anyone to talk to."

"I know it ain't much, but you can talk to me anytime you want," O'Riley said, placing a hand on Jim's broad shoulder. "I know what you're going through. I been through some pretty tough times myself."

An attractive blond walked over and reached for Jim's hand. Their eyes locked for a moment.

"Jean, this is the man I told you about, the one who took my report at the police station. Joe O'Riley, this is a good friend of mine, Jean King."

"Nice to meet you," Jean said with a smile and a firm handshake.

O'Riley smiled at the shapely young woman. Her blond hair was pulled back and pinched with a barrette. A black linen jacket matched well-creased black linen slacks, coordinated with a lightweight black-striped silk blouse. A Prada purse hung from her shoulder. As he gazed into her blue-green eyes, his heart fluttered. "Do I know you from somewhere?"

"I don't think so," Jean replied, shaking her head. "I know I'd remember a police chief if I met one."

O'Riley turned to Jim. "Hey, how's that old car of yours? Still running like a top?"

Jim's face relaxed. "I tell you what. I'll take you for a ride in it sometime soon."

O'Riley nodded. "Sounds great. I'll give you a call and we'll get together. In the meantime, if there's anything I can do . . ."

"You've done quite enough just by coming. I won't forget this," Jim said, shaking O'Riley's hand.

"You two take care," O'Riley said. "Nice to have met you," he added, nodding to Jean.

As he headed for his car, O'Riley jingled the bulky key chain in his pocket, mulling over Jim's murder accusation of a candidate for president and his narrow escape from death. Maybe connected. One thing was certain. It sure would be nice to bloody Adam Baldwin's nose again after all these years. Figuratively speaking, of course.

*

The old shoeshine man gripped the thick wooden brush handle as the horsehair bristles flicked across O'Riley's shoes. Overcast skies and a cool front had knocked the temperature down to a pleasant sixty-six degrees.

"Looks like we might have an early winter if this keeps up," O'Riley said, a box of doughnuts in his lap.

"It don't make no matter to me. I'm thankful every day just to be alive," E. replied, pulling out the buffing rag.

O'Riley stifled a yawn. "Let me ask you something."

"If I knows the answer, I'll tell ya."

"It's funny but, for all the years I've known you, you've never told me what your real name is."

E. looked directly into O'Riley's face. "I kind of been keeping it a secret."

"Edward? Erwin? Elvis, maybe?"

"People did start thinking that back in the fifties, when Presley come along. My real name is Ephraim, Ephraim Crowder."

"That ain't too bad," O'Riley said, nodding. "Has a nice ring to it."

"I prefers to have it stay a secret, if you'll keep it that way for me."

"Water under the bridge," replied O'Riley. "E. it will remain."

"People gots all sorts of secrets locked up inside 'em. Some let 'em out, others don't. I'm like a bartender—I listens to people as I shine, then they're off to solve their problems on their own. Some tell me things they won't even tell their wife. Like I'm their best friend or somethin'." He hung the buffing rag back in its spot on the worn metal stirrup.

"Here you go," said O'Riley. He handed E. the customary five-dollar bill. "Doughnut?" he asked, opening the box to reveal eleven strawberry-filled and one powdered sugar.

A smile touched E.'s face. "I sees you're messin' with Driscoll again."

He took a strawberry-filled one, eyeing the solitary powdered doughnut.

"Gotta keep things popping up in Homicide," O'Riley said. "Nothing like a little friction to keep certain people ornery."

Within minutes, O'Riley was on the second floor.

"Never fear, boys," Sergeant Harris announced, as O'Riley pushed through the swinging doors. "The cholesterol fairy has come to make sure we start our day off right with a healthy dose of fat."

Four detectives grinned broadly and greeted the former chief. One kept staring at an autopsy report in silence.

"Ah, Sergeant Driscoll," O'Riley said, putting down the box. "I'm glad to see you're having one of your better days. Always smiling, always so cordial. Such a joy to be around."

Driscoll cupped a hand over his eyebrows as if to make O'Riley disappear.

"What is it today?" Harris asked.

O'Riley reached down and opened the box, tilting it at Harris. "Strawberry jelly-filled and one powdered sugar."

Harris cocked his neck, squinting. He held a lone forefinger in the air, savoring the question-and-answer routine they had perfected over the years to tease Driscoll.

"Yes, Harris?"

"How come you always bring that one odd doughnut? If you've got eleven chocolate, you bring one glazed. With eleven custard, you might have one jelly. What's the deal?"

"Harris, my boy, have you forgotten? Driscoll here's a bit odd, so I'm always wanting to make him feel special. Like today. I got him a powdered doughnut just in case he forgot to powder his nose on the way to work."

The detectives broke into laughter as Driscoll walked over to O'Riley.

"How would you like this doughnut stuffed up your ass, old-timer?" Driscoll said, picking up the powdered ring and bringing it close to O'Riley's face.

O'Riley waited a split-second, arching his eyebrows. "It's your dough-nut. You make the call. If I were the doughnut, I'd much rather be going *in* my asshole than coming out of yours."

The other detectives oohed. Driscoll shook his head in disgust and, with a barely audible huff, stalked away, doughnut in hand.

O'Riley walked over to Trevor Mills's desk and sat down. "Share some-thing with me, Mills. What's the status of that explosion over on Devon Way last Friday?"

Immaculately dressed, as always, Mills looked over from his com-puter screen and tightened the knot in his Italian tie. "Word's come down that ATF said it was an accidental gas explosion."

"Accidental? Any details?"

Mills arched his back, stretching his broad shoulders. "Not a one."

O'Riley shook his head. "That just don't make sense."

Mills shrugged. "Whattaya want? We're up to our elbows with mur-ders anyway. ATF told the chief it was gas. Case closed. Yesterday is history and tomorrow's a mystery."

Still shaking his head, O'Riley got up and went over to a vacant desk to call an old friend, Al Parker, a former ATF special agent who had become an ATF inspector when he reached the special-agent retirement age of fifty-seven. With O'Riley's help, Parker's son, Bill, landed a job with the police department in Charlottesville, Virginia, in 1973. Surely Parker would have more details to give him.

The line rang three times before a receptionist answered. She put O'Riley on hold. An excited voice picked up.

"Joe! How you doing?" said Parker. "Seems like ages."

"Yeah, it has been."

"What's going on?"

"Al, I need a favor."

"Joe, you name it."

"You know the explosion over on Devon Way last Friday?"

117

"Hell, yes. Really made the news."

"What'd the ATF guys find out?"

"A gas line problem."

"From where?"

"They're not sure."

"Not sure? Holy shit, Al, ATF must've had twelve men over there. It looked like a goddam Treasury Department convention. What's the deal?"

"The deal, Joe, is that it was a gas leak of unknown origin ignited when the owner of the house lit a cigarette. End of story. Case closed. Got it?"

O'Riley took a breath.

"You still there?" Parker asked.

"Yeah, I'm here." Something wasn't right.

"Look, Joe. You want to meet me for a drink after I get off work?"

"Sure." This made more sense. "Where?"

"The Belmont Grill on Poplar sound good?"

"What time?"

"How's six straight up?"

"Book it. See you then. Oh, Al," O'Riley said.

"Yeah, Joe."

"Be sure to bring your drinking shoes."

*

All nine parking spaces at the Belmont Grill were filled, so O'Riley parked across the street.

He stared at the aged, rectangular building with its front brick facade and wood-on-wood sides, all painted a bright shade of green. The red awnings covering the three picture windows in front and the three small windows on the east side made him think how the building had a look of Christmas to it all year long, especially in the abnormal coolness of this late summer Tuesday evening.

He got out of his car and while he waited for the light to change, he remembered when the building had been a Cities Service gas station back in the 1940s. He thought of the night Will and Jenny had announced their engagement. They had stopped for gas on the way home after eating at the Davis White Spot.

The traffic light changed and O'Riley hurried across the street. Al Parker was waiting for him in a booth by the front window.

"How ya doing, you old war-horse?" the lean Parker asked, firmly grasping O'Riley's hand.

O'Riley laughed. "Not bad for a retired cop trying to get into trouble."

"You put on a little weight since I last saw you?" said Parker.

"You know how cotton is," O'Riley replied with a grin, patting his firm stomach. "Always shrinking."

Al Parker looked more like a middle-aged accountant than an ATF inspector. His clothes, while neat, looked like they'd been ordered from a catalogue. A blue button-down shirt, heavily starched even at the end of the day, hung stiffly from his narrow shoulders. His thin face sported wire-rimmed glasses, and he had a short-cropped, grey head of hair with a greying moustache that made him appear older than his sixty-one years.

A slender young waitress came over. "What'll it be for you two gentlemen?"

"Just bring us a couple of shots of Bushmills straight up," Parker said. "And a glass of ice water for my friend, if memory serves me well."

"Two shots each or two total?" the waitress asked, arching her faint brown eyebrows.

"Each," Parker replied, "and don't stray too far. We'll probably be needing a few more, if I know us."

The waitress turned toward the bar, her long brunette hair flowing behind her, almost touching the top of the short, cut-off jeans that barely concealed her tight backside. Minutes later she returned with the drinks.

"On a serious note," O'Riley said, "to the resolution of the truth."

They pinged their glasses.

"To its resolution," Parker said, flinging the liquid into his thin mouth and wincing. Then he looked around cautiously. "Look, about that explosion on Devon Way—you were right," he said quietly. "I just couldn't talk on the phone about it. A Fire Department bomb squad investigator found something suspicious right off the bat."

Both men tossed down second shots.

"Somebody had loosened the fittings on the gas line where it entered the stove from outside. They'd bent the line until they got a break in it. Looks like they also blew out the pilot light in the attic water heater, so the gas could build up."

"Did the cigarette make it blow?"

Parker shook his head. "That was the official word. What they really found was an unopened pack of Marlboros and a brand-new Bic lighter. Tests showed it had never been lit. Not once. Then, of course, there's the other stuff."

"Which is?" O'Riley said.

"The explosives expert found remains of an incendiary device behind the stove. Whoever set this thing up had plugged the heating element from a hand-held hair dryer into a timer. The timer was plugged into a wall socket behind the stove. The element was sitting in a white ceramic coffee mug that had a few ounces of gasoline in it, also behind the stove. Once the timer went off, the heating element sparked the gasoline."

"Whammo," O'Riley said.

"Right. On top of that, you know what else they found?"

"I give up," O'Riley said, shrugging.

Parker motioned to the waitress, holding up two fingers. He looked back at O'Riley and leaned across the table, lowering his voice even further. "The phones in the house had all been tapped. And they found bugs all over in the rubble. A real electronics convention. There must have been one in every room. Somebody knew *everything* about that couple. Where they were going, where they had been, when they last took a leak—the whole works."

He paused as the waitress placed two shots in front of each of them. Cold droplets of condensation ran down the side of the water glass and dripped onto the tablecloth as O'Riley hoisted it to his mouth, chasing the coolness down his throat with a swallow of warm whiskey.

"This thing is big, Joe—*real* big," Parker continued. "I don't know who wants it covered up or why but, take my word for it, it's out of your league. I've never seen anything like it in all my years working for Treasury. The cover-up order must have come from the Secret Service. He paused, stroking his moustache. "You know who's behind it?"

"Just a hunch, Al. Just working on a hunch."

"Well, if you keep it up, you better have a pistol on you," Parker said. "Fully loaded."

"I got it right here," O'Riley replied, tapping the bulging right pocket of his khaki pants.

"If word gets out that you know what I've told you, I'd lay odds you'll need it."

O'Riley's eyes narrowed. "Don't worry about me, Al. I'll be fine. One thing I know is how to be discreet."

19

Adam Baldwin was sitting at the foot of the elegant canopy bed as the antique brass mantle clock in the presidential suite of The Plaza Hotel chimed softly. His white silk pajamas with navy piping clung to his freshly showered body as he waited for his wife to come out of the bathroom.

On this, the third night of the Democratic Convention, Baldwin had been nominated as his party's candidate for President of the United States. As he scanned the walls of the dimly lit room, he replayed the events of the most historic night in his life.

He thought of the celebration dinner with his family and top aides at The Palm, his favorite restaurant. Also his grandfather's favorite. The two of them had enjoyed many a meal there when Franklin Hart traveled to meet him in New York during Baldwin's college days at Harvard.

He reflected on the thrill shared by his family, gathered in the presidential suite's sitting room, when his nomination became official. The cheering had reached a crescendo when Baldwin's delegate total reached only five votes below the required number for nomination. State upon state passed in order to give the candidate's home state the honor of putting its native son over the top.

"The chair recognizes the head of the Tennessee delegation," the party chairman shouted into the microphone. The throng grew quiet as delegates strained to hear the words that Adam Baldwin and his grandfather before him had dreamed of for so long.

"Madam Chairman," the diminuitive balding delegation leader said, "the Volunteer State of Tennessee, home of Presidents Andrew Jackson, James K. Polk, and Andrew Johnson, casts all its votes for *the next* President of the United States from Tennessee, Senator Adam Baldwin!"

A deafening applause rang in Baldwin's ears as he sat, spellbound. His wife's voice brought him back to reality.

"Don't start without me," Doris Baldwin said from behind the closed bathroom door, her voice sultry.

The thought of making love as the Democratic Party presidential nominee was intoxicating. Of course the bottle of Perrier-Jouët champagne they had just shared magnified his passion. Baldwin had purchased the flowered, green glass bottle in 1979, vowing to drink the contents only when he became a presidential nominee. He had begun to worry that he would never taste the fruits of victory, but now his fears were laid to rest. And the sexual desires of Doris Baldwin would soon be laid to rest as well.

The door to the bathroom slowly opened, revealing a nude form silhouetted in the doorway, the best figure money could buy. Facelifts, breast implants, a tummy tuck, and liposuctioned thighs had left Doris Baldwin with a chiseled, sculpted body that could pass for that of a well-toned forty-year-old. She was stunning, wearing only her wedding ring, earrings, and a bracelet on each wrist, all encrusted with pave diamonds. Her azure eyes, full of anticipation, sparkled like the gems that adorned her body. "Now for the most memorable event of your nomination night," she said as she glided across the shadowy room and slipped under the covers.

Baldwin stirred with excitement. He jerked off his pajama bottoms, flinging them across the room, and slid under the cool sheets until the warmth of his body met hers.

He slowly caressed his wife's firm breasts and covered them with kisses before moving his right hand down her soft, slender abdomen. She spread her legs as he inserted his index finger and began to gently massage. She closed her eyes.

"Oh, Adam," she whispered as she reached down between her

husband's legs and eased him in. In a few moments her legs locked behind him.

Baldwin fell into his usual fantasy—that he was making love to a famous newswoman. Barbara Walters, Jane Pauley, Phyllis George, Jessica Savitch, Diane Sawyer, Deborah Norville, Kathleen Sullivan, Maria Schriver, Connie Chung, Paula Zahn, Joan Lunden—in his mind, he had had them all over the years. Tonight it was Katie Couric.

With each thrust, his visualization became more vivid. Beads of perspiration turned to streams of sweat dripping down the sides of his face. He puffed repeatedly, visibly winded.

"Honey, we can stop if you need to," Doris said, breathing heavily.

Baldwin responded by picking up the pace.

With a final thrust, he climaxed, then collapsed beside his wife.

"My God!" Doris said, eyes fixed on the ceiling, an arm draped across her forehead. "We need to get you nominated more often."

"No shit," Baldwin replied, rolling onto his back. "No shit."

He leaned over and kissed her gently. Soon they drifted off to sleep, unbothered by the muffled noise of taxis and cars speeding down Fifth Avenue.

Baldwin dreamed of walking along a freshly paved road with a forest on each side. The sun was brilliant through the foliage. Down the road, a man waved. Gradually his features became visible. Flowing white hair, black-framed glasses, and finally his round face.

"Grampa!" Baldwin yelled, rushing up to him.

"I've been wanting to see you for a long time, Adam," Franklin Hart said, grinning as he embraced his grandson.

"I finally made it. I'm running for President."

"I know," his grandfather said as they walked down the road. "I've been keeping up with you. You've put all the advice I gave you to good use. Just like I knew you would, Adam. I'm proud of you, boy."

"Will you walk with me for a while?" Baldwin asked. "I have so much to tell you. And I want any words of wisdom you can give me. Words to help me win the election."

"I'm sorry, Adam," his grandfather said, pulling a gold pocket watch from his vest and clicking it open. "My time is up. You have to travel down the rest of the road by yourself."

"But Grampa—"

"I have no choice," Hart said. "My advice to you, Adam, is to beware of one thing . . ."

"Grampa, don't go!" Baldwin screamed as he disappeared.

"One thing . . ." echoed through the treetops.

"What is the one thing?" Baldwin called out. "What must I beware of?"

Suddenly the sky darkened as a humid wind kicked up. Then the road narrowed into a dirt path. Leaves turned brown and fell to the ground around Baldwin, leaving barren branches whipping above.

Rain swirled, falling in torrents, accompanied by loud rumblings of thunder and flashes of lightning. Baldwin ran as fast as he could, but his soaked grey suit weighed him down. He yanked off the coat and threw it to the side, his feet splashing in the mud. A bolt of lightning struck a tree to his right with a deafening crack, blinding him in its brilliance.

Baldwin lunged to the side of the path, seeking refuge at the base of a large, old oak. Gasping for breath, he buried his face in his hands as more lightning flashed, like a strobe light in a pitch-black room.

"You'll never be president," a shrill voice said above the din of falling rain.

"Who said that?" Baldwin yelled, looking up into the flashing darkness.

"You'll never be president," the voice repeated.

Baldwin looked around, bewildered, as rain dripped down his face, unsure where the female voice was coming from.

"Look at me when I talk to you, you murdering son of a bitch."

Baldwin's eyes filled with terror as the muddy ground began to move. Two bony hands reached up and a badly decomposed body, clothed in a shredded maroon-flowered dress, slowly emerged from the muck. A sickening stench of decaying flesh burned his nostrils, gagging him.

The bloated figure rose, strips of pale, worm-infested skin hanging from her limbs. She thrust herself free from her unmarked grave and pointed a bony finger in Baldwin's face. "You'll never be president because it's now my turn to dispose of you!" she yelled, staggering toward him, arms outstretched.

"Noooooo!" Baldwin shouted, bolting up in bed. Sweat covered his face. The red numbers on the bedside clock showed 3:17 A.M. Disoriented, he didn't know where he was. Dallas, Pittsburgh, Seattle? Then he remembered. New York. The nomination. The Plaza.

"Honey, what's wrong?" Doris said, awakened by her husband's outburst.

"Nothing," he whispered as he took a deep breath, heart still pounding. "Just a bad dream."

20

"All right, you slick-talking moron," O'Riley said, leaning back in his recliner, "let's see what kind of crap you're gonna shovel to get yourself elected." He clicked on the television with his remote and set it on top of the day's crumpled newspaper.

The buttery aroma of fresh popcorn filled the room. O'Riley munched on a handful as his German shepherd sat at attention on the worn tan carpet, waiting for an occasional piece to come flying his way.

"From NBC News," the television announced, "the Democratic National Convention continues."

"As you can see behind me," the stylishly dressed newsman said, "this convention crowd has been whipped into a frenzy as they await the arrival on stage and the acceptance speech of Democratic presidential nominee, Senator Adam Baldwin of Tennessee."

Cameras panned the sea of bodies bobbing up and down on the floor of the Jacob Javits Convention Center before zooming in on a massive beige podium and the red, white, and blue donkey poster across its front. The blue-carpeted stage, surrounded by a three-foot-high wood railing mounted atop thick, bullet-proof plexiglass, stood before a backdrop draped with alternating red and white vertical stripes two feet wide. White stars three feet in height on a navy border ran vertically down each side of the stripes. Two giant JumboTron monitors flanked the flag-colored backdrop, giving every delegate a close-up view of the podium.

"Before Senator Baldwin delivers his speech," the newsman continued, "let us examine what lies ahead after this carefully orchestrated flag-waving draws to a close this evening.

"The Democratic Party you see before you tonight has come a long way in the past eight months. At the beginning of this year, pundits said there was no possible way the Democrats would be able to hold on to The White House. But with the emergence of Adam Baldwin as the consensus candidate to lead the Democrats, the polls began to move drastically.

"At the conclusion of the Republican Convention last month in San Francisco, Republican nominee John Titus held a slim forty-eight to forty-five percent lead with seven percent undecided. Given the normal boost that every convention gives its candidate, Senator Baldwin will most likely have a slight lead in the polls as the curtain closes on the Democratic Convention later tonight.

"Although Adam Baldwin possesses a distinguished public service record, he faces in John Titus a formidable foe well-versed in the game of politics. A native of the Chicago area, Titus completed his undergraduate studies at Yale University before attending the Stanford University School of Law where he graduated first in his class. Upon returning home to Illinois, he soon tossed his hat in the political ring and was elected as an alderman for the city of Chicago. Working his way up the political ladder, he was elected mayor of Chicago and, four years later, won the governorship of Illinois in a landslide vote. Upon completion of his second term as governor, he was appointed head of the C.I.A. and subsequently, became Secretary of State during Ronald Reagan's second term, remaining in office throughout George Bush's presidency. The fifty-five-year-old Titus strikes a compromise between those who say that our departing president was hindered by his relative youth, while his Democratic successor, Adam Baldwin, occupies the other end of the spectrum."

The newsman cupped his left hand over his ear to muffle the suddenly deafening cheers of the delegates. "As you can see," he continued, "Adam Baldwin is now ready to give one of the most important speeches of his life, a speech in which he will set the tone for his campaign and his hoped-for presidential success."

The tumultuous roar continued as Baldwin moved to the podium. He waved to the crowd, flashing his charismatic smile, his full head of hair shining like silver under the blazing convention hall spotlights.

"Thank you, thank you so much," he shouted into the microphone. The crowd noise rendered his voice inaudible. "Thank you," Baldwin repeated, "thank you."

"C'mon, you hot dog," O'Riley said as he tossed the last pieces of popcorn to Bullet. "Get on with it." He frowned at the screen, face hard, laser eyes on the candidate.

The convention atmosphere was charged. Thousands of red, white, and blue balloons lay in the rafters, awaiting the crowning of the new Democratic Party king.

Chin tilted upward, Baldwin bellowed, "I am proud to accept your nomination for President of the United States."

The crowd roared. Then a gradual hush fell over the convention floor as all eyes were fixed on the figure at the podium, spellbound, as if waiting for a sorcerer to work his magic.

"I pledge to you that I will devote every effort of my mind and spirit to lead our party back to victory and our nation to greatness. We know it will not be easy to campaign against a man who has spoken so eloquently from both sides of his mouth concerning most every issue. The Republican candidate is running on a platform that says you, the American people, deserve a better standard of living. I know we can do much better. The very tenets of the Democratic Party, which we hold so dear, are based on our committed effort to move our nation forward. In just about every one of its administrations in the last fifty years, the Republican Party has said 'No' to employment, 'No' to education, 'No' to housing, 'No' to funding for distressed areas of our inner cities, 'No' to welfare programs, 'No' to the environment, and 'No' to adequate aid for the elderly and infirm."

Baldwin paused as he slowly scanned the convention floor. His voice, though measured, then filled with passion. "I come out of a Democratic Party which, in the past century, has given us Woodrow Wilson, Franklin Delano Roosevelt, Harry Truman, and John F. Kennedy, all of whom initiated and supported programs in the areas I mentioned. Which point of view do you want to lead our country, Republican or Democrat? To the American people, the answer should be as clear as a piece of fine crystal. The Democratic Party, under my leadership, will move on these issues.

"America is known as a melting pot for people from all parts of the globe. Yet, for all our differences, we must realize that the fate of any nation rests on the bond of common trust between that country's citizens and those who have been entrusted to lead the country. My campaign for the presidency, and my term as the highest elected official in the land, will be remembered as an era of renewed trust between the American people and their officials. The citizens of the United States were lied to about radiation from nuclear testing in the 1950s, Vietnam in the 1960s, Watergate in the 1970s, Iran-Contra in the 1980s, and campaign finance scandals and sexual improprieties in the 1990s. There will be none of this deception during my administration. On that point I give you my word."

O'Riley shook his head and leaned back in his chair.

Baldwin finally drew to a close, taking a deep breath, voice rising, forty-five minutes after he began. "Join with me tonight to bring about a national victory as we strive to insure an Adam Baldwin presidency. Together we will signal an America safe and strong for all of our people. The light we put forth in the pursuit of this end will shine around the world. May God bless you and the United States of America!"

The convention hall erupted with deafening applause that grew louder when vice-presidential nominee, Byron Hornaday, walked on stage. The two clasped hands and raised them high as the convention hall became a sea of placard-waving bodies. At that moment, thousands of red, white, and blue balloons rained down into the outstretched hands of the delegates, followed by a blizzard of multi-colored confetti.

"Look at that," O'Riley said out loud as the candidates were joined by their families. Weary, he flicked the television off.

"What worries me more than a lousy, lying murderer is a lousy, lying murderer with power. And that, I'm afraid, is exactly what we have on our hands."

21

Jim pulled back the parking brake of the Model A, got out, and crossed the street to Joe O'Riley's house. September had held on to the oppressive humidity of the summer. At eleven o'clock, the temperature was a muggy eighty-three degrees.

He stood at the foot of the walkway leading up to the front porch and stared at the greying stucco house, its sloping yard lush with ivy and shaded by two huge oaks.

A brilliant flash of light suddenly blinded him. As he regained his sight, the house that stood before him looked different. It now glowed a freshly painted white and the oak trees were much shorter. Grass dotted the yard, mixed with small patches of ivy. But as quickly as it had appeared, the image vanished. Jim rubbed his eyes. The house was once again grey with age.

He realized he had been there before. He knew it. A chill ran through him as he rang O'Riley's door bell.

"Thanks for coming by," O'Riley said, as the door creaked open. He was wearing a white t-shirt and grey jogging pants. "Excuse my looks," he said. "Just got out of the shower. Been weeding those damn ivy beds all morning." He showed Jim into the living room, brushing his still-damp hair with a wave of his hand.

Jim settled into the couch across from the white marble fireplace. The room's furnishings, tasteful and uncluttered, looked as if they had been in the same place for years. Deep grooves in the Oriental rug formed a moat around the coffee table and every chair leg.

"How's things going?" O'Riley asked.

Jim shrugged, lips pinched. "It's tough. When something bad happens, you can usually bounce back. It's different when you lose a child. It's always lurking in the back of your thoughts. You just do the best you can." He paused. "What have you been up to?"

"Plugging along. Sometimes I lose track of what day it is. I see you drove your Ford," O'Riley said, scratching his chin. "That ain't the only car you own, is it?"

Jim shook his head. "I brought it because you liked it. Usually I drive an Olds Ninety-Eight. I have a little daytime date after I leave here. Wanted her to see it too."

"That woman from the funeral home?"

"How'd you know?"

"I saw the way you were looking at her. You don't have to be a detective to figure that one out. You two serious?"

"We haven't known each other very long. We're taking things slowly. We have quite a bit in common, though."

"I can imagine," O'Riley said. He pulled a clear baggie full of Cheerios from his pants pocket.

"What's with the cereal?"

O'Riley popped a few into his mouth. "Gotta watch my weight." He tapped his tightened stomach twice with his fist. "You ain't the only one with a girlfriend, you know. Mine just happens to be out of the country."

"Ran her off, did you?" Jim said, grinning.

"She's a teacher," O'Riley replied. "Exchange program in France. She'll be back before Christmas."

Jim nodded. "That ivy out front is really thick."

"That's the idea, right?"

"What I mean is . . ." Jim paused. "I mean—the ivy has grown thicker since I last saw it."

Deep wrinkles creased O'Riley's forehead. "You pulling my leg?"

"No, really. I just flashed on how everything must have looked years ago. The house was whiter. The two trees out front were a lot smaller. And the yard had just a few clumps of ivy. I saw it clear as day. Then it vanished."

"You some kind of psychic?" O'Riley said.

Jim shook his head. "Just a regular guy. Well, I used to be, at least. Before the treatments."

O'Riley paused for a moment. Maybe this guy was a nut case after all, he thought to himself as he thrust his hand in his right pants pocket. No pistol. It was in his khakis upstairs. "Treatments?" he asked. "Like electric shock therapy or something?"

"Experimental drug treatments."

"What for?"

"My memory. That's why I lost my job. I kept forgetting things. The doctors diagnosed me with early-onset Alzheimer's. I entered an experimental treatment program at St. Jude."

O'Riley breathed a sigh of relief. "How'd these treatments affect you?"

"The drug was supposed to stimulate some kind of memory cells in my brain. Crazy as it may sound, it's almost like I can recall things that happened to me in a previous life."

"Like you're rejuvenated?" said O'Riley.

"You mean reincarnated?"

"That's what I meant. Damn, you correct me just like a friend of mine used to do when I was a youngster. So, you think you've been reincarnated?"

"I know that's weird, but I can't think of another explanation. Some sight or sound seems to trigger a vision from this earlier life. One was a murder, something I must have witnessed in that life."

O'Riley mulled this over as he felt the top of his head. Almost dry. "I remember stuff . . . memories."

"With a bright light?"

"No bells and whistles. I just remember."

"With my visions, it's different," Jim said, looking down at the floor.

O'Riley arched his eyebrows. "These treatments. Is the doctor's name Morgan?"

"How the hell did you know that?"

"We're casual acquaintances. I'm familiar with his line of work, you might say." O'Riley remembered the David Lancaster serial killer case.

Bullet suddenly barked at the back door.

O'Riley got up. "Hold on a sec. I need to let my dog in."

Moments later, O'Riley returned with ninety pounds of black and tan fur at his side. The dog lifted his nose and sniffed at the stranger.

"Don't mind him," O'Riley said. "He looks mean but there ain't a bad bone in his body. The only thing he's ever bitten is his dinner."

Jim held out a hand and the dog eased toward him and licked his forefinger, tail wagging. Jim rubbed the thick fur under the shepherd's neck. "You must like me," he said softly. "You're a good dog, Bullet, good dog."

The animal's ears perked up.

"What did you just say?" O'Riley asked.

Jim glanced at O'Riley. "Good dog?"

"No, before that. Bullet."

"It just came out."

O'Riley leaned back in his chair, shaking his head. "That's the damn dog's name. How'd you know? My first dog was named Bullet and he was a shepherd. Just like this one. I had him when I was a kid from the early 1940s until he died in 1952, a few years after I became a cop." He cocked his head to one side. "What kind of game are you playing?"

Jim stood up, face flushed. "I'm not playing games with you, but strange things have been happening in my mind. And after what happened to my daughter, I'm afraid to tell anybody about it but you and Jean King. They would think I was nuts. You probably feel that way already."

"Take it easy," O'Riley said, motioning Jim to sit back down.

O'Riley had always been able to peg a suspect in an interrogation. He could spot a liar in the time it took to light a cigarette. He knew Jim was telling the truth. He could see it in his face. There was something else he couldn't figure out. But he knew he could trust him.

"Trust is a two-way street," O'Riley said. "What I'm about to tell you is gonna be hard for you to swallow. If you want to tell your lady friend, that's all right. Just don't let it go any further." He took a deep breath. "That explosion at your daughter's house was no accident."

Jim's eyes widened. "The police, the fire department, the ATF. They all agreed it was a natural gas explosion."

"Oh, they're right about that. It was a gas explosion all right. What they didn't tell you is that it was a deliberate gas explosion."

Jim shook his head, a puzzled look spreading across his face.

"I been a cop a long time. When you've been around as much as I have, you develop a kind of sixth sense about situations. I got an idea who's responsible."

"Who would want Sarah and David dead?"

"Maybe not them," O'Riley said.

"You mean me?"

"You know of anybody who doesn't like you?"

"I don't think I have an enemy in the world. You don't make many enemies selling clothes at Oak Hall—"

"Oak Hall," O'Riley said. "That's where you work?"

O'Riley flashed to his youth, driving Will Harrison's Model A with Jenny Adair in the front and Will in the back. The pungent odor of engine fumes tinged the air.

"Hurry," Will pleaded. "Mr. Halle said if I'm late for work, don't even bother coming in. One minute after ten and I'm history."

"Aw, he's just playing with you," Joey said as he maneuvered through the Main Street traffic. "You make straight-A's and you're the class president next year. How many stock boys have credentials like that?"

Will leaned forward from the back seat and pecked Jenny on the cheek. "Don't let that mug get you in any trouble today."

She tweaked Will's nose. "I'll keep him in line."

"Hit it," Joey yelled.

Will flung the door open, stepped onto the running board and jumped from the still-moving car. As he ran down the sidewalk past Woolworth's to Oak Hall, Joey *ah-oo-gahed* twice on the horn. Will waved without looking back.

Jim's reply brought O'Riley back to the present. "Used to work. I'm on leave."

"You're kidding," O'Riley said.

"No, why?" Jim asked.

"That's where my friend worked—you know, the one who had the Model A when I was in high school. I can't believe all these coincidences." O'Riley took a deep breath. "Back to you. You ever threatened anybody?"

"Never."

"You ever been perceived as a threat to anybody?"

"Joe, what are you getting at?"

"I'm trying to get you to see this on your own. That explosion was meant to kill you, not your daughter and her husband."

Jim frowned. "Who would want to kill me?"

"How do you think Adam Baldwin feels about you?" O'Riley asked, rubbing the bridge of his nose.

"He wouldn't know I exist. I just told you what I saw in my vision. I didn't say go arrest him. How would he know who I am?"

"Anytime a person makes so much as a disparaging remark about someone running for president, the local police zip word to the Secret Service."

"You mean the Secret Service was told about me after I gave you my report?"

"That very day. We had to. Regulations."

"So Adam Baldwin does know who I am."

"Count on it," O'Riley replied.

"Wait. You think Adam Baldwin is behind the explosion?" Jim shook his head. "No way. He's running for president, for crissakes."

O'Riley's eyes narrowed. "Say you found out that some guy, a nut case for all you knew, accused you of murdering somebody fifty years ago. If you didn't do anything wrong, you'd blow it off and not worry about it, right?"

Jim nodded. "No-brainer."

"But what if part of what this guy said was true? Even the tiniest bit? What if you *were* somehow involved in a murder? What would you do?"

"Get rid of the accuser."

O'Riley nodded. "Now you're popping. Adam Baldwin wanted you out of the way. Your daughter and son-in-law were just a mistake."

"But how did he know where I was supposed to be?"

"I got a close friend with ATF. He said they found listening devices in the rubble. And they found a timer and part of an incendiary bomb."

Jim clenched his fists. "If he was in this room right now, I'd kill the bastard! I swear it."

"Easy," O'Riley said. "That's what got you in this mess to begin with. You just didn't know it."

Jim puffed his cheeks, burying his face in his hands. "Now what?" he said, looking up. "Will he send somebody else after me?"

"I don't think so, at least not right now," O'Riley replied. "He's won the nomination. He's about as high profile as it gets. He doesn't want anything negative to surface. If that accusation of yours kept coming up, you might have a problem. He's concentrating on the presidential race. You're just a forgotten blip on his radar screen."

"What can we do?"

"Not much, I'm afraid, about the explosion. What we have to do, if we want to get even," O'Riley said, gritting his teeth, "is bring the son of a bitch down. If what you saw in your vision is true, we're gonna have to prove it, and that ain't gonna be easy."

"I'll have to leave that to you," Jim said. He stood up to go. "But I might have somebody who could help."

"That lady friend of yours?" O'Riley said. "Please, not today. I'm already on sensory overload. Tomorrow'd be better."

Jim nodded, managing a weak smile.

"I can't figure all these strange happenings out. The old car, you describing my front yard years ago, calling my dog by name, working at Oak Hall—even correcting my vocabulary." O'Riley shook his head as Jim headed for the door. "And the way you honk that horn . . . what makes you do that?"

"Always have," replied Jim. "Just feels natural. Makes people smile." He winked. "See you tomorrow."

The next morning, O'Riley walked briskly toward the entrance of the St. Jude Children's Research Hospital, pausing to pay homage with a brief prayer at the statue of St. Jude, patron saint of lost causes.

Inside, the lobby resounded with a constant din of conversations, doctors' pages, and the occasional crying of young children, most with cancer. O'Riley stopped for a moment to adjust the collar of his blue blazer, awkwardly turned up atop his yellow plaid shirt. Standing in the center of the six-story atrium, he felt like a small ship awash in a sea of sickness.

After a fast elevator ride to the fourth floor, O'Riley took a wrong turn before finding the correct section. "Doctor Morgan?" he said, poking his head into a cluttered office.

"Ah, O'Riley," the doctor replied, peering over the top of his black-framed glasses. "Come in. Right on time, as always."

"Just like a train," O'Riley said, firmly gripping the young doctor's bony hand. "In the old days." He sat in a brown tweed swivel rocker and crossed his legs.

"Wouldn't know about that. Never been on one. I'm a child of air travel."

O'Riley glanced around the office, admiring the dark wood paneling behind an array of diplomas, certificates, and honorary plaques. "I had a helluva time finding you. Went to the old office down the hall."

"My cubbyhole," Morgan said. "Have a little success and they give you a bigger office."

"Looks like you jumped straight from high school to the NBA."

The diminutive doctor shrugged. "Talk of Nobel Prize consideration for my memory drug does wonders around here. They want to keep me from wandering off." He gripped the arms of his glasses and, holding them up to the light, inspected them for smudges. "How about you? Chasing any more serial killers?" He returned the glasses to his hooked nose.

O'Riley shook his head. "Nah. Just clopping around like an old horse avoiding the Alpo factory."

"Sometimes old horses are best at pulling wagons around. They already know what to do."

O'Riley nodded.

Morgan leaned forward, elbows resting on a mountain of files stacked haphazardly on his desk. "Pleasantries aside, I would guess you've come for more than a discussion of the benefits of aged equines." He arched an eyebrow, throwing his ponytail behind the back of the white lab coat that hung limply from his rounded shoulders.

O'Riley managed a faint smile. "I need the lowdown on one of the participants in your most recent experimental study. Hale's his name. Jim Hale."

"Is he in trouble?"

"No, no," replied O'Riley with a shake of his head. "He's a friend of mine. I'm just checking out some information. Might help out in an investigation I've gotten myself into."

"I remember him well. Good looking guy about fifty. Blond hair. Diagnosed with early-onset Alzheimer's. Know the difference between that and late-onset?"

O'Riley frowned.

"It's an age thing—a line of demarcation. It's early-onset if the patient is younger than fifty-seven. Late-onset if he's older." Morgan wheeled around in his chair, brown ponytail dancing behind his balding head. He opened a walnut file cabinet the color of his desk and pulled out a manila folder, studying its contents. "Hmmm. Mr. Hale's MRI showed no perceivable brain atrophy but his EEG did reveal some moderate and diffuse slowing of brain activity. Still remember our last discussion of Alzheimer's?"

O'Riley shifted in his chair. "In general. But I thought mostly older people, like in their seventies or eighties, got it."

"Not so," replied Morgan, making a steeple with his fingers. "We're now finding that the number of diagnosed cases of people in their forties and fifties with Alzheimer's is rapidly increasing, striking many at the peak of their careers and affecting their child-rearing years. As you know, the disease left untreated is characterized by a progressive and irreversible deterioration of brain function. This deterioration can include a variety of symptoms but, at the time of the study, Hale's situation was characterized only by intermittent short-term memory losses." He paused. "Remember the name of my experimental drug?"

"Alzheimerone," O'Riley replied, puffing his chest. "No second z. I made that mistake one time too many."

"Remember the procedure?"

O'Riley leaned forward, one eye squinting. "Refresh me."

"Patients are sedated intravenously with ten milligrams of Valium. For a few I may use Ativan. We make a three to four millimeter incision in the upper groin area and insert a fourteen-gauge needle. A catheter is threaded through the femoral artery into the aorta and then to the carotid artery for direct brain access."

O'Riley cringed. "Glad it ain't me."

Morgan half-smiled. "It's quite painless. The Alzheimerone is then infused into the bloodstream, which rushes the drug to the brain. Once there, it targets cells in the areas believed associated with memory, stimulating them just as bodybuilders use steroids to enhance muscle growth. Only takes about forty minutes from start to finish."

O'Riley pulled a small note pad and pencil from the chest pocket of his blazer.

"In my studies following administration of the Alzheimerone, most of the participants with Alzheimer's, even those in advanced cases, showed marked improvement of not only short-term memory but long-term as well. Very importantly, the advancement of the disease ceased almost entirely. The most remarkable breakthrough," continued Morgan, the pitch of his voice rising, "is the discovery of new cell growth found during autopsy in five patients. New cell growth. Neurogenesis. That's what's piqued the interest of the Nobel Prize committee."

O'Riley's forehead wrinkled as he scribbled on his pad.

"The question is, we don't know if the new cells are functioning once they're produced and, if so, are they performing normally? That's the big question."

"Any side effects?" O'Riley asked, still scribbling.

"Physically, no. Creatively speaking, yes. Quite a few patients report that they seem to experience short bursts of scenes playing out in their minds, like a dream or a vision."

"How long would one of these last, on average?"

"Varies. Some say a few seconds. Others up to several minutes."

O'Riley stared at the doctor, feeling the thrill of interrogation surge in his veins. "How'd they describe it?"

"Like a movie in one's mind. Pretty fascinating."

"Vivid?" O'Riley resumed jotting notes on his pad.

"Again, it varies," Morgan replied. "Some are black and white. Others see color. Sometimes with sound. Other times not. There's no real pattern I can discern. Seems to run the gamut. But not everybody sees them by any means. I found it to be predominantly those who were open to the possibility of previous lives."

"You mean reincarnation?" O'Riley thought about the case of serial killer David Lancaster. The medical examiner, he remembered, after discussion with O'Riley when Morgan's studies were in their infancy, purposely left out the findings of new cell growth from the autopsy report. Only O'Riley, Trevor Mills, and the medical examiner, Brian Davenport, knew the truth.

Morgan nodded slightly. "Also those who didn't believe in reincarnation but had a strange feeling that certain likes and dislikes they possessed, habits even, weren't learned but were innate from birth. Inexplicable nuances."

"Such as?"

"Your man Hale, for one."

O'Riley's hand froze.

"He doesn't believe in reincarnation. But he said he always had a love for antique cars. As long as he could remember. Model A's. Said he went out and tracked one down when he turned forty. Got behind the wheel and felt like he was riding a bicycle. Knew just what to do."

O'Riley cocked his head to one side.

"Another one's a woman he got chummy with at session's end."

"A blond?" O'Riley said.

Morgan nodded. "She had a thing for passenger trains. Never been on one but felt like she had." He slipped his glasses off, again holding them up to the light, then positioned them firmly back on his nose. "I found the concepts of reincarnation and predetermined preferences so alluring I used them as added parameters for the thirteen adults in my most recent group, the one Hale was in. It was my largest to date."

"What's large?"

"Double that of the past. Twenty. Divided into four groups."

"And they were?" O'Riley asked.

Morgan touched a finger to his jaw and looked at the ceiling, shutting one eye. "Five children who have or have had brain tumors; five individuals—two children and three adults—who lost memory as the result of vehicular accidents or falls; five adults with early-onset Alzheimer's; and five adults with late-onset." He glanced over at O'Riley, eyes wide. "Any other questions?"

"One." O'Riley's hunch nagged at him like a worry that keeps popping up, even during sleep. "Do you believe in reincarnation?"

Morgan considered O'Riley's question with skepticism that showed on his thin face, shrugging dismissively. "I would love to but, being a man of science, I just can't see it."

O'Riley stood up, his knees making a popping sound. He spotted a full-color, three-dimensional chart of the human brain on one wall and walked over. "Let me run with this for a second."

Morgan nodded, toying with his ponytail.

"Say your drug causes new cell growth. And say this neurowhatever—"

"Neurogenesis."

"Say these neurogenesis cells are functioning. If it occurs in the part of the brain controlling motor functions, a paralyzed person might develop movement, right?"

Morgan's mouth formed a crooked smile, acknowledging a reasonable possibility.

O'Riley tapped the brain chart twice. "And say it occurs in the part of the brain controlling memory. Memory loss ceases. People even regain memory function. Isn't that what you think is going on?"

Morgan nodded.

"Well, what if there is such a thing as reincarnation? Maybe it doesn't happen to everybody, just some people for whatever reason."

Morgan snorted.

O'Riley held his hands up, palms facing the doctor. "Just a hypocritical—"

144

"Hypothetical."

O'Riley's forehead creased. "That's what I meant. Hypothetical. Say these people don't know they had previous lives. But *they're* the ones predisposed like you said to have certain likes and dislikes that they can't figure out. Hell, all of us have likes and dislikes. Maybe some of us just aren't as perceptive about it." He walked over to the doctor's desk, hands on the edge, and leaned over. "Say your drug causes new cell growth in the memory portion of the brain in these people, enabling them to see flashes of previous lives? What if these creative bursts are the real McCoy?"

Morgan leaned back, his small frame dwarfed in his oversized chair. "Farfetched but interesting. If I could prove that, the Nobel for medicine is a gimme. I'm on the cover of every magazine in the country. *Time's* Man of the Year."

O'Riley's eyes widened. "What are the chances? One in a hundred? One in a thousand?"

Morgan frowned, stroking the side of his cheek with a forefinger that ended up on the tip of his pointed chin. "Try one in a million. Maybe a lot higher."

"C'mon, Doc," O'Riley said, jingling the keychain in his pocket. "I can get better odds than that from Publisher's Clearinghouse."

"Just an opinion," Morgan replied, "but I tell you what." His eyes crinkled as he broke into a wide grin. "You find this person and we'll get a white lab coat with Dr. O'Riley on it. We'll even share the cover of *Time*."

"Deal," O'Riley said with a handshake in parting. At the doorway he turned. "There's a saying in law enforcement you need to remember, Doc."

Morgan's eyes begged for the answer.

O'Riley winked. "Never make a promise you can't keep."

22

Jean stared hard at the double-gabled house as she closed the door of Jim's Oldsmobile. "Amazing. Just what I saw. Only older."

Jim put his arm around her as they walked up the steep concrete steps. "Just one more thing that'll knock O'Riley for a loop."

They paused at the screen door when O'Riley motioned for them to hold on a minute while he finished a phone call.

"Oh, don't worry about me. Things are real quiet," O'Riley said, winking at Jean and Jim as he spoke. "None of those Frenchmen are hittin' on you, are they?" His lips formed an arching grin. "Well, they're gonna get more than they can handle. Miss you too, honey. Love you. Bye now." He hung up and walked across the living room.

"Checking up on you, is she?" Jim said.

O'Riley opened the door, still dressed in the same blazer and yellow plaid shirt he had worn to the doctor's office, not a hair on his freshly combed head out of place. "It's the other way around. Had to tell her goodnight. It's bedtime in Paris." He looked outside. "No Model A?"

"Too hot," Jim replied. "We needed air conditioning. Where's the t-shirt and jogging pants?"

"It's not often I get called on by an attractive woman. Clean up nice, don't I?"

Jim grinned. "You remember Jean?"

"Of course." O'Riley shook her hand and then Jim's. "Come on inside."

146

"Where's Bullet?" Jim asked.

"Took him to the vet to get a bath this morning. He has to be dipped for fleas once a month. Can I get you two something to drink?"

"No thanks," Jim said as he and Jean sat on the green velvet couch covered with tan pillows.

"Well," O'Riley began, nodding at Jean, "I guess Jim told you what we think about the explosion on Devon Way."

"As incredible as it sounds," she replied, "I'd have to agree."

"And this treatment business. You in on it, too?"

"That's where I met Jim."

"You look a little young to have been in the program."

"I lost part of my memory in a car wreck. My college years."

"Do you have an occupation?" O'Riley asked.

"I'm a photographer. I live with my parents so I won't starve." She laughed. "Actually, they live in Florida half the year."

"When was the accident?"

"Just after I graduated from Virginia. In 1984."

"Charlottesville, right?"

Jean grinned. "Most people aren't sure where UVA is."

O'Riley winked again. "We detectives get around." He paused for a moment. "The accident. What happened?"

"I went through the windshield. Almost died. When I came to, I had no recollection of college. Nothing. Four years, gone. I agreed to get involved in an experimental treatment a doctor at St. Jude had come up with. They hoped the drug would help restore my lost memory. Jim was in the same group." She glanced at Jim, squeezing his hand.

"Doctor Morgan's group," O'Riley said.

Jean leaned forward. "You are good. Do you know about his research?"

O'Riley nodded. "Sometimes I think I know more about it than he does," he said with a wide grin. "I guess it worked on you, too."

Jean's blue-green eyes brimmed with enthusiasm. "I was with my mother and suddenly I started remembering everything about my years at Virginia. Everything. Memory after memory popped into my head. Then, a strange thing happened."

O'Riley cocked his head. "What happened?"

"My mother's glasses broke just after she turned our car onto Goodwyn. I slid over into the driver's seat. This vision of a fight between a boy and a girl in an old maroon car flashed into my head. It was the same vision as Jim's—only he's seen it twice. A boy smashed a girl's head against the car window. The boy was young Adam Baldwin."

O'Riley stared at the couple, thoughts shooting through his mind like an out of control pinball machine. Was this accusation against Baldwin on the level or a hoax? Maybe they were a couple of hired con artists who had checked into his background. Came up with a story a gullible retiree would love to believe. Then there was the incident with Jim's daughter.

"You sure this isn't some kind of screwy con game you two are pulling on me?"

"My daughter's death was not part of some game," Jim replied.

"I know," O'Riley said, wincing. "I'm sorry. This just all seems a little too coincidental." He ran a hand through his hair. "Jean, does my house seem familiar to you, too?"

"I'd never seen it before I drove up today. Not in person, anyway," she replied. "But it flashed in my mind a few days ago. I had no idea whose house it was until Jim picked me up yesterday. I started describing it in detail and he about fell on the floor." She laughed. "He said he had just been at that house."

O'Riley crossed his arms. "Did you see anything else?"

"A day later, I saw a vision of what looked like the back of the same house." Jean closed her eyes, hands folded in the lap of her lightweight grey slacks. "There was an old grill made up of white stones in the middle of the yard, with a concrete bench on each side. It backed up to an old shed just big enough for a car to fit inside."

"I'll be damned." O'Riley stood up, motioning to Jean and Jim. "Follow me."

They walked down the hallway and through the tidy kitchen, its appliances and counters gleaming like a display in a showroom. "Close your eyes, Jean," O'Riley directed at the back door, taking her by an elbow down five cracked concrete steps. "I won't let you fall."

The afternoon sun felt warm on her tanned face.

"Now open," O'Riley said.

"That's it!" Jean said. "That's what I saw."

Before her stood an outdoor grill made of jagged white stones with a rusted metal grate still in place. To the left and right were two curved concrete benches. Behind the grill was a rickety green shed.

"When I was a kid, I used to eat out here all the time with my two best friends." O'Riley smiled. "And that old shed still looks about like it did when it was new. My father won a 1934 Ford sedan in a Hav-A-Tampa cigar contest. Only thing he ever won in his life. He built that shed with his own two hands to keep the car out of the weather."

"There's more," Jean said after they returned to the living room. "At the funeral for Sarah. The cemetary . . ." She glanced over at Jim, who looked down at the Oriental rug and closed his eyes. Squeezing his hand, she went on, "I'd never been there. Yet it seemed so familiar—as if I'd been there many times before."

O'Riley was standing by the white marble fireplace, hand in pocket, jingling his keys. "Memorial Park?"

Jim looked up at O'Riley. "Elmwood."

O'Riley's mind slipped into high gear. He thought of his many visits to Elmwood with Jenny Adair to put flowers on his father's grave. Of Dr. Morgan and his research. Could Jean have been Jenny Adair? And Jim Will Harrison? Had Morgan unknowingly stumbled onto a link to past lives?

"I'm not sure what to make of all this," O'Riley said, wanting to believe in his heart what his head said wasn't possible. "It's uncanny. You two remind me of Jenny Adair and Will Harrison."

"Who were they?" Jean asked.

"The two best friends I ever had in my life, up until I got married. They got killed in a car crash in Overton Park in 1949. We were just kids. Graduated from high school earlier that year. I tell you, I wonder . . . sometimes I think . . . ." He paused, staring out the window at splotches of sunlight dancing through the trees.

"That we might have been them," Jim said.

O'Riley's face relaxed. He glanced at his watch. "Oh, jeez. I gotta pick up Bullet before the vet closes."

"We need to get going anyway," Jim said.

Outside, Jean fluffed her pink silk blouse and said, "What should we do about Baldwin?"

"If the two of us come out and accuse him of murder," Jim said, "are people going to say we're—"

"Crazy?" O'Riley interrupted. "Damn right. It's gonna be hard to convince folks when you say 'Oh, by the way, we saw him do it in our *previous* lives.' We need proof. Or you may as well keep your visions to yourselves and get on with your lives." He paused. "Let me think about it. I got an idea."

*

Over the next few days, O'Riley came up with a plan to test a theory he had. The first stage involved Jean; Jim would be next.

A week later, O'Riley picked up Jean and they drove down Poplar Avenue.

"Things sure have changed around here in the last sixty years," O'Riley said, pointing to the upscale Chickasaw Gardens residential area on the right. "I remember when they first started building homes in there when I was a kid. Late 30s. And see East High School over there on the left?" He pointed at the massive school and its huge, arched entryway majestically situated on an expansive tract of land. "That used to be nothing but cotton fields. So was the area further up, where Poplar Plaza is now."

The Lincoln cruised down Poplar, passing Oak Court Mall. O'Riley continued his running commentary as Jean listened intently. The wind blew through the open car windows, tousling her curled blond locks like some mischievious sprite.

"Behind Schnucks Supermarket used to be Colonial Country Club," said O'Riley, pointing. "And near the Dan West Garden Center up here used to be Mr. White's lumberyard. See how close it is to the Norfolk Southern Railroad tracks? The train would stop to pick up lumber to take to downtown merchants. They called it White Station. That's where they got the name for the road up ahead—White Station."

Jean laughed. "You're just a living, breathing history book of Poplar Avenue's past, aren't you?"

O'Riley grinned. "Haven't thought about this stuff in years. Next to the lumberyard, in a little yellow building, was the Maypop Inn. If it was illegal, you could buy it there. Fireworks, liquor. And on the left was a public golf course next to a Cities Service gas station where the Belmont Grill is now."

As the Lincoln approached the Poplar and White Station intersection, O'Riley braked as the traffic light flashed quickly from yellow to red.

"It's time we start a little experiment on you, Jean. Then we'll pick up Jim and get him involved."

"Experiment?" Jean said, tilting her head. "Is that what this mysterious outing is all about?"

"Oh, it'll be fun. We're just gonna try to jog your memory a bit. You remember anything about this area from when you were little?"

"Sure. Especially here. On that corner where Starbucks is was The Tropical Freeze. It was the last bit of civilization before leaving Memphis. After that it was fields and land except for Memorial Park. My father used to take me out to The Tropical Freeze on Sundays during the summer. I can see it now. Looked like a little South Seas hut. Hula-type music would blare on loudspeakers as you picked out some fancy tropical sherbet or ice cream concoction. The passion fruit freeze was my favorite. I think the place closed in the mid-60s."

"I remember that," O'Riley said, slowly accelerating when the light changed. "There used to be a restaurant called the Davis White Spot up here on the right, not far past Poplar and Estate. Ring a bell?"

Jean shook her head. "Never heard of it."

They pulled into a parking space at an apartment complex next to a Cadillac dealership. O'Riley switched off the ignition. "Let's take a little stroll."

"What are you up to?" she asked, smiling.

"You'll see. Just my investigative nature."

They walked down Poplar in the relative cool of early afternoon. O'Riley pulled a pink Dinstuhl's candy bag from his pocket.

"Here," he said, "have one of these."

"What are they?" Jean asked, peering into the sack.

"Something special I had Mr. Dinstuhl make up for me. They're little balls of flavored liquid covered by a clear sugar shell. You suck on it like a peppermint and then, bam! The liquid comes out."

"I've never seen these before," Jean said, passing over the orange, purple, and yellow spheres in favor of a red one.

"I knew you'd pick cherry."

"How'd you know that?"

"You've got a thing for cherry—just like Jenny Adair. Come on, let's go this way."

They strolled from the sidewalk across a spacious slope that separated the apartments from the dealership showroom. Thick green grass and a lone massive tree offered a respite from the noisy traffic on Poplar.

"Let's take a seat over here," said O'Riley, motioning to a worn concrete bench under the tree. "Now close your eyes, breathe deeply, and just let your mind wander. Then tell me what you see."

"I can't really see anything, Joe," she said, starting to open her eyes.

"No, keep 'em shut," O'Riley said. "Concentrate on relaxing."

Just then the sugar coating dissolved just enough to release the cherry liquid into Jean's mouth.

"Joe," she said softly, "I do see something."

"Describe it," he whispered.

"A white house with a gravel parking lot. There are swings out back, but no children. It's nighttime. I feel a coolness in the air. People are eating at white cloth-covered tables; each has a candle burning. I see two boys. Young men actually. It's as if I'm with them." She paused and took a deep breath.

"What else?" O'Riley said.

"One of the boys has blond hair and blue eyes. He's the same boy who was in the car with me in the other vision. He's wearing a navy blue jacket. The other one is wearing a navy jacket, too. The second boy's eyes are brown and so is his hair, with a reddish tint to it. Like auburn brown. He has a small scar on his left forehead." Jean's eyes opened wide as she turned to O'Riley. "Just like you!" She covered her mouth with one hand.

O'Riley shook his head. "This just gets more weird all the time. It's like days of view."

"You mean _déjà vu_, don't you?"

"Damn, you're as bad as Jim," O'Riley said, smiling.

"I'm sorry, Joe, I didn't mean to make fun of you."

"It's nothing." He patted her shoulder. "I'm just a retired detective with an identity crisis of my own. I think half of me must be crazy and the other half is as smart as Sherlock Holmes."

Jean grinned. A stiff breeze then blew through the tree limbs, creating an eerie, whooshing sound.

"You know what happened on that night you just saw?" he asked, a chill snaking up his back.

"Tell me."

"Will and Jenny said they were gonna get married. I remember it like it was yesterday. I toasted the two of them and told 'em they were the best friends a guy could ever have. Will then toasted me and said, and I'm quoting because I never forgot it, 'To our special friendship, our special tie that binds. May we feel it not only now but in the decades to come.' I'll be damned if he wasn't right 'cause after all these years, I'm feeling it again . . . with you and Jim."

Jean gently took O'Riley's hand. "We're feeling it with you, too, Joe." She smiled and kissed him lightly on the cheek.

"We better pick up Jim," O'Riley said, blushing. "We got a little more experimenting to do."

Ten minutes later they pulled into Jim's driveway on Lynnfield Road.

"I wondered when you two would get here," Jim said, squeezing into the front seat with them.

"You sure you don't want to get in the back?" said O'Riley. "It's a helluva lot roomier."

"No, cozier this way," Jim replied, taking Jean's hand.

"I don't know if I can stand this much coziness," O'Riley said, easing over.

"What've you two been up to?" Jim asked as O'Riley backed into the street.

"Reliving the past of the three of us. His, mine, and me," Jean said, nodding at O'Riley.

Jim cocked his head, squinting.

"His, mine, and Jenny's," she explained. "I remembered a place where Joe had been with Jenny and Will when they announced their engagement. There were two young men. One was the same one in the car with me when I flashed to that murder. The other was Joe."

Jim stared over, blue eyes wide.

"Now," O'Riley said, "I got another something up my sleeve. We'll get you involved in this one, Jim. First we have to drive a ways into town."

The Lincoln barreled around the southern leg of Interstate 240 as the sun peeked through grey clouds. O'Riley slipped on a pair of Ray-Bans to stifle the glare, watching daytime Memphis pass. In a few minutes he veered onto the Lamar Avenue exit ramp.

At that moment, Jean noticed a small silver chain dangling from O'Riley's neck as it caught the sunlight.

"What's that?" she asked. "A Saint Christopher's?"

O'Riley reached for the shimmering silver object on the chain with his right hand, steering with his left. "It's an old coin. I probably shouldn't polish it like I do. Ruins its value. It's mainly sentimental anyways."

"*Pax vobiscum*," Jean said.

Suddenly O'Riley was standing outside Central Station in downtown Memphis, dropping Jenny and Will off to catch the train.

"I still can't believe you two are really going away to college."

"Look," Will said, "it's only New Orleans. It's not like we're going to Africa." He then nodded to Jenny, who pulled a small white box from her purse.

"Go ahead," she said, smiling at Joey. "Open it."

He fumbled with the red ribbon, then slowly lifted a silver link chain with a small silver coin attached. "Wow!" He paused for a second. "What is it?"

"It's a good-luck necklace, moron," Will said.

"I know that, you sap. I meant, what kind of coin?"

Jenny took the necklace and carefully placed it around his neck. "It's a Roman denarius. *Pax vobiscum* for as long as you wear it."

Joey frowned. "What's that mean?"

"Peace be with you."

Then the memory vanished. "That's what Jenny said when she gave it to me," O'Riley said, glancing at Jean.

"That was just the first thought that came to mind when I saw it," Jean said. "*Pax vobiscum. Peace be with you.*"

O'Riley quickly pulled over in front of an abandoned warehouse and rubbed his eyes, trying to gather his thoughts.

"Look," Jim said, "I know this isn't easy to understand. You can imagine how unsettling all this has been for Jean and me. The truth is, I'm not Will. I'm Jim Hale. The way I figure it, people don't come back just like they were in the past. Most of the time, they probably don't even sense a previous life. It's just that parts of a previous life, one in which you knew me, keep popping up. Same with Jean."

"I'm not Jenny Adair now," said Jean, shaking her head, "but in a past life, I must have been."

O'Riley took a deep breath, shifted into forward gear, and pulled slowly away from the curb.

"Does this road lead where I think?" Jean asked, looking at the abandoned warehouses and businesses that lined the street.

"Wait and see," O'Riley said with a weak grin.

He steered the black Continental down a bumpy old road, as countless vehicles had done for over a hundred years. The desolate buildings with their crumbling walls and broken windows provided a grim prelude to the community of death that lay at the street's end.

"This is it," O'Riley said, pointing to a black, wrought-iron sign that spanned the single-lane bridge entrance.

"I had no idea it was this large," Jean said as she scanned the sprawling hills covered with mausoleums and large stone monuments. "At Sarah and David's funeral, my thoughts were on other things."

"We aren't staying too long, are we?" Jim asked quietly. He stared off in the distance toward his daughter's grave, squeezing Jean's hand tightly.

"I know it's hard on you," O'Riley said. "We're almost there." He eased to a stop on one of Elmwood's winding, narrow roads.

156

They got out and O'Riley pointed at two small markers before them, one grey marble, the other white. He read aloud the inscription on the grey headstone.

Patrick Joseph O'Riley
A Servant of the Law and the Lord
February 1, 1891—March 15, 1947

"Let's do like before, Jean," O'Riley said softly. "Close your eyes, and tell me if you see anything."

Jean stared at the inscription for a moment before shutting her eyes. A gentle breeze suddenly swept through the trees, making goosebumps on her arms and bare shoulders. "I see . . . this exact spot," she said slowly, "only the trees are smaller. There are flowers at the grave."

"What kind of flowers?" O'Riley asked.

"Easter lillies—no, poinsettias." She paused. "Now lilies—fading back to poinsettias."

"Son of a bitch," O'Riley said.

Jean looked over at him, eyes wide.

"You've been here before," O'Riley said. "A long time ago."

"I don't feel I've been here before," Jim said. "Other than for Sarah."

"Ah," O'Riley said, a finger pointing skyward, "you wouldn't. Will Harrison never saw my father's headstone. He hated cemeteries. Jenny would come out here with me at Easter to put lilies on the graves. And at Christmas, poinsettias. Even other times, so I wouldn't have to come alone. Your turn, now. Give it a shot."

Jim nodded and stared at the grey headstone as he closed his eyes. A slight breeze jostled the loose sleeves of his shirt.

"Whattaya see?"

"Nothing."

"What do you mean, nothing?"

"I mean nothing—black."

Jim then opened his eyes and looked over at the thinner white headstone.

Louise O'Riley—An Angel On Earth
February 4, 1905—April 5, 1936

Jim slowly closed his eyes. He quivered slightly, hands balling into fists.

"There are people all around. Many in police uniforms. It's overcast—there's a light drizzle falling. I'm standing next to a boy who has rusty brown hair and a scar on his left forehead . . ." Jim quickly opened his eyes. ". . . just like yours."

O'Riley shook his head, staring down at his mother's grave. "This is the only headstone Will Harrison ever saw. He never came out here again after my father's funeral."

Jim turned to Jean. "You must have been the brown-haired girl I saw standing on the other side of Joe. The same girl who was in the car with me on Goodwyn." He reached over and took Jean's hand.

O'Riley shook his head. "Nobody, and I mean nobody, would believe this."

"What next?" Jean asked.

"What next?" O'Riley jingled the keys in his pocket. "I'll tell you what's next. We're gonna figure out a way to solve that murder."

23

"Top of the morning to you, E.," said O'Riley.

"And the rest of the day to you," the shoeshine man replied, white teeth shining bright in the morning sunlight.

O'Riley glanced over at the untended stand on the sidewalk. "What are you doing over here on the steps?"

"Settin'."

"I can see that." O'Riley laughed as he sat down next to him.

"Just gittin' a different perspective on things," E. said, pinching his chin. "Ain't nobody gonna mess with my shine stand whiles I can still see it."

"I guess you're right," O'Riley said, raising his voice above the honks and revs of morning traffic.

"It keeps your mind sharp all week long when you do some deep thinkin' on Monday morning."

"You think so, eh?" O'Riley rubbed a knuckle across his lips. "I've got a question. You believe in reincarnation?"

"You mean coming back from the dead, like ghosts?"

"No," O'Riley replied, scratching his jaw. "I mean somebody dies, then maybe a few days or a few years go by, and he or she is born again into another body. They're a different person, but sometimes they remember bits and pieces from a previous life."

The old man arched his grey eyebrows. "That sounds pretty crazy to me, Joe. I do believe in ghosts, though."

"You ever seen one?"

"Sure have," E. replied, slapping the knee of his stained brown pants. "My uncle Jasper come back one Christmas Eve night and told me I better put that bottle down and go buy my wife a present."

"Bottle?"

"Jack Daniel's. I drunk a whole damn fifth that day."

"And you saw your dead uncle Jasper? Hell, if I drank a whole fifth of anything, the only thing I'd see is the back side of my eyelids."

E. nodded. "He was real! Been dead twenty-three years but he give me the best advice I ever got. If I hadn't staggered into that pawn shop at closing time and bought that Timex, my wife would've shoved my black ass up the chimney and told me not to come home 'til I had Santa Claus with me."

O'Riley laughed as he stood up and patted E.'s shoulder. "On that note, I'll leave you. Give my regards to your uncle Jasper next time you see him."

"Don't be joking like that," E. said. "You might see him 'fore I do."

Once inside police headquarters, O'Riley didn't make his customary left turn up the staircase to Homicide. Instead he continued straight down the long corridor past the Vice Squad to a narrow, seldom-used stairwell and hurried down two flights to the basement. A thick musty odor hung in the air.

He then went straight to a massive wooden desk at the end of the floor, glimpsing the steel-grey file cabinets that housed the unsolved homicide and missing-person files.

"Where's Captain Schmidt?" O'Riley asked the baby-faced officer at the desk.

"Off for a couple of vacation days," the officer replied. "Said he needed some rest. You're Chief O'Riley, aren't you?"

"Yeah, how'd you know?"

"We had to memorize the names and pictures of past chiefs for our academy final. You were an easy one because of that little scar on your forehead."

O'Riley scowled. "Didn't your mama ever teach you it's not nice to discuss abnormalities in a person's appearance?"

"No, sir. I mean, yes, sir. Sorry, sir," responded the young man, his face so red his freckles disappeared.

"I need a favor, if you will."

"Yes, sir?"

"I want to take a look at the unsolved missing-person files from 1949."

"Sorry, sir, I can't let you see those without written authorization from Chief Perry," the officer replied.

"What do you mean I can't see it?" O'Riley bellowed.

The officer's head dipped. "Again, sir, I'm sorry. It's new policy. Why don't you go upstairs and ask Chief Perry to okay it? I'm stuck here for the next six hours."

O'Riley cracked a smile. "What's your name, son?"

"Larsen, sir. Howard Larsen."

"You keep up the good work, Larsen," O'Riley said, his voice echoing as he headed back to the stairwell. "Don't give in to people no matter how ornery they act and you'll go far in this organization." He disappeared into the darkness leading upstairs and added in a whisper, "Little bastard."

In a few minutes O'Riley was sitting across the desk from Charlie Perry.

"Why do you need to be nosing around in those files?" Perry asked, tilting back in his soft leather chair. "With all the regulations we have now, do you know how many forms we'd have to fill out just to get that 1949 file out of the archives dungeon? You didn't have to screw with this much paperwork when you were chief. Besides, I'm supposed to report the names of anybody wanting to view any archives prior to 1950 to the Secret Service."

O'Riley belched under his breath. "The Secret Service?"

"Yeah," Perry said, stroking his greying moustache. "Some agent, name of Stafford."

"Why would they want you to do that?" O'Riley asked, knowing the real reason.

"Has to do with security for a presidential candidate is what he told me. When those guys get involved, I just follow directions and get out of the way. I have enough problems as it is." Perry pushed his tortoise-shell glasses back up the bridge of his nose. "Look, if you think you might be onto something sometime, let me know. I'll take care of it personally."

"I don't want to take up any more of your time, Charlie," O'Riley said, standing up, nerves jingling like his key chain. "You're a busy man. Don't work too hard."

"Don't you work too hard," Perry replied, an arm on O'Riley's shoulder as he escorted him out of the office.

"Well, look who the cat drug in," Sergeant Driscoll said as O'Riley approached Homicide.

O'Riley's eyes narrowed. "Don't mess with me today."

Driscoll shot a crooked smile at the former chief. "Who in the hell elected you king?"

"Not king. Vice president of sex and music."

"What's that supposed to mean?"

O'Riley glared at him. "If I want your fooking opinion, I'll whistle."

Driscoll crossed his long arms. "No doughnuts? What gives?"

"I don't want 'em taken for granted. I'll bring enough for everybody next time," O'Riley said, abruptly turning to leave, "except you."

"What's gotten into him?" Mills asked. "He's usually in a pretty good mood."

✳

Early that afternoon, O'Riley sat in his small den with Jean and Jim.

"I appreciate your coming over on such short notice. Can I get you something to drink?"

"Water's fine for me," Jean said.

"Do you have a Coke?" Jim asked.

"Diet or high-octane?"

Jim smiled. "High-octane."

O'Riley vanished to the kitchen, returning a few moments later. He placed the glasses, Coke fizzing, on the coffee table in front of them. "I ran into a little hitch in my plan to get a picture of the girl I think you might have seen Baldwin kill."

"What kind of hitch?" Jim asked, taking a sip.

"A Secret Service agent is keeping tabs on anybody requesting information about police files prior to 1950. They're saying it deals with the security of a presidential candidate," O'Riley said, making quote marks with curled fingers. "What does that sound like to you?"

"Like Baldwin is a little concerned," Jean replied.

"And wants to keep tabs on anybody who might be onto him," Jim added.

O'Riley nodded. "I'm gonna get that file, but it may take a couple of days. I want to make sure a certain guy I trust is on duty in the old records area. In the meantime, plan B. I've come up with another experiment. Spent about an hour in the attic digging through a mountain of dust to come up with this one."

"Oh, no," Jean said, laughing, "not another trip back in time."

"Not quite," O'Riley replied. "This will test your memory of the visions you've already had. Keep your batting averages up like they've been and we'll have a positive I.D. on the victim in a matter of minutes. Maybe something more." O'Riley stood up. "I should've thought of this earlier. Jim, you come with me. Jean, you stay here and relax. Watch the news or play with Bullet, if you can wake him up." He tilted his head toward his dog, asleep in the corner. "When Jim finishes, I'll call for you."

The two men walked down the hallway and into the dining room. There lay thirty small pictures of high school students from the late 1940s, fanned out on the glossy rosewood dinner table.

"I cut these out of my high school yearbook. No names, just faces. Look at each one real closely and tell me if any of 'em look familiar," O'Riley said.

Jim studied each one carefully. "They look so much older than high school seniors," he said. The boys had slicked-back hairstyles and most of the girls wavy, shoulder-length hair.

O'Riley hovered over the table, one hand resting on the annual's faded green cover. "What can I say? Kids these days grow up quicker. Back then we were naive but looked older." He paused for a few moments. "Recognize anybody?"

"Four people."

"Which ones?"

Jim pointed to Adam Baldwin. "This one, of course. Same picture I saw in *Time* of him during his high school days. He's the one who committed the murder in my vision. No doubt about it. And this one," he said, picking up the photograph of Allison Tucker. "She was the girl who was murdered."

O'Riley's heart fluttered. After all these years. The mysterious ball of yarn that was Allison Tucker's disappearance was finally unraveling. How had she disappeared with no trace? Buried? Dumped in the river?

"What about the third?" O'Riley asked.

Jim held up the picture of young Joey O'Riley. "You," he said. "This is who I saw standing next to me last week in my vision at Elmwood."

O'Riley's left eyebrow arched. "Lastly?"

"This girl. She was the one in the car with me." His finger rested on the picture of Jenny Adair.

"I knew it! Now we're getting somewhere. Jean!" he yelled. "Your turn."

Bullet trailed behind her as she entered the room, promptly curling into a worn spot of carpet in a corner of the dining room.

"Look through these pictures and tell me if you recognize anybody," O'Riley said, spreading the pictures once again.

Jean carefully examined each picture, moving around the table for a better look as Jim and O'Riley held their breath.

"Three guys and one girl look familiar. This one murdered the girl," she said, picking up the photo of Adam Baldwin. "And this is the girl he killed." Her neatly manicured nail rested on the smiling face of Allison Tucker. "And this guy is who I'm in the car with on Goodwyn, and the one who was at the table at the Davis White Spot." The picture was Will Harrison. "This last one," she said, holding up Joey O'Riley's photograph, "is the other boy I saw at the White Spot. The one with the scar. You."

"I'll be damned," O'Riley said as he sat down in one of the chairs.

Jim and Jean sat down with him at the table.

"This is too much," O'Riley said. "You two drop down out of nowhere like the damn tooth fairy and give me the answer to a case I couldn't solve my whole career." He looked down at the floor, massaging his greying temples. Then he looked up. "Now comes the hard part. We still don't have any witnesses. Or any evidence. For those of you keeping score, that means no case for the home team."

A few days later, O'Riley burst into Homicide, taking refuge from the overcast, drizzly skies. His raincoat, slick with water, shone under the bright fluorescents.

Ken Driscoll shot a wicked glance at the former chief. "What'sa matter, O'Riley? Finally got enough sense to come in out of the rain?"

Trevor Mills, at his corner desk punching a computer keyboard as though playing the piano, looked up.

O'Riley pulled a box of doughnuts from beneath his raincoat and turned to Driscoll. "Do you always have to be so rude?"

"Yeah," Driscoll replied, "I do. Deep down you like it."

O'Riley's sheepish smile confirmed that the sergeant was right. But the kid didn't stand a chance. He'd give him a ten-second reprieve.

The other detectives stopped attacking the files and loose papers left on their desks from the day before. Harris focused on O'Riley's white cardboard box.

"Hey, Harris," O'Riley said, "I noticed E. ain't outside. Nothing's wrong with the old guy, is it?"

"Who you kiddin'?" Harris replied. "That old buzzard's healthy as an ox. Had to get his dentures looked at. Irritating his gums or something. He'll be back tomorrow."

O'Riley passed the doughnuts around, purposefully avoiding Driscoll. "You got that recommendation for Driscoll's transfer to Internal Affairs?" O'Riley yelled to Harris as he approached Driscoll's desk.

"Yeah, Chief," Harris replied loudly, ready to play the foil. "It's here somewhere." He shuffled the papers on his desk as he bit into a doughnut. "Got it!" he said as he handed a piece of official police stationery to O'Riley.

"Hmmm." O'Riley nodded. "Works well when under constant supervision and cornered like a rat in a trap. Sets low personal standards and consistently fails to achieve them." He paused.

"Isn't there more?" Harris asked, grinning.

O'Riley nodded. "In closing, although one-celled organisms consistently outscore Sergeant Driscoll on IQ tests, he should still go far and, the sooner he starts, the better. Signed, Joseph O'Riley, former Memphis Chief of Police."

A wave of subdued laughter rolled through the department.

Driscoll jumped from his seat, grabbing a handful of files, and walked toward the door. "Funny, O'Riley, funny," he said, his balding head tinged red. "Why don't you go have your prostate checked? Better yet, let these guys do it for you. They seem to be easily amused by assholes."

Laughter closed around him as Driscoll stormed out.

"Hey, Mills, you ever look at that TV show, *60 Minutes*?" O'Riley asked.

"Yeah, sometimes," Mills replied, biting into his doughnut.

"Takes Driscoll an hour and a half to watch it."

Harris chuckled. "I hate he missed that one."

"Do me a favor and repeat it when he gets back. Have a great day, gentlemen." O'Riley winked, gave a casual salute, and walked through the door, heading straight to the basement with four remaining doughnuts in the box under his arm.

Emerging from the dimness of the dingy staircase, O'Riley spotted the rotund figure of his old friend, Captain John Schmidt, at the antique precinct desk. Schmidt had been on the force over forty years. Although honest and hard-working in his prime, he never possessed the special inner drive that propelled some officers to the top ranks of the department. His high rank was mainly due to the regulation that promoted every thirty-year veteran to the rank of captain, deserved or not.

Schmidt was surveying his murky realm as if he were a corpulent king on his throne, lord of a subterranean world of police artifacts. "Joe O'Riley," he bellowed as the former chief emerged from the shadows. "What brings you down to the dark depths of my domain?"

"Doughnuts, Smitty," O'Riley replied, placing the white box on the high desk. "Not that you need 'em."

Schmidt patted his large midsection. "I can always use some dough-nuts. The guys up in Homicide say they been seeing you about every week. I was wondering when you'd make it down here." A grin spread across his pudgy cheeks. "You must need a favor. I may be fat, but not between the ears."

"Yes I do. The unsolved missing persons files from 1949."

"You gotta be kidding. What for?" Schmidt ran a hand across the top of his head, bald with only a few strands of grey brushed back from his forehead.

"I've got a hunch. There might be something in the file I can use," O'Riley said. "Help me out, will you?"

Schmidt squinted, round face wrinkling like a prune. "Aw, Joe, I can't do that. Nobody can get anything out of here without clearance. You know that. Besides, Chief Perry sent word down that nobody should come in here without him personally knowing about it. He wants the log sheet on his desk first thing every morning."

"Smitty, Smitty, Smitty," O'Riley whispered, "this hunch I'm working on is a *big* secret. Nobody can know about it. Not even the chief. Not yet."

"Sorry, Joe. Can't do it."

"Smitty, how far back do we go? Thirty-five, forty years?"

Schmidt shut one eye and scratched the back of his thick neck. "Forty plus a few. You took me under your wing when I was a rookie in Homicide in 1956."

O'Riley spread his hands. "Think of all those cases you helped me with. The Chickasaw Gardens decapitation early in '57, the Hollywood killer later that year, the doctor who threw his wife off the fire escape at the Parkview Hotel in '62—why, even the hippie ax murder by that flower child tripping on LSD in 1970 out at the lake in Audubon Park. You were always there to help me when I needed it."

Schmidt's chair creaked as he leaned back, his hands folded, propping up his sagging double chin. "I know it, Chief, but—"

"And the bottles of Bushmills we've been through. I'd need a calculator."

"Yeah, but—"

"My father, Paddy, was a policeman's policeman, as you well know from all my stories about him. He had an old Irish proverb I want to share with you, Smitty."

"Always remember to forget
The things that made you sad,
But never forget to remember
The things that made you glad.
Always remember to forget
The friends that proved untrue,
But don't forget to remember
Those that have stuck by you."

Schmidt stared into O'Riley's brown eyes for a few moments, then pushed back in his chair and stood up. "Ten minutes, Joe, that's it. And if anybody accuses me of letting any unauthorized people down here, I'm gonna deny it to the hilt."

A smile spread across O'Riley's face. "You're a saint, Smitty, a real saint."

Schmidt stepped down from behind the desk and lumbered to the file cabinets lining the wall on his left. "I hope you've been eating your Wheaties," he said, opening a drawer labeled 'Missing Persons 1939 to 1949—Unresolved.' He grunted as he lifted a bulky volume from the drawer and dropped it with a thud onto a small table next to a short desk lamp. "Have at it, Joe. Ten minutes, no more."

O'Riley quietly sat on a small wooden stool and flipped through the unwieldy book. He quickly found the report on Allison Tucker at the end of the 1949 section. Straining, he carefully read the notes, hoping something might jump off the page at him, something that would lunge out and bite him on the ass.

Allison Tucker. Date of birth, 10-13-32. Height 5'4". Weight 110 lbs. Brunette hair, slight build. Petite. Daughter of Robert and Miriam Tucker. Residence, 587 South Belvedere. Date missing, 12-29-49. Investigated by Flannery, Abbott, and O'Riley.

Subject last seen by parents early evening 12-29-49. She said she was going out with a friend, Lisa Mitchell. Mitchell girl never saw her and denied making any plans to be with her that night. Reported to have been wearing a maroon wool dress with flower designs, as that is the only item the parents know to be missing. No sightings, no leads.

O'Riley flipped the page to find another entry in the Tucker file by a Sergeant Adamson on 12-30-50. "Damn," he mumbled, "didn't know about this."

Negro male, thirty-six years of age, reports he saw the missing girl, whom he recognized from a picture in *The Commercial Appeal* with the story about her being missing for one year. Says he saw her on the night of her disappearance wearing a maroon flowered dress. Witness is most likely reliable since that fact was never released to the public. He said she was in the company of a college-age, Caucasian male, but the witness was unable to describe the male or the car that the suspect was driving, other than that it was 'a fancy car that looked dark.' Sighting took place on Goodwyn off Southern Avenue where witness is employed as a yardman. Further investigation by Flannery and Abbott turned up no additional information.

O'Riley's mouth dropped as he read the last notation on the report.

Name of witness is Ephraim Crowder.

24

The next morning at 7:45, the glossy black door to Charlie Perry's office creaked open. Joe O'Riley stood in the doorway.

"Charlie, you told me to let you know if I was onto something and you'd take care of it. That time has come a little sooner than I thought," O'Riley said.

"I'd say a helluva lot sooner," Perry replied.

"Remember, just me and you. Nobody else for now."

"You have my word," the chief said. "I'll drop into Homicide at nine o'clock. Give you enough time?"

"See you then."

"Wouldn't miss it for the world," Perry said with a wink.

A few minutes later O'Riley pushed through Homicide's doors with E. at his side. The old man had a portable shine box under his right arm.

Driscoll was puffing on a cigarette in the corner, a cloud of wispy white smoke surrounding his desk like fog around an island. "To what do we owe this honor?" he said, looking up. "His highness has graced us with his presence for the third time this week." He took a final drag on his Camel and drained the last of a Coca-Cola.

"What brings me here today," O'Riley replied, "is that, instead of doughnuts, E. here is gonna shine everybody's shoes. My treat. Mills, Harris, Crosby, Norton—all of you, even Driscoll. And while he's at it, Driscoll, he'll even buff your head. No extra charge."

"You know, O'Riley, sometimes you aren't such a bad guy," Driscoll said, smiling. "When I get older and grumpy like you, I'll try to be generous every now and then too."

After tackling every pair of shoes in sight, E. finally took a seat outside the Mystery Room, where suspects and witnesses were often questioned.

"You've worked pretty hard, E.," O'Riley said, patting the old man's stooped shoulders. "Let's go in there and take it easy for a bit, away from all the commotion."

E. took one of three chairs at the small conference table. The sparsely furnished room contained a phone, a chalkboard mounted on the wall, and an electric clock on the opposite wall. The clock pointed to nine on the dot.

This is it, O'Riley said to himself, another chance after years of retirement to show the chief and the other cops what I can do.

Out of the corner of his eye, O'Riley spotted Perry. The detectives quickly picked up their pace as the chief entered, feverishly punching keys on their computers, creating a din like the clatter of tap dancers in a vaudeville show.

"Hey, Chief," O'Riley yelled through the door, "everybody's had a shine except you. Come on in here. I think E. has one with your name on it."

When Perry was inside, O'Riley closed the heavy wooden door to the sound-proofed chamber behind him. Less than five minutes later, the chief's black Gucci shoes were as shiny as a mirror.

"How many is that, E.?" O'Riley asked.

"Total of ten. At two-fifty each, that's twenty-five smackers. I gave the group rate." He held out his calloused right hand and rubbed his thumb and forefinger together. "Pay the man!"

"This should cover it," O'Riley said, slapping a fifty-dollar bill into his outstretched palm.

"Well, I don't see Mr. Grant too much. But I am on intimate terms with Mr. Washington. Mr. Lincoln and me are pretty tight, too. Anything else I can do for you gentlemens 'fore I go?" he said, dentures flashing.

"There is one thing, E.," O'Riley replied, motioning to a chair. "You better get comfortable."

"I don't likes the sound of that. Do we got a problem?" he said as he eased into the hard wooden chair.

"No problem at all, E., that the truth won't solve," Perry said. He smiled at the puzzled shoeshine man.

"I happened on an old missing-person file yesterday involving a case I've been trying to resurrect," O'Riley said. "It has to do with a girl named Allison Tucker. She turned up missing in December of 1949."

E. stared at the beige floor. The bald crown of his head reflected the fluorescent lights above.

"Seems a witness showed up about a year later," O'Riley continued. "He had seen her on the night she vanished but couldn't remember what he had seen too well. Any of this sound familiar?" He paused for a few moments. "And," O'Riley added, "he went by the name of Ephraim Crowder. He'd be close to ninety if he was still alive."

E. looked over at O'Riley, his brown eyes the size of golf balls, beads of perspiration dotting his brow. He rubbed his fingers together.

"What were you doing at the scene?" O'Riley asked.

E. straightened up in his chair. "I was the yard boy for the Shermans. I stayed late that night doing some fix-up work on a fountain in the front yard."

"The yard boy?"

"Yessir, I was. That's what they called it back then. Today I'd be a handyman. I did just 'bout anything they'd ask me to do. Cut the yard, trim hedges, work the flower beds, cut firewood, paint, tinker on their cars, drive 'em around town, fix up around the house—you name it. They's good folks. Gave me a job right after the Depression that kept me and my family going when other peoples had nothing. I'm grateful to 'em."

"What happened to the girl that night?" O'Riley said.

"I was working on that fountain when I seen a car pull up near the drive. It parked near the street light so's I could see pretty good. The boy got out, and the girl did, too. She was a little thing with brown hair and a pretty smile."

Perry got up, planted a foot on his chair, and rested an elbow on his knee. "How far away was this fountain from the street?"

"Oh, I reckon about a hundred feet."

O'Riley frowned. "Then how, may I ask, did you see that pretty smile so clearly?"

E. hesitated, throat twitching. "It's like this. I ain't no peeping tom or nothing, but that boy would always bring girls up to that same spot and mess around with 'em. Kissing. More if he could."

"So when he was walking around with the girl, you moved closer to see better?" Perry asked.

"Yessir, I did. Close up behind some hedges."

"What'd you see next?"

"After they walked around for a few minutes holding hands, they got back in the car. A whiles later it looked like they was scuffling. The girl tried to get out of the car, and the boy pulled her back. She grabbed at his neck and hit at him. Then he smacked her head upside the door. I heard the glass break. The girl didn't move at first, but all of a sudden, she started flapping around like a big ol' catfish on a cane pole. Then she didn't move no more. The boy upchucked a few minutes later and drove off." E. took a deep breath and slowly exhaled, his gaunt face relaxing.

"Did you see any other people? Any cars?" the former chief asked.

"Another car looked like it went after him. An old Ford. Model A. Had a boy and a girl in it. They'd been parked on the side of the road doing the big shimmy in the back seat before the other couple drove up."

"How did you know the girl had been killed?" O'Riley asked.

"I didn't that night. But, two days later, I seen a picture of a girl in the paper who was missing. It was the girl I seen."

"Could you identify the car you saw and who the boy was?" Perry asked.

"I *know* who it was!" E. wiped sweat from his upper lip. "The car was one of them sports cars. Looked like something out of the future. Like from one of them Flash Gordon serials. It was maroon. And the boy, everyone knew him."

"How so?" O'Riley asked.

Perry pursed his lips as if he had bitten into a lemon as he waited for the answer.

"It was the mayor's grandson—Adam Baldwin."

A smile spread across O'Riley's face. A real witness had finally emerged after all those years.

"E.," Perry said, "why didn't you come forward with this whole story before?"

"That's easy to answer now but not back then—times is changed. Back then, nobody said nothing that Mayor Hart could get on you for. Who do you think people would have believed—a black yard boy or the grandson of the mayor? They'd a pinned the murder on me. No sirree, I had my job to think about. And my family."

"Why are you telling us all this now?" Perry asked. "You could have remained silent and refused to answer our questions."

E. glanced at O'Riley and took another deep breath. "Chief Joe and I been talking a lot lately. Having a lot of heart-to-hearts. I'm an old man. I want to have a clean slate when I meets my maker. I want to be able to say I done what's right. I'm a Democrat myself." He pointed a crooked finger at his chest. "But what's right is right, and Mr. Baldwin should pay for what he done." He straightened his back, shoulders forward, proud to have set the truth free.

"Are you willing to testify as to what you saw that night, E.?" O'Riley asked.

"Yessir, I am. Ain't nobody can threaten me now. My family and friends is all gone. I'm close to being dead myself."

"If you don't mind," Perry said, leaning forward, "we'd like to put you under police protection."

"In a nice hotel?" E. said.

"Of course."

"With room service?"

"All you can eat," Perry promised.

"And one of them jacuzzis?"

"You name it, E.," O'Riley added, "it's yours."

"No way," Jim said later that afternoon as he and Jean sat on the sofa in O'Riley's living room. "The old guy *really* witnessed the murder?"

"Described it just like you and Jean did. The car, the fight, the girl's head smashed against the window. Saw it all. Even a Model A Ford following the Cord as it drove off down Goodwyn."

Jean leaned forward. "Can't you use his testimony to get an indictment against Baldwin?"

O'Riley shook his head, face tightening. "It's tough to build a case on a single witness, especially one that old. The grand jury would question his credibility without any evidence. More so if the alleged perpetrator is someone of Baldwin's stature." He fell silent and drew a breath. "If we just knew where the bastard drove off to that night. Finding the remains of our missing girl would put us in high cotton."

"So what do we do?" Jim asked.

"We ain't gonna give up, that's for sure," O'Riley replied. "Just be on guard. Wary of strangers. Watch out for anything out of the ordinary."

"Why's that?" Jim asked.

"Do you want a chance to *really* get Baldwin?"

Jim nodded. "That goes without saying."

176

"Well, with every reward comes a risk."

"How so?"

"Chief Perry and I came up with a plan. We're gonna find out just how serious a threat Baldwin thinks you are."

"Me?" Jim said, pointing both hands at his chest. "I thought we had a real witness now."

"We do. But we don't want Baldwin to know who it is. We've got him hidden away like a mummy in a tomb over at The Peabody Hotel. Hardly a soul in the department knows about it. Just Perry and the three undercover guys guarding him. Tomorrow, Perry's gonna let it leak that there's a witness to the 1949 slaying of a girl in Memphis and that a very important politician has been implicated in the crime. Believe me, word's gonna travel fast through the grapevine to Baldwin's top aide. A guy named Tom Stafford. He told Perry he was Secret Service, but he's a former agent. Nice little connection for a politician to have, ain't it?"

"So where do I fit in?" Jim asked, eyebrows arched.

"If Baldwin suspects somebody's coming after him again, it's gonna fan the flames. He'll think the witness has to be you. Who else has brought this murder up? If any hanky-panky starts up from his end, it'll lend us more credibility."

"In other words, it might be open season on me again?" Jim shot a worried look at Jean.

"Might be?" O'Riley rapped the side of his head with his knuckles. "Anybody home? How do you think a honeybee would feel if he thought it was your hand groping around in his hive?"

Jim stood up. "All right, all right," he said. "I get the picture."

"This isn't just getting in the way of somebody's business deal. This is interfering with the dream of a lifetime."

Jean reached up, clutching Jim's hand, nervously tapping a foot on the floor. He rubbed his temple and eased back down on the couch.

"But don't you worry. I'm gonna make sure you're safe. I got a friend who does surveillance work on the side. I'll line him up to keep an eye on you. He's good. He'll spot any strange goings-on." O'Riley paused for a moment, looked down at the worried couple, and cleared his throat. "There is one problem. I know you and Jean have been seeing a lot of each other. Better take it easy for a while. The less anybody sees you together, the less danger for Jean."

Jean's shoulders tensed, oval eyes opening wide.

"I don't mean to scare you, Jean," O'Riley said. "They're not after you. You don't know nothing as far as they're concerned. I'll be keeping pretty close, if that'll make you feel better."

"It would," she replied, nodding. "A lot."

He looked over at Jim. "You keep any money around the house?"

"Yeah, I do—in case of an earthquake."

"How much? Two, three hundred?"

"A thousand dollars."

"A thousand dollars! You planning on a 6.8?"

"Just in case," he replied, with a quickly vanishing grin.

"Well, then, just in case, keep it on you at all times. This might involve getting you out of town. Could be short notice. Any cities you have friends in?"

"Not really," Jim replied, shaking his head.

"Any place you want to visit? Los Angeles, maybe?"

"I don't think so," he said. "Too spread out. Besides, no need leaving one earthquake zone for another."

"San Francisco?" O'Riley asked.

"Ditto."

"New York City?"

"Don't think so."

"You think about it and let me know. It ain't something we gotta figure out today."

"Are we still going to that restaurant?" Jean asked, eager to change the subject.

"I don't see why not," Jim replied, squeezing her hand. "We need to make the most of our time together before word gets out." He stood up and helped Jean with his strong right arm. "Want to join us, Joe?"

"Nah, I'll leave you two to yourselves." He walked them to the door, one hand in his pocket, jingling his keychain. "Remember. Be cautious of everybody after this weekend. You can trust yourselves, me, and the guy I'll have watching you. His name is Reynolds. Rich Reynolds. He's a good-looking older guy," O'Riley said with a wink, "like me."

Within minutes O'Riley had Reynolds on the phone. "Glad I caught you at home, Rich," O'Riley said, holding the receiver to his ear with a shoulder. "Whatcha been up to?"

"Oh, not much, Joe," his old friend replied. "I hang out around the house with the missus. That is, when I'm not farming."

"A farmer? You gone nuts in your old age? You couldn't even grow weeds in that patch out back you called a garden."

"Old age, my ass. I'm five years younger than you. I'm a farmer, I tell you. King of the honeydews."

"Heard that one," replied O'Riley. "Honey, do this. Honey, do that."

"Still sharp after all these years. Must be why you made chief and I retired a captain. What's up?"

"I got a job for you if you're not too busy farming."

"Let me wipe the mud off my boots and you'll have my undivided attention," Reynolds replied with a laugh.

O'Riley quickly laid out the situation, warning that trouble was a possibility. He had thrown Reynolds a lot of investigative jobs in the past and he had always been eager to oblige.

"I still have a permit to carry my nine-millimeter Glock," Reynolds said. "And I ain't afraid to use it if the situation warrants."

"That's what I like to hear."

"I do have one conflict. Starting Monday is fine but I have a meeting Tuesday at five to close on a piece of property I'm selling. Won't take long. I can be back on the job by six-thirty."

"Shouldn't be a problem," O'Riley replied. "I'm not really expecting anything to happen for at least a week or two. If at all."

"Usual rate?"

"That and all the Bushmills you can drink on Saturday nights."

"You always did overpay," Reynolds said, laughing.

25

Adam Baldwin had just finished his room-service breakfast of Eggs Benedict as he placed the white linen napkin beside his plate, pushed back from the table, and stood up to stretch. He wore a dark Zegna suit, purple Hermès necktie, custom-made white shirt—easy competition with the Hollywood luminaries he would soon be addressing.

The slowing economy and growing unemployment figures nagged at him. The American influence was suffering abroad. President Benson had been ineffectual. His vice president the same, a spineless yes man. An experienced older candidate was sure as hell better than the Republican nominee, John Titus. The virus running rampant through Baldwin's veins would only die when he achieved his place in The White House. But an obstacle remained.

Information received the previous night weighed on his mind. He nervously paced the carpet in the Century Plaza's Royal Suite, stopping for a moment in front of a gilt-framed mirror to tighten the knot in his tie. He winced, his hand aching from shaking hundreds of hands the day before.

Just then there was a double knock on the door, followed by a high-pitched squeal.

"Come in, come in," Baldwin said, a wide grin veiling his worries as a towheaded boy dressed in dinosaur print pajamas darted across the room. "That's my boy!" He reached down and hoisted his three-year-old grandson, Adam III, above his head.

"We just wanted to say goodbye," the tall, broad-shouldered man trailing behind the youngster said.

"Good to see you, son," Baldwin replied, shifting his grandson from right shoulder to left. "If only for one night."

"Do spider, Bumpaw," the child pleaded.

"Bumpaw has work to do," Adam Jr. said. "We'll have plenty of time for spider after our vacation when Bumpaw gets home to Memphis."

"Don't be silly," Baldwin said. "There's *always* time for one more spider." He sat down, sinking deep into the fluffy couch with his grandson sprawled in his lap.

At that moment, Tom Stafford entered, moving quickly past the Secret Service detail in the hall, and greeted Adam Jr. with a firm handshake. "Spider again?" he whispered.

Adam Jr. nodded. "Kid's got him wrapped around his finger."

Baldwin's left hand was high in the air. Fingers slowly descending, he wiggled them menacingly and began to sing:

The itty-bitty spider came from up above.
The itty-bitty spider looked for one to love.
The itty-bitty spider turned happy, full of joy.
The itty-bitty spider jumped on the little boy!

Adam III screamed in delight, his tiny body convulsing with laughter as his grandfather tickled his stomach. "Do again! Do again!"

Adam Jr. reached for his son. "Bumpaw has a busy day. Kiss him goodbye."

The corners of the youngster's mouth drooped. He whimpered, round face wrinkling.

"Momma's waiting for us in our room," Adam Jr. said. "You want to go see Mickey Mouse today, don't you?"

A sparkle settled into the boy's steel-blue eyes.

Baldwin planted a kiss on Adam III's forehead and traded goodbyes with his son.

"Keep the old man out of trouble," Adam Jr. said as he passed Stafford on the way out.

Stafford grinned. "That's what I'm here for." He turned toward Baldwin as the door slammed. "We better go, Adam. Don't want to be late."

Baldwin looked at Stafford dead on, face hard. "Screw the prayer breakfast and the church service too, goddammit. I can be a couple of minutes late. This crap from last night has my stomach in knots."

"What's your read on the situation?" Stafford asked. "You think Hale is the witness they're talking about?"

"Absolutely," Baldwin snapped. "Who else could it be?"

"But he wasn't even alive in 1949."

"Open your eyes, Tom. It's a goddam smokescreen."

"What's his motive? He's never tried to extort money from you, has he?"

"This isn't about money. It's about image. That jerk's gonna put my hard-won public image up for inspection with his accusations, and my bid for the presidency will go up in smoke," Baldwin said, his blue eyes lit like a fuse on a firecracker. "They think I'm a trophy-caliber swordfish that swallowed the whole line. They want to yank me out of the cool Atlantic where I'm minding my own business and make me sail through the air over and over, fighting for every goddam breath, until they reel me in and spread me out on deck."

"He's a nobody," Stafford said, throwing his palms toward the ceiling. "Who's gonna believe him?"

"The public doesn't give a shit! Who are *you* gonna vote for? A Republican who goes around kissing babies or a Democrat accused of murder?"

Stafford nodded.

"This thing's getting out of hand. I'm not basing my campaign speeches on damage control. I will *not* let some crazy Memphis bastard ruin this for me." Baldwin plowed a hand through his thick grey hair, pondering. Suddenly he snapped his fingers. "You want a motive? I'll give you a motive. It *is* money. Probably straight from the Republican National Committee in unmarked hundred-dollar bills. Plenty of 'em."

"What next?"

"You're my top aide," Baldwin said. "What would *you* do?"

"I would take care of the situation," Stafford replied. His eyes locked onto Baldwin's with the icy stare of a judge signing a death warrant.

Baldwin hadn't invented the rules of politics but was a master at bending them to his advantage. After all, his grandfather had often compared politics to war. Casualties occur. Nature of the business. Like stepping on a bug. Just make sure it's somebody else who does the stepping. He smiled. Not a pleasant smile.

"Last time you got pissed off when I misunderstood," Stafford said. "You're saying to—"

"You know damn well what I'm saying, Tom! How about I punch it in Braille for you? I want Hale out of the picture." Contempt flashed across his face. "I don't mean next month or next week, either. If you have to go through friends of his to get him, so be it. Use whoever you have to. I don't care. Just do it. Any room for misunderstanding now?"

Stafford shook his head.

"Then you can skip the prayer breakfast and the church service. I'll meet you back here for the luncheon and speech to the Screen Actors Guild. Send Baxter up. He can go with me while you take care of business. Any questions?"

"Not a one," Stafford said, turning to leave. "Give 'em hell at lunch. Only stop of the campaign where everybody's dressed in two-thousand-dollar suits." He winked. "Just like you."

Baldwin checked the knot in his tie again as the door closed, pleased about the polished appearance that had become his trademark. He walked over to the balcony door and looked down at the palm trees lining the street below, their fronds scarcely moving in the dry, motionless air. He then lifted his eyes for a sweeping view of Beverly Hills, Century City, and the surrounding smog-shrouded hills of Los Angeles.

"It's like my grandfather used to say, Hale. If you're going to play hardball, you damn well better bring your glove."

26

Monday marked an end as well as a beginning for Jean King. She dreaded both as she waved, watching Jim drive away.

The end to the most glorious weekend of her life was bad enough. The beginning of her forced separation from Jim compounded the pain stabbing at her heart.

Together for three days straight, they openly shared their likes, dislikes, and innermost thoughts. For him, she softened the loss of his daughter, listening as he poured out memories to ease the anguish. For her, he opened eyes long shut to the richness of a relationship filled with tenderness, laughter, and love.

Was this separation really necessary? Surely not. Even Joe said nothing might happen for a few weeks. Nothing might happen at all. Probably just a needless precaution.

She sat on her front doorstep, elbows resting on the knees of her tight blue jeans. The crisp morning air, full of pine and evergreen, blended with the woodsy scent of Jim's cologne, still lingering on her neck and face. She inhaled deeply and closed her eyes, thoughts drifting back to the night before.

She felt the coolness of the bedsheets dissolving with the warmth of their bodies; the touch of his kisses on her breasts, then moving slowly down; the arousal as they joined, becoming one, lost in shared ecstasy.

Jim's face, staring into hers, blazed in her memory, his blue eyes aglow. "It was as if we had been there before," he said afterwards, gently moving a fingertip along her cheek to her chin, then tenderly pressing his lips to hers.

"We have," she had whispered, nuzzling the soft curves of her body against his taut chest as he drew her closer, wrapping his arms tightly around her. They eased into sleep, hands intertwined.

Jean opened her eyes and sighed, longing for his touch. But suddenly another memory crowded into her thoughts. Not of Jim but of a vision she had experienced over the weekend as they strolled down a secluded road in Overton Park. The burial site. Youthful Adam Baldwin digging frantically. A young tree, growing crooked in the dim light. She had to find it.

She gathered her photography gear, swapped her red long sleeve knit for a blue chambray shirt, and pulled on her hiking boots.

Within a half hour she was trampsing through the woods on the east side of the park with her Gitzo tripod over her shoulder and Sinar view camera tucked away in her green canvas backpack.

Leaves and twigs crunched under foot as she explored the dense undergrowth. She moved through the towering trees for an hour, then two, constantly framing scenes. Nothing looked familiar.

Tired and thirsty, she finally sat down on a tree stump near the Overton Park pavilion and reached for her water bottle. Just then, a crooked tree, basking in the sunlight, caught her eye. Clumps of blue flowers hugged the ground at its base.

She craned her neck, mind racing. Could this be it? She took a spot meter reading, then a quick shot. After replacing the 210 millimeter lens with a 75 millimeter for a wider view, she covered her head with a black cloth behind the bulky camera and clicked shots from various angles.

Uncovering her head, she nodded, her thin lips forming a slight smile. This was more than just trees and underbrush. The windswept and weatherbeaten landscape spoke to her, telling its story without uttering a sound.

27

On Tuesday afternoon, Jim returned home with two bags of groceries just before Rich Reynolds drove off for his real estate transaction, the first time in two days he had not been under surveillance. Hoping to take the Model A for a spin when Reynolds returned, he parked his Oldsmobile at the curb instead of the driveway. As he went in the house, Jim noticed three yellow Memphis Light, Gas & Water service trucks parked down the street, not unusual since there was frequent maintenance on the electrical wire towers that ran behind the subdivision.

Minutes later, he heard the front door chime. Through the peephole Jim saw a stocky man with a pot belly wearing a white hardhat imprinted with the multi-colored MLGW logo. The man yawned and scratched at his thick, dark beard.

"What can I do for you?" Jim said through the door.

"There's been some gas main surges down the street. They're causing a few leaks, especially in some attic water heaters with loose connections," the man replied. "As a precaution, we're checking all gas appliances."

"Is it really necessary?"

"You wanna take a chance on getting your ass blown to kingdom come, be my guest. That'll just get me home five minutes quicker. I got twenty more houses to check. Yes or no?"

Jim glanced out the living room window as another MLGW truck slowly drove past. The guy looked on the level.

The deadbolt clicked. "Come on in," Jim said, opening the door. "You can't be too careful these days."

"I know all about that," the man said. "My car got stolen from my own garage a month ago."

"How long will this take?"

"Four or five minutes, tops," the man replied.

Jim winced at the man's sour smell as they walked into the hallway. He tugged on a cord to expose the pull-down stairs to the attic.

"Wanna watch? Maybe you could take my job and I'll retire," the man joked, climbing the rickety ladder.

"Don't think so," Jim said, feeling more relaxed. "I'm all thumbs when it comes to home maintenance."

For the next few minutes, the only noise Jim heard was the occasional slight tapping of metal on metal.

"That's got her," the man said as he eased down the stairs, slapping his hands together to knock off the dust. "Surges or no surges, you're in good shape now."

"Can I get you a beer for the road?" Jim said, trying to make up for his initial lack of hospitality.

"They'd fire my ass in a heartbeat for drinking on the job."

"Won't tell a soul," Jim said as he walked into the kitchen, grabbed two beers from the refrigerator, and handed them to the MLGW man.

"Thanks, pal," he said with a smile, stashing them in his grease-stained plaid shirt as Jim let him out.

As Jean opened the door, the wind swept her blond hair across her face, molding her knit top and slacks to her body.

"Four-thirty," she said, smiling. "Right on time. Come in."

"You talked to Jim today?" O'Riley asked, crossing the threshold.

"I'm not bashful about burning up the phone lines. I talked to him about three o'clock. He was going to the grocery. He wishes he could join us for dinner but he understands about keeping his distance."

"You ready?"

"In just a minute. First I want to tell you something that happened over the weekend. Saturday. Jim was pretty excited about it."

"Another vision?" O'Riley asked, brown eyes widening.

"Another vision of young Adam Baldwin. He was standing in a group of trees. It was dark. He had a shovel in his hands and was digging."

"Would you recognize the place if you saw it?"

"Sure," Jean replied, penciled eyebrows arching. "Especially now that I've photographed it."

"You're kidding," O'Riley said.

"Follow me," she replied.

She led him to several rooms that had been converted into a photography workshop and gallery at the back of the house.

"So this is Ansel Adams Central, eh?" O'Riley said.

"Not quite," she replied, laughing. "But now you get to see what I do. This is where I show my work." One room's white walls were covered ceiling to floor with color and black and white landscape photographs, all matted in white and framed with sleek black wood.

O'Riley carefully examined two snow-capped mountain shots and another of a vast, flat field of swaying wheat. "35 millimeter?"

"I take *real* photographs," she replied, shaking her head.

"So do I. Got a Canon Sure Shot. Takes great pictures of my dog," O'Riley said, laughing.

"Those are snapshots, Joe. For photographs in an exhibit, you know, art gallery quality, you need a lot of fancy equipment." She pointed to an open door. "Like the things in there. My studio. Come on in."

The next room was full of cameras, tripods, and high-tech lighting equipment. O'Riley let out a high-pitched whistle. "Bet that stuff cost a pretty penny. You ever had any exhibitions?"

"Two," she replied. "The most recent was six months ago at the Jack Kenner Gallery in Overton Square. Showed about forty photographs but only sold a few. The Memphis market's not quite there yet." She paused. "That's what aspiring artistic photographers are supposed to say if not many photos sell. Actually, some of my best work is hanging on company walls across the United States and Canada. Gets thrown out every year."

A puzzled look spread over O'Riley's face.

Jean grinned. "Calendars. Brings in enough money to live on. I put them together for companies wanting an environmentally-friendly image. I've traveled quite a bit on my own. National parks. Canada. Alaska. Even played with the idea of starting my own calendar production company. *In Decent Exposures*. Catchy, don't you think?"

O'Riley laughed. "Yeah. They'd go just perfect in plain brown envelopes. The guys down in Vice would love 'em." He ran his hands through his hair as he examined another wall of landscapes. "You develop these yourself?"

Jean pointed to a third door. "The dark room." She opened it and turned on the light.

"Holy cow," O'Riley said. "This *did* cost a forture. Looks like the one down at headquarters." The tight room was crammed with vats, chemicals, trays, paper, lights, processing machines, and a color enlarger.

"Initially expensive but it pays for itself in the long run. If I had to rely on outside development, it would *really* cost me."

O'Riley shook his head as they walked back into the gallery. "And I sized you up as a delicate flower, needing somebody to watch over you, living with your momma and daddy."

Jean smiled. "I guess you detectives aren't always right."

"Hazards of the trade," O'Riley said, nodding.

"I'm afflicted with only child syndrome," she said, making quote marks in the air with her fingers. "My parents are getting up there. Someday, when they're gone, I'll know I was always there for them. Besides, with their living half the year in Florida, I have plenty of time to myself."

O'Riley was staring at a black and white cemetary scene filled with worn, broken headstones. "You like color or black and white best?"

"I only do color for the calendars or for special requests. In my mind I'm a black and white landscape artist. In a view camera like mine, the image the photographer sees is upside down and backwards. Your Canon shifts the image internally so what you see through the viewfinder is what you get in your photos. It's not that way with my equipment. The way I see the world is not the way you see it."

O'Riley's eyes narrowed, trying to visualize what she meant.

Jean held up her hands, making a square, thumb to thumb, forefinger to forefinger. "I've been adjusting the world all my life to the view camera. Making little snippets from a larger view. These visions I've been having—that's why I think I see them more sharply, more clearly even than Jim. My mind's trained that way. When I have one, it's like I'm framing for a photograph. I see more than the center. I notice the periphery, too. I see things others wouldn't notice."

O'Riley arched his eyebrows.

"Take a movie, for example. A Clint Eastwood shoot 'em up. You have two guys standing in the middle of a dusty street in a western town. You focus on the two men about to draw. I see the men but *much* more," she said, her face animated. "I notice everything on the screen—the color of the buildings lining the street. How many horses are tied up to posts. People peering out of windows. Even what they're wearing. Sunshine or clouds in the sky."

"Same thing me and the Homicide boys do at a murder scene, I guess," O'Riley said. "Most people see a body and a bunch of blood. We notice position of the victim, items in the room, stains on the walls, floor, ceiling. That kind of stuff."

"Exactly," Jean said. "*That's* how it was with the crooked tree. I caught it in my periphery. Same shape as the one from my vision. Just

192

larger." She walked over to a dark brown antique table, picked up an eleven-by-fourteen-inch photograph, and handed it to O'Riley.

"That's right near the Overton Park pavilion," he said, eyeing a sliver of the structure's sloping roof that lined the right border. "Been there since about 1911. I know right where this is."

Jean touched her chin. "You think it might be where—"

"Allison Tucker was buried." O'Riley jingled his key chain. "Can you hold out a bit longer for dinner while we take a little drive over there?"

"Lead the way," she said, as they walked to the door.

In less than fifteen minutes, O'Riley's black Lincoln was entering the heavily wooded section of the park where the roads became narrow and winding, lined with trees and underbrush that had remained largely untouched since the 1920s.

O'Riley turned to Jean, after looking at his gold watch. "Here it is, close to six o'clock, and it's already getting dark."

Suddenly there was a flash of oncoming headlights as a car headed straight for them. "Joe! Watch out!" Jean yelled.

O'Riley jerked the steering wheel to the right, barely avoiding a red Acura. "Damn these narrow roads!"

"I'm scared, Will," Jean said, her voice full of fear. "What are we going to do?"

O'Riley pulled to a stop on the side of the road.

Jean clutched her left arm and began to sob, crying uncontrollably as O'Riley put his arm around her. "You're all right, doll—everything's okay."

She glanced up, quickly regaining her composure. "I just saw myself die," she said, her expression pensive, haunted. "I was with that same boy. Will Harrison. We were being rammed by a car. Knocked right into a tree—that's the last thing I saw before I . . . before we . . ."

"What did the other car look like?" O'Riley asked.

Jean tucked a curl behind her ear. "It was maroon. The hood was rounded on top and the car had lots of shiny chrome. And the windshield—

it was split into two panes. It was the car in my vision on Goodwyn, Joe. It was Adam Baldwin's."

O'Riley felt heat rush to his face.

Jean pointed straight ahead to a fork in the road with a massive black oak at its center. "That's the spot. That tree."

One glimpse shot O'Riley into his past. The tree was much smaller then, with Will's charred, smoldering Model A wrapped around its trunk. He felt Mike Kelly's arm around his shoulder.

"It's sad to lose loved ones, Joey. You and me, we been through this before. It's okay to cry, 'specially if you're an Irishman. It shows you got compassion in your heart."

O'Riley's stomach clenched as the memory faded. He looked down, covering his eyes with his left hand.

Jean placed her hand on his shoulder.

At that moment O'Riley slammed his fist on the dashboard, temper exploding like a long-dormant volcano. "We'll never be able to prove that son of a bitch was responsible for Jenny and Will's deaths, but by God, he's gonna pay for the girl's. That demon's gonna have a stake driven through his political heart before this is over and I'm just the one to do it!"

"I'm glad I'm on your side," Jean said as she leaned back in her seat.

"Me too," O'Riley replied, his anger subsiding.

O'Riley pulled back onto the road and drove toward the pavilion.

When they reached the eastern edge of Overton Park, Jean said, "Something stands out about one of my earlier visions—the burial one. It's different from the others. Everything seemed bathed in an eerie, blue light."

O'Riley's lips formed a knowing smile. "There's a place near the pavilion that's completely covered in forget-me-nots every year. Just like kudzu. They'd have been dying out in late December, but I bet a flashlight shining on 'em would make things look blue."

A few minutes later, the Lincoln rolled to a stop at the side of the road. The Overton Park pavilion loomed through the trees on the right. Nearby was a large, crooked white oak, towering over a sea of blue forget-me-nots.

"This is it, Joe," Jean said. "It's the corner of my photograph—the part I enlarged. The place I saw in my vision."

"You know something, Jean?"

"This is where we might find some evidence?"

"Damn straight."

They both nodded as O'Riley reached for his cell phone to call Jim and Charlie Perry.

"Battery's dead again," he said with a scowl. "How 'bout we finally get that dinner? We can go to Ronnie Grisanti's. It's not far. The owner and I go way back. We can use his office phone and tell Jim about our discovery. Then I'll get Perry on the horn so we can set up a little digging exercise tomorrow morning." O'Riley winked. "My morgue buddies. I also have a couple of old friends at the FBI I need to get in touch with. It's about time I called in a few favors."

28

The doorbell woke Jim just as he was settling in for a nap. He rubbed his face, sat up on the blue quilted bedspread, slipped on his shoes, and went to the front door.

Peering out the peephole, he spotted another MLGW workman. Back again. He unlocked the door and opened it wide. "Yes?"

"Sorry to bother you, sir," the muscular, middle-aged man said. "We got a busted water main down on Macleod. We've been out here wrestling with it all afternoon. We'll have to be shutting off the water to everybody here on Lynnfield until we get it fixed. Just wanted to let you know."

"What the hell is wrong with this neighborhood?" Jim said gruffly. "First the gas and now the water."

"Gas?" the workman replied, a frown on his face.

"One of your guys came by here around four o'clock and told me about gas line surges. He went up in my attic to make sure my water heater connections were tight. A guy with a black beard."

"Look, I'm the crew supervisor and there ain't been one gas problem out here all day. Besides, MLGW's been cracking down on beards."

Jim's heart jumped as he remembered the tapping sound while the repairman was in the attic. "We gotta get out of here!" he yelled, grabbing the workman by the shirt and pulling him across the small front yard.

"Are you nuts?" the workman shouted as they bolted across the street, taking refuge behind a towering maple.

The MLGW man shook himself loose, breathing heavily.

Suddenly the house exploded, intense heat whipping by them like a sandstorm in the desert. Shards of wood and brick hurtled in every direction, ricocheting off the surrounding houses and cars. A fiery mushroom jumped skyward, illuminating the overcast sky. A second blast shot the washer and dryer into the air. They crashed into the street, grinding to a stop against the curb. The Model A lay on its side in the neighbor's front yard as an expanding shroud of thick smoke blanketed the area.

"Fool me once, shame on you; fool me twice, shame on me," Jim murmured through clenched teeth as he stared at the wreckage. Everything he owned was either ashes or on fire, everything except the clothes on his back and his car in the street.

"It's a good thing you didn't turn off the water—the fire department's gonna need it," Jim said over his shoulder as he ran for his Oldsmobile.

"Hey!" the MLGW man yelled. "You can't leave."

But Jim was already inside his dust-covered navy car. He raced the engine and screeched off.

He barrelled east onto Quince from Lynnfield, realizing there were only two people he could really trust—Jean King and Joe O'Riley. Everyone else was suspect.

He passed the Lichterman Nature Center and glanced in his rear-view mirror, noticing a royal blue Mercedes not far behind him. Near the traffic light at Quince and Ridgeway, a pumper truck, a hook and ladder, and an ambulance roared past, sirens wailing.

The Mercedes edged closer. Was it tailing him?

As he approached Poplar Avenue, he decided to find out. A wrong turn down a secluded road would be the last wrong turn of his life. He had to stay around other people. Safety in numbers. And, he had to come up with an escape plan. A damn good plan, damn fast.

He quickly pulled into the crowded lot of the Malco Ridgeway Four cinema and parked, hustling to a pay phone in the lobby. He spotted the blue Mercedes parking near his car just as Rich Reynolds drove into the theater lot. What was he doing here? The ringing phone line clicked in his ear.

"City-Wide Cab," said a female voice in a slow, Southern drawl.

"I need a cab, please," Jim said, breathing hard.

"Where are you, sir?"

"Have him come to the office building at 5885 Ridgeway Center Parkway. Next to the Ridgeway Four."

"What's your name, please?"

He paused a moment, not wanting to give away his identity.

"Sir, it's not a trick question. I just need your name," the dispatcher said.

"Sorry. It's Harrison. Will Harrison." He drummed his fingers on the side of the black pay phone. "And tell the driver I'll meet him at the lobby entrance."

"We'll have him there in about five to ten minutes. Have a nice night, sir."

"Thank you."

Jim inserted another fifty cents. He dialed O'Riley's home number and then his car phone. No answer. The change clinked into the coin return. He fished it out and dialed Jean's number as he noticed no one had gotten out of the Mercedes.

After the fourth ring, Jean's answering machine clicked on.

"Jean, I'm calling to say I'm fine. I wasn't in my house when it blew up. I'm being followed by some people, I don't know how many, in a blue Mercedes with tinted windows. I tried to call Joe but couldn't reach him. Listen to me carefully. I'm going *roamin'* where it's *always light* outside. I won't be Jim anymore. But you will know who I am. I love you so much."

Jim sighed deeply, placing the receiver on the hook as an emptiness gripped his chest. He walked over to the box office window, purchased a ticket, and then bought a Coke. After weaving through the crowded lobby, he slipped into the screen one theater, tossing his ticket stub for screen two into a trash can.

Jonny Custer lowered his binoculars and dropped them on the white leather seat of the blue Mercedes. "I lost the son of a bitch in the crowd, Moose. Goddammit!" He banged the steering wheel with his right hand. His thin, close-shaven face, with olive skin stretched taut like a hand forced into a doctor's latex glove, turned red with anger. "I'm going in. Keep an eye on things."

Custer slammed the door, flicked a half-smoked cigarette to the ground, and snuffed it with a pivot of one of his shiny Ferragamo loafers. He walked toward the movie theater, his oily black hair slicked back, clinging to the sides of his head, accentuating a receding hairline.

He and Moose Carson worked as a team. A classic hit-man duo of brains and brawn. The slender Custer neatly balanced by the sloppy, ill-mannered Carson. Working out of Philadelphia, this was their first job in Memphis, and they stuck out like a couple of professional wrestlers at a Southern Baptist convention.

Jonny Custer never killed with his bare hands. A .357 Magnum bullet right between the eyes was his trademark. No back of the head stuff. He wanted his victims to see what they were getting. Cold-blooded and never remorseful, at thirty-four he was responsible for twenty-one unsolved murders across the United States.

Moose Carson, on the other hand, had never killed with a gun. The brute strength of his hands was all he needed, occasionally augmented with a garroting wire or baseball bat. He loved torturing victims into talking before Custer opted to put them out of their misery. Broken fingers, arms, and kneecaps were often found during autopsies of their victims. On eight occasions, Carson had done the job by himself. Five broken necks, two garrotings, and one decapitation were on his resumé, and he was only thirty-two years old.

A former offensive lineman for the University of Miami Hurricanes team that dominated college football at the end of the 1980s, Carson maintained a weight four times his I.Q., keeping himself toned with rigorous daily workouts. His devotion to his body came at the expense of his neglected teeth, the few that hadn't been knocked out during fights in high school or during his abbreviated college career.

Seen as a rising star during his sophomore year, with first round NFL draft potential, he was banished from the squad when he paralyzed a Nebraska defensive lineman in the Orange Bowl, breaking his opponent's neck with a violent uppercut to the chin. He was subsequently kicked out of school for a number of brushes with the police, the last a one-year jail sentence as an accessory in a cocaine distribution ring. After his release from prison, he hooked up with Custer on the recommendation of a former inmate. Always one to stand out in a crowd, he suddenly seemed to drop from the face of the earth.

They lacked creativity but didn't discriminate, working for anybody willing to pay the fee. But the buyer beware. Once paid to do a job, it was done. The next day, the table could be turned, victor becoming victim. No loyalty to people. Only greed.

Results were guaranteed. Terms non-negotiable. Two hundred fifty thousand up front, the same amount upon completion. For a husband and wife, they didn't even charge extra. Killing women was a bonus, like a free game on a video machine.

Custer entered the lobby. The caricature of the well-dressed hit man as portrayed in movies always seemed humorous to him, yet he failed to see the humor in his own reflection in the shiny ticket window. "Hello, little lady," he said, eyeing the young brunette behind the glass partition. He smiled, revealing teeth yellowed by years of smoking. "I hope you can help me out."

The high school girl's eyes twinkled as he spoke. "I'll try," she replied, tugging at her braided ponytail.

"I was supposed to meet a guy here for a movie but he forgot to tell me which one."

"That wasn't very nice of him, was it?" the girl said, looking sympathetic.

"No, not at all." One side of his mouth twisted upward as he looked directly into her green eyes. "If I wasn't such a nice guy, I just might have to kill him. He was wearing a navy sweater with squiggly thingies on it. Do you remember him?"

"Would he have been on the phone for a while?"

"Yeah. Probably trying to call me. My car phone's been on the fritz."

"He bought a ticket for screen two."

Custer's tight face wrinkled. "The Disney movie?"

"That's the one."

"Isn't that for kids?"

The girl nodded. "I'm afraid so."

"Gimme a ticket. That's why there's .38s and .357s."

"Excuse me?"

His thin black eyebrows arched. "I said, that's why there's chocolate and vanilla."

The young girl handed him a ticket stub and change from a twenty-dollar bill.

"Keep it, honey."

Her ponytail swung side to side. "Sir, I can't. We're not allowed to—"

"Keep it," he insisted with a wink. "Buy some liner for those beautiful eyes of yours."

She slid the money into her vest pocket as he waved and entered screen two.

At that moment, Jim was pushing through the seldom used outside exit door of screen one, which connected to a walkway behind the building. He bounded up a flight of concrete steps and ran along the back of the dimly lit parking lot amid the muffled sounds of cars and trucks speeding down Poplar Avenue.

When he reached the building next door, he glanced back at the cinema parking lot. He doubted he'd been seen. A black-and-white City-Wide taxi stood in front of the building's lobby. Jim grabbed the door handle of the cab.

"Shit!" the chubby, grey-haired black driver shouted as a toothpick dropped from the corner of his mouth. "You 'bout scared me to death. I thought you'd be coming out the lobby."

"I used the back," Jim replied, panting as he slid onto the seat and slammed the door. "I was in a hurry."

"Where to?"

"The airport. I got a plane leaving in forty minutes," Jim said, hoping the lie would get the driver moving. Fast.

"Hold on," the cabbie said, as if challenged to a drag race. He jammed down the accelerator, leaving a cloud of white smoke in the parking lot. "My friends don't call me leadfoot for nothing. You pay the speeding ticket if we get caught?"

"All night long."

At the airport, Jim stared at the departing flights monitor as he inched toward the ticket counter. It was 7:40.

Flight 555	to Los Angeles	DEPARTS	7:50 P.M.
Flight 636	to New York-LaGuardia	DEPARTS	7:55 P.M.
Flight 826	to Atlanta	DEPARTS	8:00 P.M.
Flight 979	to Las Vegas	DEPARTS	8:10 P.M.

An attractive Northwest agent handed the man in front of Jim a ticket as she motioned for him to move forward.

"Hi," he said, nervously glancing around.

"Hello, sir," the agent replied. "Where to tonight?"

"Las Vegas."

"That flight starts boarding in ten minutes at gate B3. Do you have any luggage?" she asked, brushing her dark hair from her face.

"No, I hope it's a short trip."

"A spur of the moment round trip is our worst fare. Eight hundred and sixteen dollars, to be exact. Is this an emergency?"

"It's a matter of life or death," Jim replied.

"Financial life or death?" the woman asked. "Planning on some gambling?"

Jim shook his head. "No, real life or death. I just need a one-way ticket. The return's up in the air. Whatever you can do," he said, a pleading softness in his voice, "I would be most grateful."

The agent glanced at her screen, quickly tapping the computer keyboard. "There are quite a few empty seats." Her mouth eased into a smile. "How does two hundred sixty-eight dollars sound?"

Jim nodded. "I really appreciate that."

"Name, sir?"

"Harrison. William Harrison."

"May I see some identification?"

Jim pulled out his wallet and flashed a photo I.D., covering his name with a finger.

The woman smiled again. "Window seat or aisle?"

"Aisle, as close to the bulkhead as possible."

"17D is the closest I have."

"I'm thankful for whatever," Jim said, handing her three one-hundred-dollar bills.

"Have a nice flight, Mr. Harrison." She winked, handing him his ticket and change. "I hope everything works out okay."

"Thank you," he said with a grin.

He went straight to the weapons detection scanner in Concourse B, passing quickly through.

His stomach growling with hunger, he spotted a Baskin-Robbins ice cream booth next to his gate and ordered a strawberry cone. Just as he took his first bite, everything vanished in a burst of white light that soon faded, revealing Will's Model A bumping to a halt in the gravel parking lot of a small restaurant near the Poplar Avenue viaduct. He walked in, greeting the owner, Mr. Meadows, by name. The enticing aroma of fifteen-cent steakburgers grilling over an open flame hung in the air.

Mr. Meadows handed him a toasted waffle cone filled with a thick glob of ice cream loaded with chunks of strawberries grown on the farm behind the restaurant.

"What do you think?" the old man said.

Will's mouth filled with a burst of sweet flavor. "Fortune's doesn't hold a candle to your Angel Food. Not even close."

"Mister, are you all right? Your cone's dripping down your hand."

Jim instantly snapped back to reality as his vision focused on a red-haired boy of four or five with big blue eyes staring at him. "So it is," he replied, wiping his hand with a napkin. "I must have been daydreaming. Thank you, young man."

The small boy smiled and continued down the row of chairs in the waiting area, dragging a worn, brown teddy bear behind him.

Once the call to board was made, Jim jumped up to be first in line and they were soon on their way.

The jet engines screamed as the airliner accelerated down the runway. It nosed up into the darkened sky and began to glide over the city, banking to the left on a westerly course. Just before ascending above the clouds, Jim looked down on the bright, twinkling lights of Memphis. Would he ever hold Jean in his arms again?

29

"I knew I shouldn't have eaten dessert," O'Riley said, puffing his cheeks as he slowly exhaled. "That white chocolate créme brulee with sun-dried cherry sauce put me right over the edge."

"Me, too," Jean said. "I probably gained three pounds."

O'Riley frowned. "No way. You ate like a sick bird. Must've left half that sea bass. No wonder you have such a good figure."

"Let's give that new battery for your car phone a try," she said, dialing Jim's number. "Still that out-of-order beeping. What if something's wrong?"

"I ain't worried. Rich Reynolds is watching him," O'Riley replied, pulling to a stop in front of Jean's house. "Probably just a phone-line outage."

They hurried to the front door in the chilly night air.

"Want a cup of coffee to warm you up?" she asked, noticing a blue Mercedes parked down the street.

O'Riley looked at his watch. "I better be getting home. It's almost nine. This has been a tiring day for both of us."

Jean leaned over and kissed him lightly on the cheek. "Thanks for everything, Joe. It's been enlightening." She unlocked the door, stepping inside.

"Enlightening for us and for Mr. Baldwin. I'll call you in a little while to make sure you're okay."

"That's sweet—you don't have to."

"I know," he replied with a smile. "G'night."

Jean went to the kitchen and filled a glass with tap water, checked the back door, and hurried down the hallway to her bedroom. She placed the glass on a cork coaster on her bed table and tuned her clock-radio to a classic rock station.

The melancholy strains of The Moody Blues' *Knights in White Satin* erased the silence in the room as Jean began to undress. She slowly unfastened the buttons of her jacket and slipped it gently from her narrow shoulders. Unhooking the metal fastener at the waistband of her tan pants, she let them drop to the floor as she pulled the pink cotton turtleneck over her head. She twisted her neck hard to one side, then the other, popping it twice, her blond hair skipping across her shoulders. Dressed only in black lace bikini panties and matching bra, she finally pressed the button on her answering machine.

She gasped when she heard Jim's voice. "I wasn't in my house when it blew up." Her right hand flew to her lips. "I'm being followed by some people, I don't know how many, in a blue Mercedes with tinted windows." Jean's eyes widened. The car parked down the street. "I tried to call Joe but couldn't reach him. Listen to me carefully. I'm going *roamin'* where it's *always light* outside. I won't be Jim anymore. But you will know who I am. I love you so much."

As the machine clicked off, a wave of dread engulfed her.

"Awww, ain't that sweet," said a voice in the doorway. "I love you so much." A well-dressed man eased into the bedroom, a .357 Magnum in his hand.

*

O'Riley's Lincoln was less than a mile from his home when the car phone rang.

"Hello?" the former chief said.

"Joe, this is Rich. Where the *hell* have you been? You didn't answer your phone."

"Battery was dead."

"I'm parked in front of your house."

"Why ain't you at Jim's?"

"You want the good news or the bad news?"

"The bad news."

"I ain't at Jim's house 'cause it ain't there. Blown to smithereens. The good news is, he's okay."

"God Almighty," O'Riley said, slapping a palm to his forehead.

"But more bad news. I don't know where he is. I know he went into the Ridgeway Cinema for the 7:15 show and didn't come out. Left his car in the lot. Two goons were tailing him. One went inside and couldn't find him. Then he called in his sidekick to help. They came back outside, scratching their heads with their thumbs up their ass. These guys looked like professionals, and they weren't from here, guarantee that. They hopped into their car, a blue Mercedes, and screeched off—in a hurry all of a sudden. I lost 'em right after they zig-zagged from Poplar onto Central."

"Holy shit, Reynolds, I gotta go. I'll get back to you."

O'Riley spun his car around as he dialed Jean's number. After four rings, her machine came on. She was in trouble. And it was his damn fault. He punched numbers again. The phone rang twice. Charlie Perry picked up.

"Charlie, O'Riley here. I need big-time help again and I mean *quick*. It's an emergency." Adreneline shot through his body, firing the blood in his veins.

"Name it, Joe."

"I need some SWAT guys on the double."

"SWAT's the county special unit," replied Perry. "The city changed theirs to the TACT unit a few years back."

"I don't give a shit if they call it the Goldilocks Search and Destroy Team. I need six, eight, whatever, over to 333 Haynes at Central. On the corner. The girlfriend of our supposed witness, Jim Hale, is being held by a couple of hit men. I'll bet my life on it. If TACT sees a blue Mercedes parked anywhere near the house, they're inside for sure. I'll be there in five, six minutes. Got it?"

"By the time you get there, they'll be in high gear," Perry promised. "One thing," he said, pausing.

"Yeah?"

"I'm in up to my asshole with you on this thing. I expect you to fill me in from here on out."

"You pull this off and you got it," O'Riley snapped, clicking off as he raced toward Jean's house with the speedometer pushing seventy.

*

"The name's Custer, no relation to Little Big Horn," the man said, zeroing in on Jean with his deep-set, dark eyes. "We've been real nice up to now but you haven't given us jack." He grabbed her arm and pulled it up behind her. "Talk to me," he growled.

Jean winced, staring at the floor.

"Where is he?"

"I . . . don't . . . know," she stammered, her voice a toneless whisper.

"Wrong answer." Custer tightened his grip.

"Owww," she moaned. Her cheeks, red as the rest of her contorted face, puffed out.

"You better think of something or I'll rip it out and let you carry it to the next room," Custer said, yanking her arm.

She let out a gasp, fainting as Custer caught her around the waist. "Help me, dammit," he barked at Carson.

The ox snatched Jean up like a weightlifter picking up a barbell.

Regaining consciousness, Jean felt powerful arms gripping her, squeezing across her breasts and under her chin. Moments later, sitting upright on the couch in the living room, she hoped she'd just had a bad dream. But reality stared at her from the intruder's face, only inches from her own. She cradled her sore arm against her chest, silent, frighteningly aware that she was still in her undergarments.

"For the last time," Custer warned, "where's your boyfriend?"

"I told you, I don't have any idea," she replied, hands trembling.

"Somehow I knew you were gonna say that. You know, if I was a betting man, and I am, I'd say your lover boy has skipped town."

Just then Jean recalled Jim's message. He had said *roamin'* where it's *always light*. Roamin' as in Roman. Always light. Neon. Caesar's Palace. Las Vegas. That *had* to be it, she thought.

"You ain't saying nothing, pretty lady. I guess you want me to think he didn't want you to know. I'm afraid I'm gonna have to call *bullshit* on that one," Custer screamed, his face turning red. "Moose here don't like to be lied to, do you, Moose?"

Carson shook his head, scowling as he sat down on the couch next to her. He rolled a toothpick from one side of his mouth to the other, then clenched down with his teeth, the toothpick snapping. "The first time I killed a guy," he said, his foul-smelling breath right in Jean's face, "I felt nothing. Just doing my job. The first time I killed a woman, it was different. I liked it. I kinda look forward to it now." He reached over and cupped her left breast in his hand.

"Stop, you're hurting me," Jean pleaded, tears rolling down her cheeks.

Carson smiled stiffly. "Lady, you don't know the meaning of the word hurt. I'm just warming up."

∗

O'Riley pulled up with his headlights off and parked behind three unmarked TACT unit vans down the street from Jean's.

"Who's in charge?" O'Riley asked.

"Allendorfer," the officer replied, motioning to a man in the shadows. "The short guy."

O'Riley walked over, offering his hand. "I'm Joe O'Riley. What's the situation?"

"We're about to go in. Been monitoring the conversation. The two abductors and the hostage are in the living room, just inside the front door. One of the guys is starting to get abusive. The other one's holding a .357."

"What's the plan?" O'Riley asked.

"We'll set off two diversionary explosions, flash-bang grenades, in the dining room next to the living room. Then we'll knock down the door."

O'Riley glanced over at the other four members of the assault team, none of them over five-nine. "Don't you need some bigger guys?"

Allendorfer pulled on his stocking mask and goggles. "My little friend here has a way of making us shorter guys seem over six feet tall," he said, patting the MP-5 submachine gun in his hand. "You need to back up and take cover inside that white van over there, if you don't mind. Just in case."

A two-man diversion team stood at the side of the dining room window, grenades in hand. The five-man assault team lined up single file, facing the front door, the lead gripping a battering ram. The four behind him held MP-5's in ready position.

All wore identical black, ripstop fatigues with the coiled cobra patch of the Memphis Tactical Apprehension and Containment Team sewn on each shoulder. Black bullet-proof flak jackets protected their chests. Black stocking masks and fire-retardant Nomex gloves covered their faces and hands, shatter-resistant goggles protecting their eyes. Drop holsters strapped to their thighs contained nine-millimeter Smith and Wesson handguns.

Allendorfer held second place in the assault team line as he adjusted a tiny microphone in his ear, waiting to give the signal.

*

Carson grabbed Jean's hair and snapped her head back, brandishing a baseball bat in her face.

"Quit sniveling, you bitch," he yelled. "Where is he?"

"I . . . don't . . . know," Jean repeated.

Carson slapped her with his powerful hand, knocking her to the floor.

At that moment, two grenades smashed through the dining room windows, followed by a flash of light and a deafening explosion. Instantly, the front door flew open from the force of the battering ram. The team members button-hooked through the doorway, took aim, and squeezed their triggers.

The rapping cadence of deadly five-shot bursts from the MP-5's echoed in the room. Custer and Carson's chests exploded, their bodies wildly convulsing. The beige wall behind them splattered with red. A team member lunged at Jean, covering her with his body as the reflex of Custer's right trigger finger pulled off a single shot of the Magnum. The bullet blasted a gaping hole in the glossy hardwood floor.

"Two Zulu down!" Allendorfer yelled. "Hostage secured."

The five-man assault team was immediately joined by three other squad members and they fanned through the house.

Within minutes, Allendorfer gave the signal that the house was secure. "Signal Sierra," he yelled.

Paramedics from an ambulance that had just arrived bolted in, two to the bullet-riddled men and one to Jean.

"D.O.A. on this one," the paramedic examining Custer said.

"Same here," Carson's examiner added.

Jean was covered with a blanket as she sobbed, face in her hands.

"Joe," Jean cried, as O'Riley rushed in. She stood up and wrapped her arms tightly around him, burying her face in his shoulder.

"Everything's gonna be just fine," he said, gently rubbing her back. "We better get you cleaned up." He shook his head. "I never shoulda left you alone in the first place."

"You couldn't have known."

"If anything happened to you, I'd never get over it. Not to mention Jim would kick my ass."

Just the mention of Jim's name softened the ridges in Jean's cheeks as she pulled the blanket around her and hurried to the bedroom.

O'Riley's eyes followed her until she was out of sight and then looked around the blood-stained living room, surveying the carnage as investigators traced the path of every bullet fired from the TACT unit's MP-5's.

Suddenly he glanced over his shoulder.

Detective Trevor Mills, natty in a black camel hair sportcoat, was staring at him.

"Don't you ever dress down?" O'Riley asked.

"Yeah," Mills replied. "In the shower." He arched his blond eyebrows. "Anything you want to share with me? Like how in the hell this whole thing came about?"

O'Riley took a deep breath. "Just between you and me?"

Mills nodded, zipping his lip with a finger.

"The hit men were going after Jim Hale, the guy who gave me that statement about seeing Adam Baldwin murder a girl back in the late 1940s in a vision."

Mills pursed his thin lips. "And you believe him?"

"Get this. Both Hale and his girlfriend—Jean King, she lives here—were patients in memory drug experiments at St. Jude."

"Like David Lancaster?"

O'Riley shook his head. "It ain't the same. That was more extreme. With radiation in addition to the drug. They just got injections. They don't turn into anybody else. They just see things. Visions. Flashes. Whatever. They saw the same thing. Baldwin murder the girl."

Mills squinted, tilting his head to one side.

"What if this drug promotes new cell growth under certain circumstances? What if it not only stimulates memory cells but also enhances the growth of new cells that might reveal a past life?" O'Riley paused as Mills clicked his tongue against the roof of his mouth, thinking.

"I know, I know," O'Riley said, rolling his eyes. "Bear with me."

Mills held up his hands, palms facing O'Riley, his voice an octave higher. "Whatever you say. After last time, even against my better judgment, I'd follow you into a burning building."

O'Riley smiled. "We have a real witness to the murder. The old shoeshine man who's been right in front of our noses for decades. We have him in protective custody. Baldwin's people, or whoever it is behind this, think our witness is Hale. They were responsible for that house explosion earlier tonight, too. Know whose house it was?"

"Hale's," Mills said.

"You've been doing your homework. Remember the Devon Way explosion? Hale's daughter. He was supposed to be there when it happened. These guys went after Hale's girlfriend when they lost Hale. As of now, nobody, not even the girl, knows where he is. That ain't all. I think I know who Baldwin killed and where the body's buried."

Mills took a deep breath. "When I grow up, I want to become a detective, just like you."

"There's more, smart ass. The Secret Service was real interested in knowing if anybody was getting access to our old files. Turns out our Secret Service contact is a former agent who just happens to be Adam Baldwin's top aide."

"Don't you think you ought to let the federal boys in on this one?" Mills said.

O'Riley stroked his chin. "I already notified the Justice Department."

"What next?" Mills asked.

"We're gonna dig for the remains in Overton Park in the morning. I lined up our friends from the morgue."

"Davenport and Sims?"

O'Riley nodded. "Maybe Webster, too."

"What time?"

"Nine o'clock, straight up. Join us?"

"Got no place I'd rather be."

30

Jean was finally able to relax on the couch in the den as O'Riley faced her in his green tweed recliner.

"I'm glad as hell this day is over," O'Riley said, nodding at the time displayed on his RCA console: ten minutes before midnight. "I deserve some Bushmills tonight. How about it?"

"I just might have a sip," Jean replied, her eyes regaining a hint of blue-green sparkle. "To calm my nerves."

"To the guardian angel who was on your shoulder tonight," O'Riley said, as their glasses pinged. "May he or she watch over you always."

"And over Jim," she added, lifting the glass to her lips.

"Don't you worry, he'll be all right," O'Riley said, emptying his glass. "And you'll be safe in my old downstairs bedroom. Bullet can stay with you. He'll enjoy sleeping near a good-looking lady for a change."

O'Riley poured another shot and downed it in one rapid, fluid motion.

"You don't like that stuff much, do you?" Jean said with a smile as she ran a hand down a lapel of her pink terrycloth robe.

"Even an old Irishman's nerves can get a wee bit frayed, me little lass," he replied, the alcohol rushing to his head. "Another shot?"

"No thanks. I'm having fun just watching you."

"You know, if you'd feel better, I can leave this down here for you," O'Riley said, picking up his pistol.

She shook her head. "I've never used a gun."

"Well, you probably won't have to, but at least you'll know where one is. See this?" he said, pointing to a red dot on top of the gun's handle. "That's the safety. Push this little lever," he said, as the weapon made a clicking sound, "and you're ready to shoot. See? No red dot." He clicked the safety back into place and handed the gun to Jean.

"It's not very heavy," she said, gripping the dark blue firearm in her right hand.

"Just like a camera. Aim and shoot. That's all there is to it. Wham, bam, thank you, ma'am." He smiled, feeling lightheaded. "You might be a regular Annie Oakley and not even know it."

Jean handed the gun back. "Don't hold your breath."

"We'll leave it stashed back here in the den, right next to my car keys," O'Riley said, placing the gun in a cabinet next to the stereo system. "You'll know where it is if you need it."

"What about you?"

"I'm like a boy scout—always prepared. I got another one upstairs." He poured another shot and hoisted it to his lips.

"What about Jim?" Jean asked, not sure that she wanted to reveal her hunch.

O'Riley scratched his head. "Where do you think he is?"

She shrugged. "I guess he could be anywhere."

"With that wad of cash, he can hole up for a while."

"I did the same thing." She opened her purse and pulled out nine one-hundred-dollar bills. "Just in case you and I need to travel."

"Guns and cash," O'Riley said, smiling. "We make a pretty good team. The only thing missing is Jim." He stood and walked over to the window, looking up at the sky.

"What's the matter, Joe?"

"Damn stars all have twins," he mumbled. An uncharacteristic softness crept into his voice. "It seems like my whole life, everybody I've really cared about, really loved, has been taken away from me. My mother, my father, Jenny, Will, Mike Kelly, my wife, almost even Nancy . . ." His voice trailed off. ". . . but it ain't gonna happen with you and Jim. Not as long as this body of mine can draw a breath," he said, slamming a fist on the window sill.

"Or knock down the better part of a bottle of Bushmills."

O'Riley laughed. "You know, you'n Jim're always remembering things from way back when," he said with a slight slur. "Tell you what I remember. The world didn't use to be this dangerous a place, not like today, where drugs are constant, kids get shot at school, people's houses get blown up, innocent folks get terrorized in their own homes. When I was young, smoking cigarettes at parties was the fashionable thing to do. Grass was something we mowed, pot was something we cooked in, and coke was something we drank when we got tired of root beer. Things were innocent and carefree." His face wrinkled. "The world's topsy-turvy."

Jean smiled. "If you don't put that bottle away, you won't be able to remember those good old days. Besides, you have to be in good shape for that dig in the morning."

O'Riley nodded. "I guess it takes the will of a woman to keep us rowdy men in line. Good thing Nancy's in France. She'd a kicked my butt three shots ago. You sure you'll be all right?"

Jean stood up. "I'll be fine," she said as she kissed O'Riley goodnight on the cheek.

*

Jim stared down at the sea of colorful lights coming closer and closer.

In a few minutes the plane touched down, wheels bouncing once, then settling onto the runway at McCarran International Airport in Las Vegas at 10:30 P.M., Pacific Daylight Time.

Dinging slot machines mixed with the din of human voices in the airport lobby formed a constant, frenetic noise level, like static on a radio.

He finally relaxed as he moved through the terminal and stepped onto the moving sidewalk.

"Welcome to Las Vegas," said the recorded voice of Bill Cosby. "We know you're in for a good time. Please observe the yellow line in the center of the moving walkway. If you wish to stand, please do so to the right of the line to allow those walking on the sidewalk to pass to the left."

The message was followed by the recorded voices of other celebrities: Don Rickles, Joan Rivers, Rich Little, and Tony Bennett. Wide-eyed riders moving in the same direction were full of enthusiasm, peering at the huge hotel posters lining the walls, anticipating riches that would soon be theirs. Unsmiling faces moving in the opposite direction mirrored disappointment and lack of sleep.

As Jim waited for a cab in the balmy night air, he desperately wanted to talk to Jean, just hear her voice. But he couldn't take the risk.

A Checker cab pulled up and he hopped into the back and slammed the door.

"No luggage, buddy?" the driver asked.

"Airline lost it," Jim replied. "They'll get it to me later."

"Where you headed?"

"Caesar's."

"That's still the classiest place in town," the driver said as the cab roared away from the terminal. "You a gambler?"

Jim rubbed the bridge of his nose. "Yeah," he answered, "yeah, I am. I've been gambling a whole lot lately."

31

Jean lost track of how many times she had glanced at the red numerals on the small clock radio on the nightstand. She lay under the cool, crisp sheets, head buried in her pillow, remembering how it felt to be in love.

The anticipation and rapid heartbeats. The tightness in her throat and the shortness of breath. Ever since she had met Jim. Their lovemaking had only intensified her feelings.

She looked at the clock again: 3:58 A.M. No use. She was wide awake.

She had to be with him. They could hide out together. But how?

The faint sound of a freight train horn in the distance broke the silence. "That's it," she whispered to herself as she flicked on the bedside lamp and picked up the telephone. Amtrak Train Number 59 was scheduled to arrive in Memphis at 6:02 A.M. from Chicago and depart at 6:17 A.M. for New Orleans. She reserved a sleeping compartment.

She dressed, then peered in the mirror, running a brush quickly through her hair. No time for much make-up. Just a dab and some lipstick. She'd have plenty of time on the train.

Going into the den, she found a pen and notepad and began to write as Bullet, curled up in O'Riley's recliner, eyed her curiously, tail wagging. She put the pistol and O'Riley's key ring in her purse, patted the dog on the head, and slipped out the back door into Joe's car. Within a half hour she was at Central Station.

After parking the car and hiding the keys under the floor mat, she crossed South Main Street and paused for a moment on the southwest corner of the intersection. As she stood on the cracked sidewalk next to the corner-stone of the renovated train station, a chill ran through her body.

She turned around, looking back at the corner. The red-bricked facade of the Carnevale gift shop disappeared and a gleaming white store-front took its place. Through its windows she could see cases brimming with trays of chocolates, sugar-coated fruit slices, rock candy, peppermint sticks, and multi-colored jaw breakers.

A heavy-set, white-haired woman wearing an apron stood behind the counter, weighing chocolate-covered raisins and sliding them gently into a small white bag. *Lipford Brothers Candy Company* was painted in bold, black script on the large plate-glass windows.

"Hey, lady," an old man with a scraggly beard yelled as he waved dirt-caked fingernails in Jean's face. "I said, can you spare a dollar?" His breath reeked of cheap wine.

"No, sorry, I can't," Jean blurted out as the Lipford's store vanished. She turned quickly and entered the station.

"Your name, please," the ticket agent said.

"Jennifer Adair," Jean replied.

"Let's see. Adair. Here you are," he said, fingering his gold tie tack.

She handed him a hundred-dollar bill.

"Not much change." He smiled, giving her two ones. The computer whirred for a moment, then spit out a white and blue ticket. "Just show this as you board. Have a nice trip."

Jean quickly found her way to the platform and handed her ticket to a young black attendant holding a clip-board at the entry to the sleeping car.

"Name, please?" His eyes never left the clipboard.

"Adair."

He scrolled down the listings. "Jennifer Adair?"

"That's right."

"Compartment number eight. Up the stairs to your right."

Clutching her purse and overnight bag, Jean climbed the narrow steps.

Inside her compartment, she gazed out the window at the nearly deserted rail yard. Once the hub of train travel through Memphis, the station had to compete not only with air travel but its own former image as a monument to decay and neglect.

Suddenly the flickering lights outside brightened and, in an instant, the rail yard was alive with throngs of people waving as the train eased from the station. A middle-aged couple was running slowly along the platform, mouthing words that could barely be heard over the noise of the crowd.

"Study hard, but take time to write," a grey-haired, lanky man said.

A brunette woman with him waved and called out, "We love you, Jenny. We'll miss you!"

Tears rolled down Jean's cheek as the smiling young man next to her reached out. "Don't worry, Jenny. I'm with you. We'll always have each other," Will Harrison said.

The slowly rocking train brought Jean back to reality as it approached the Central Station yard limit. The pink light of day was just kissing the horizon to the east.

Jean leaned back in her seat, heart racing, and placed a hand to her mouth. She wiped the tears from her eyes and stared out at the moving landscape of abandoned buildings and crumbling warehouses.

At that moment a sharp knock rattled her compartment door.

"Yes?"

"Conductor, ma'am," replied a skinny-faced man with wire-rimmed glasses. "Ticket, please."

With a tip of his hat, he was gone. Seconds later there was another knock at the door.

"Ms. Adair?"

"Yes?"

"My name is Alphonse. I'm the sleeping car attendant. I have your complimentary meal voucher for breakfast and lunch. Arrival time in New

Orleans should be right around two o'clock. If there is anything else you need, I'll be glad to be of service."

"Thank you," she replied, taking the slip of paper as he bowed and closed the door behind him. Jean then locked the door and drew the orange and yellow curtain.

32

Only the soft hum of the clock-radio on his nightstand and the shuffling sounds of a squirrel scampering across the roof broke the morning silence as O'Riley lay sleeping, hands resting above his head on the pillow. He was dreaming of Paris. And Nancy.

His arms were wrapped tightly around her from behind. They looked down from the Eiffel Tower at the twinkling city lights. His lips curved into a smile.

At that moment there was a loud knocking followed by Bullet's husky, rapid barks. O'Riley's eyelids fluttered as he ran his tongue around the inside of his mouth and swallowed hard. He whipped a handful of sheets to the side and reached for his robe.

"I'm coming, I'm coming," he yelled, staggering down the dark staircase, its wooden steps creaking under his weight. He stumbled across the living room, eyes burning in the sunlight flooding through the front door.

Rich Reynolds stood on the porch. Autumn leaves carpeted the yard behind him, a blanket in varying shades of red and gold.

O'Riley unlocked the deadbolt and swung open the door, letting in a rush of brisk morning air.

"What time is it?" O'Riley said, rubbing half-opened eyes.

Reynolds stepped inside. The screen door slammed behind him. "Eight o'clock."

"Geez, I overslept. I gotta be at Overton Park at nine."

"How's the girl?"

"Asleep down the hall."

"Don't be so sure."

O'Riley's eyes widened. "What the hell are you talking about?"

"She's one slick little number. Slipped out hours ago and headed straight to the train station."

"Why in blue blazes didn't you call me?"

"You wouldn't have gotten far anyway. She took your car."

"Dammit!" O'Riley said under his breath.

"She parked it near the Arcade Restaurant and took the morning Amtrak to New Orleans. I figure she knows what she's doing."

O'Riley drew a sharp breath, as if he'd taken a blow to the gut. "New Orleans." He pulled a Tums antacid from the pocket of his robe and popped it into his mouth, teeth grinding it to chalk in an instant. "Jim wouldn't go there."

Reynolds shrugged. "You got me. You just asked me to keep an eye out. I ain't a mind-reader."

"I better get my FBI boys to watch for her when she gets off that train. Want some coffee?"

"I better get on home. It'll keep me awake and the missus will just talk my ear off. This way I can fall asleep while she yaps," Reynolds said with a wink. "Keep me posted how things turn out, Joe."

"I will," O'Riley said, as Reynolds headed for the door. "And Rich," he called out, "thanks."

The big man nodded as the door closed behind him.

O'Riley turned and walked down the hallway to the den. On the table next to the Bushmills was the note he expected to find.

Dear Joe,

I apologize for leaving like this. I'm sorry not to tell you where I've gone but, it's like you said, "no clues, no news." You're a pretty smart guy. I'd take a wager you can come up a winner and find us.

Thanks for the use of your car. I'll leave it parked near the Arcade Restaurant downtown with the keys under the front floor mat.

You're a wonderful man, Joe. One of the most special people I've ever known. The three of us will be safely together soon.

With much love until then,

Jean

O'Riley's mouth arched into a lopsided grin. "Sweet girl," he mumbled.

After calling Charlie Perry to get a ride to Overton Park, O'Riley stood in front of the bathroom mirror, straight razor in hand, not liking what he saw. His brown hair, laced with grey, stuck out in all directions. Tiny veins in his bloodshot eyes looked like a map of the Los Angeles freeway.

He then took a long shower, standing for several minutes as the hot water ran against the nape of his neck. Why New Orleans? He could drive there in five hours if he didn't have the grave dig set up.

*

"How come you called me for a lift, Joe?" Perry asked, steering his Buick onto Overton Park Avenue. "Your Lincoln on the blink?"

"It's a long story, Charlie. I'll tell you about it at the dig. Suffice it to say, I was blind-sided by a bottle of Bushmills. You know," O'Riley continued, "this is a nice set of wheels you got here." He rubbed his left hand on the Park Avenue's burgundy leather front seat. "Still smells new. How many miles you got on it?"

"Three thousand, two hundred," Perry replied.

O'Riley closed his eyes and inhaled deeply. "Ain't nothing like the smell of a new car. How'd you swing this while everybody else is using Fords and Chevys? I couldn't have done it in my day."

"In your day, all you had was the Bureau of Narcotics and Dangerous Drugs. Things have changed, Joe. Hell, you see it in the papers daily. South

American drug cartels. Crack on street corners in Everytown, U.S.A. Semi-automatic machine guns used in robberies. Hit men. Mob money. You name it. We get a little extra financial help thanks to the B.N.D.D's offspring, the Organized Crime Unit."

"Oh," O'Riley said, nodding. "Now they're offering luxury automobiles because the drug business is so good. What's the grand prize if you bust a major interstate heroin ring? A week for two in Hawaii with five thousand bucks for expenses?"

"They only give us two thousand," Perry deadpanned before breaking into a wide grin.

O'Riley laughed. "You almost had me, you son of a bitch."

"Actually," Perry said, "it wasn't too hard to get this car. The federal government allows police agencies to buy equipment with confiscated drug money. All we had to do was add the siren, alarm, radio and *voilá*! Better spent on me than on a month's worth of prostitutes for some Columbian drug lord."

"Maybe I *should* come out of retirement," O'Riley said.

Perry, still grinning, stroked his salt-and-pepper moustache. "That's a great idea, Joe. We'll fix you up real nice. Tell me, do you want an automatic transmission or would you rather have air conditioning on that GEO Metro?"

"And to think I recommended you as my successor," O'Riley replied, shaking his head in feigned disgust.

O'Riley and Perry were soon looking on as four police officers, two homicide detectives, the Shelby County medical examiner, and two forensic anthropologists from the University of Tennessee Department of Pathology cleared away decades of rotting leaves and branches.

"I hope your hunch is right about this, Joe, 'cause I sure as hell put my nuts in a vice," Perry said, twirling the gold coin ring on his finger. "If this turns out to be a wild-goose chase, the mayor will probably drop-kick my ass all the way down to foot patrol on Beale Street."

"And if we turn out to be right?"

"I imagine he'll find some way to take part of the credit," Perry replied with a smirk. "Hell, I could probably run for mayor myself if we're right, but I don't play those political games. I'd settle for a guest spot on *Oprah*. She's just my type."

O'Riley grinned. "Yeah. Filthy rich."

With the brush cleared, the forensic anthropologists began their search. Each pushed a thin metal rod slowly into the ground and pulled it out, repeating the process over and over, criss-crossing the area around the crooked tree.

O'Riley turned to the medical examiner. "Hey, Davenport," he said, reaching to shake his friend's hand, "things still dead down at the morgue?"

Davenport ran a hand across his freshly buzzed scalp. "Everybody except the rats."

O'Riley hooked a thumb toward the anthropologists. "You been working with those two guys a long time, haven't you?"

"You mean the two goons?" Davenport said, motioning toward Webster and Sims. Webster peered up through his gold wire-rimmed glasses as Sims, disheveled brown hair hanging down both sides of his long, narrow face, blew a kiss at O'Riley. "Yeah, we all graduated in the same class. Been working together ever since. They took a liking to old dead bodies. I was more enamored with the fresher ones."

O'Riley grunted. "I bet I could really lose some weight if I hung out with you guys again. How do those metal things work?"

"Just push 'em in the ground," Davenport said. "Undisturbed earth has a consistent hardness to it. If the rod hits a spot that's been dug up at any time and then covered over, it zips in a lot faster. If there's a grave anywhere near this tree, they'll find it."

"Does that thing work on old graves?"

"It depends. You can find graves four or five hundred years old with probes. Either the ground's been disturbed or it hasn't. If it has—"

"Zip. The probe slides right in," O'Riley interrupted.

Davenport nodded.

The tedious, methodical probing continued for a half hour. Then, a few minutes past 9:30, Webster yelled out, "Gentlemen, paydirt. Three and a half to four feet deep."

Davenport moved in as the two anthropologists scratched an outline of a grave in the topsoil with the point of a trowel.

"When was the girl buried here?" Webster asked.

"1949," replied O'Riley.

"What time of year?" Sims asked, scratching his prominent jaw with a lanky finger.

"Winter. Late December," O'Riley replied.

"Was she wrapped up in anything?"

O'Riley shrugged. "How the hell would we know? She was a goddam missing person, for crissakes."

"It'd be great if she was," Davenport said. "Would have kept out the rodents." He paused for a moment. "If she was buried deep enough, she may even be partially soponified."

Webster's dark eyebrows arched. "After more than fifty years?"

"Maybe," Davenport replied. "If she was buried three feet deep, the soil temperature would hold at about sixty degrees year-round. Any deeper, and she'd be at fifty-five or so. Might be pretty well preserved."

Webster shook his head. "I dunno. With water seeping in and out over the years, she's probably decomposed. Most likely she was just bones after two years."

"You two guys sound like you're bickering over a date. The answer is simple," Sims said with a ghoulish gleam in his hollow eyes. "I'll take the young lady to the dance."

Webster cracked a slight smile. "There is a chance for some soponification if she was wrapped real tight in a thick blanket. I'll bet there's no clothing or blanket left, if there was even one to begin with. Fabrics are usually gone within forty-eight months, tops."

"Unless," Sims said with a grin, "she was wearing everyone's favorite—polyester!"

Webster gave him a hard look. "They didn't have it back then."

"Say," O'Riley said. "This soponiwhatever. What is it?"

"Soponification," Davenport replied, "is when fat turns into, basically, soap. Same idea as when people making lye soap mix in fat."

O'Riley sighed, combing his fingers through his hair. "All I need is the remains of a body. Bones, some teeth, maybe a little jewelry. If I want soap, I'll buy a goddam bar of Safeguard."

"If you don't mind, make mine Dial," Sims said, smiling as he turned to Webster. "Shall we?"

"By all means," Webster replied, picking up a squared-end shovel. "Let the games begin."

Sims reached for the shovel and slowly skimmed the top layer of dirt from inside the outlined area, piling it in a neat mound.

"When I'm digging for fifty-year-old buried bodies," said Sims, mimicking a television commercial, "I always take along my trusty Marshalltown brand trowel. The thick wooden handle fits snugly in my hand and the sturdy, one-piece construction of the rod with its diamond-shaped blade just can't be beat. I could dig all day, body after body after body . . ."

Webster laughed as they both dropped to their knees and started scraping the ground with six-inch-long trowels. They kept scraping for about thirty minutes as the policemen milled about under the chilly overcast skies. Sims carefully placed this dirt in a separate pile.

"I think we've hit the humus," Webster said as the pit reached a depth of five inches.

"You sure?" Sims asked. "I don't see much difference in soil color."

"Mist it," Webster said.

Sims picked up a spray bottle and quickly covered a small area of the dirt with three squirts.

"See?"

"You're right," Sims replied, noting the darker color. "The texture is a little different now."

"Phase three," Webster said. "Let's take the pit down."

The pace increased as the two anthropologists dug deeper, soon running into roots.

Charlie Perry walked over to O'Riley. "I bet you never thought we'd make it this far, Joe."

"You're right, Charlie, we have come a long way."

"I mean *we*," Perry said, pointing to himself and Deputy Chief Albert Wilcox, just arriving at the dig.

"You mean you two black guys getting the number one and two spots in the department? Let me tell you, neither of you would've made it if you didn't deserve it. I remember back in the early seventies, just a few years after the King assassination, when you two were the first black detectives in Homicide. You worked days and Wilcox nights, right?"

Perry nodded.

"I took a little heat for moving you guys up so quickly. Pissed off more than a few people. You two kicked ass, especially on the Boone and Groseclose murders. You made me look pretty good. You might say I'm color-blind, Charlie, but I still see every color in the spectrum. And I call 'em like I see 'em."

"That, Joe, is the reason you got the TACT unit last night. And it's the reason we're out here shivering our asses off in the woods today. I finally figured out what you were doing when you had E. singing like a canary downtown. Right then and there I was back in the good old days following your lead."

O'Riley smiled as he buttoned his cardigan and slipped his hands into his trouser pockets. "I could sure use some coffee. My treat."

"Hey," Perry yelled at the detectives. "One of you, c'mere."

"What's up, Chief?" Harris said as he hurried over.

"O'Riley and I need a cup of coffee. Can you handle such an important mission?"

"Where from?"

"Try the Dairy Queen down on Summer," O'Riley said. "Tell 'em to drop a spoonful of vanilla ice cream in mine. Get one for yourself, too. Anybody else? Davenport? Webster? Sims?"

"I'll take a Coke," Davenport said.

"Nothing for us," Webster replied. "Our water jugs are all we need when we're digging."

"Speak for yourself," Sims said. "I'll take a cup of warm blood if they have it." He flashed a smile at O'Riley.

"Don't mind him, Harris. He was born that way," O'Riley said as he handed the detective a ten-dollar bill.

"Damn these sonuvabitchin' roots," Webster said, frowning. He was now three feet down in the hole. He glanced at the dirt-smudged face of his black sports watch. Five minutes past noon.

"This pit's been here a long time," Sims said. "Look at the size of this baby." He cut out a thick piece of the root and studied the rings.

"Looks like about fifty years to me," Webster said.

After another thirty minutes, Webster motioned to Sims as he carefully exposed two inches of a hard, brownish object. Their wide eyes met.

"Showtime, Davenport," Webster bellowed. Davenport, Perry, Mills, and the others rushed to join O'Riley, already at grave's edge. "Gentlemen," he announced, "we have human remains."

Webster and Sims crawled out of the tight space and the medical examiner took over.

"Do me a favor, Davenport," Webster said. "Don't mess anything up."

"Hey, guys, I read the book," Davenport replied. "I don't think we need a toe tag for this one." He rubbed his finger across the surface of the bone. "I've seen enough. You two can continue. That is," he added, "if I haven't put things in too terrible a state of disarray."

Webster and Sims eased back into the pit, each carrying a slender, six-inch piece of bamboo.

"What's that for?" O'Riley asked.

"Wood is the same density as bone," Webster replied. "It won't scratch or alter bone like metal."

Everyone crowded around as they dug.

"What is it?" O'Riley asked.

"Distal humerus," Sims replied.

"A distant what?"

"In English, an elbow. A right one, to be exact. Looks like the head will be at the north end of the pit."

"You guys are good. Got age, race, and sex yet?" Davenport said, smiling.

"Don't quite know all that, but it *is* a female," Sims answered. He peered up at Davenport. "And she appears more lively than most of your dates."

Everyone laughed as the laborious process of pedestaling the remains continued. As the digging progressed, the brown-hued bones looked as if they were on display in a museum, their pedestals the dirt that had supported them for over half a century.

33

"Yes?" Jean said cautiously, feeling for the pistol under the pillow in her lap as a loud knock sounded on her compartment door. "Who is it?"

"Conductor. Sorry to bother you," a man replied. "We're about an hour from New Orleans. I have a message for you." His voice could barely be heard above the droning clatter of the train's wheels.

She glanced at the white face of her watch. Nearly one o'clock. Who could possibly know where she was? She slowly pulled the orange curtain.

"You're not the conductor who punched my ticket," Jean said.

"He got off in Jackson. I'm on for the next three days," he said, his dark eyes narrowing as he waved a white envelope in the window.

"Who's it from?"

"A Mr. Jim Hale," the conductor replied. "He said it was urgent you get this right away."

Jean's heart raced as she wrestled with her thoughts. Was the message really from Jim? But she had to take a chance. Read the message. She had no choice.

"Just a minute," she said, unlocking the door.

The man lunged into the tiny compartment and clamped his right hand across Jean's mouth, dropping the envelope to the floor. Then he slammed the door shut, locked it, and drew the curtain.

Pushing Jean onto the seat, he pressed her head firmly against the red vinyl headrest and reached into his jacket, yanking out a gleaming nine-millimeter Ruger pistol.

Her face turned ashen, eyes wide and white, as he stuck the barrel to her head.

"One peep out of you, bitch, and your head will look like Julia Child's colander. Get it?"

Jean nodded, hands trembling.

"So," the gunman said, "your boyfriend's in New Orleans." He relaxed his hand on her mouth.

She sat in silence, paralyzed.

His steely eyes undressed her. "There are things I can do to make you talk. Some would feel real good. Others not. You could slip off those pants and panties and we could have a little roll in the hay. Think of it—as the train enters Louisiana, I'll be entering you. When I'm done, you'll be seeing stars."

Jean looked down, staring at his black loafers.

"Or I could just break your nose and knock some teeth out of that delicate little mouth. Think you might be able to answer some questions now?"

Jean looked up. His black hair matched his eyes. "How do I know you won't kill me?" she said softly, her voice quivering as she slowly gripped her pistol.

"Well, you never know. But, if it'll make you feel better, I'll reserve this as a last resort," he replied, placing his gun on the seat behind him.

"He's not in New Orleans," Jean said, looking straight in his eyes.

"Then why are you heading there?" the man bellowed, his bony face turning red. He grabbed her throat with his left hand, his right a clenched fist, cocked to deliver a blow to her face.

The train's whistle drowned the sudden pop of the pistol. Jean watched in horror as the man's eyes grew round and large, like two yolks sunnyside up. He reeled back, clutching his chest. He tried to speak but only a slight gurgling was heard as pink saliva bubbled from his lips, slowly trickling down the side of his chin.

The man's lifeless black eyes, fixed open, shone like marbles. A darkening wetness stained the chest of the blue uniform and quickly spread, dripping onto the chair's red, yellow, and black upholstery.

Jean cupped a hand over her mouth, the pungent smell of gunpowder permeating the air, burning her nostrils.

Her thoughts drifted to the time when she was fishing with her father at Horseshoe Lake in Arkansas. She was seven. Her first time. Her only time. Squealing with joy when she caught a big catfish. Her father throwing it into a white styrofoam ice chest, continuing to fish off the dock. She stared, unable to pry her eyes from her catch.

It flopped around on its frozen bed, gasping for air. Soon it was still, barely panting. Moments later, it lay dead, eyes wide open. Just like the gunman.

She sat motionless for several minutes, sick with shock, trying to calm down. Trying to keep her heart from pounding out of her chest. She listened for the sounds of anyone who might have heard the gunshot. Passengers in adjoining compartments. The real conductor.

Part of her prayed for help to come. Help that would rescue her from her nightmare. The other part, terrified and untrusting, hoped it would not.

But no one came.

Jean finally stood up, dropping the pistol to the floor. Hands shaking, she slumped back down, her face covered with desperation.

Fear gave way to remorse. She had taken a life. But in an instant the remorse turned to relief she had not been the victim.

She gathered her thoughts. Once in New Orleans, she would get off the train and go straight to the airport. Hopefully she would be gone long before the body was discovered.

Her quivering hands began to steady.

The train was now barreling through the bayous outside New Orleans. Spanish moss hung from the trees, many of them cypress, their trunks spread wide at water level.

Soon the train came to a stop in the shadows of the Louisiana

Superdome. Bright sunlight blazed through the window onto the body. Jean shuddered at the metallic smell of the blood as she drew the window curtain so no one could see inside. She quickly picked up her purse and overnight bag, stepped into the narrow corridor, and pulled the door closed behind her.

She first dropped the gun, wrapped in a newspaper, into a trash barrel. To avoid the long line at the taxi stand, she hurried toward Loyola Street in front of the terminal. She waved, quickly attracting the attention of a green and white Liberty Bell Cab.

"Don't like them cab lines, do ya?" said the driver, a large black man who hopped out to open the door. He then slammed the door and jumped back into the driver's seat. "Most of them folks in the terminal line are going to hotels here downtown and I can't make much money on them. Where you headed?"

"This is your lucky day," Jean replied. "The airport."

"That's what I like to hear. Music to my ears and my pocket book. This is your lucky day, too."

"How's that?"

"You ever been here before?"

She shook her head. "Can't say I have."

"Well, you're in for a treat," the driver said, turning right onto LaSalle. "My name's Bill Parks, taxi driver and tour guide extraordinaire. No extra charge." He grinned.

"That's Dr. King's statue," Parks said as the cab turned from Martin Luther King Drive onto Claiborne. "And, of course, you know the building over there."

"The Superdome," Jean replied, relaxing into a smile.

"Attagirl," Parks said as the cab accelerated onto Interstate 10.

"Been driving long?" Jean asked, noticing the colorful Mardi Gras beads dangling from the rear-view mirror.

"Thirty-three years. This here's my own car. A 1998 Oldsmobile Delta 88. They don't make 'em no more. I got a hundred-ninety-eight thousand on it. It's my baby. This car's been overhauled, white-walled, relined, refined, scuffed, buffed—you name it. It's had more face-lifts than a seventy-year-old in Hollywood. Speaking of Hollywood folks, Clint Eastwood and Sharon Stone have been fares of mine. Sat in the same spot you're in."

"I could sure use Dirty Harry right now," Jean said.

"Couldn't we all," Parks said, laughing, "couldn't we all. Look at the building on the left. That's the *New Orleans Times Picayune*—best newspaper in town."

The downtown skyline shrank as the cab roared down the interstate. Cemeteries filled with row upon row of mausoleums bordered the road, transforming the highway into a thin thread of life running through a metropolis of the dead.

"That's Lakeside Cemetery on the right," Parks said. "And that's Lake Lawn over on the left."

"I've heard everybody is buried above-ground here," Jean said, rolling her window down enough to let a breeze wash across her face.

"Have to," Parks said. "New Orleans is below sea level. The ground's too soft to bury people in. You either get planted inside a mausoleum, cremated, or shipped somewhere else. What's your name, ma'am?"

"Jean," she replied. "Jean Howard."

"Nice to know you, Jean. You call me Bill. For these few minutes we'll be good friends. That okay with you?"

"To be perfectly truthful, you've been the one sunny spot in a pretty stormy day."

"A lot of folks tell me that same thing," Parks said, flashing two gold front teeth. "This here is Metairie we're entering now. It's a suburb of New Orleans. Won't be too much longer to the airport."

Soon they reached Kenner and veered off to the right onto Airport Road. Traffic was thick, but Parks weaved in and out of lanes like a bumblebee drunk on nectar.

"There it is," Parks said, pointing. "What airline?"

237

"Northwest probably. I'm looking for the fastest way to get where I need to be."

"Where's that?"

"Nothing personal," Jean said, "but as far away from here as I can get."

"Northwest is on your right, under that green awning," he said, as the taxi rolled to a stop. "That'll be twenty-one dollars, Jean."

She handed him a twenty and a ten. "The extra is for the conversation—even if it was free. Thanks." As he helped her out, the eighty-degree heat hit her square in the face.

"Thank you, Jean. I hope you end up wherever it is you want to be!"

She threw the straps to her purse and bag over her shoulder and entered the terminal. Within minutes she stood in front of a Northwest ticket agent.

"Where to today?" the man asked.

"Las Vegas, as soon as possible."

"Name, please?"

"Jean. Jean King," she replied, feeling brave.

"Could I see a picture I.D. please?"

The computer spit out boarding passes seconds after the agent completed punching his keyboard. "Ms. King, we have you on Flight 1263 to Minneapolis leaving at 2:55 P.M. from Gate A1, connecting with Northwest Flight 711 to Las Vegas. That will be three hundred and eighty-three dollars."

She handed him four hundred-dollar bills.

"Gate A1 is behind you to your right," the agent said. "They're boarding right now."

Jean was a study in paranoia as she sank into seat 12C. She didn't know who to trust. O'Riley's words came back to her. Trust no one but himself and Jim.

She glanced at the people seated near her, eyes constantly in motion, darting about the cabin as the airplane taxied toward the runway, its engines whining.

An older lady in seat 12A was engrossed in a romance novel. The woman in 12B appeared about forty-five. She talked with a slight accent and sported neck-length red hair held back with a black headband. Seats 12E and 12F across the aisle were taken by a mother and daughter, a large woman in her fifties and an attractive twenty-year-old. None seemed threatening. And no one seemed to notice her.

"Flight attendants, prepare for departure," came over the intercom. The whirring of the jet engines increased and the plane lurched forward, pushing Jean into her seat. The bumpy sprint down the runway soon became a graceful glide into the skies.

Jean looked out the window with the eyes of a photographer at the sun-drenched, billowy, white cumulus clouds that hung like huge cotton balls over a bright blue canvas. How easy her life had been, so uncomplicated before her treatments at St. Jude, she thought. She had been as carefree and innocent as those clouds dancing on the massive stage below her.

Never again.

34

"Hey, O'Riley," yelled Webster as the pedestaling reached its third hour. "I got a question."

The former chief and Charlie Perry were just finishing Big Macs in the front seat of Perry's Buick. O'Riley stuffed the last bite into his mouth, wiped sauce from his lips, and turned to Perry. "I hope those two gravediggers ain't trying to get me to puke 'cause I just might do it."

He got out and walked over to the edge of the pit. Sims was snapping pictures.

"You said you might know what this girl was wearing, right?" Webster asked, scratching at his chin.

"Yeah," O'Riley replied. "We think she had on a maroon dress with a floral design."

"You might find this of interest." Webster pointed to a green area on the hip bone. "There's no dress left to speak of, but this spot of green could be significant."

"It appears to be the remains of a pocket," Sims added. "With a few pennies in it. This bit of fabric turned green but was preserved due to the oxidation of the copper."

O'Riley's brow wrinkled. "Copper preserves fabric?"

Webster nodded. "You better believe it. Copper preserves just about anything. Sims and I were working on a turn-of-the-century grave found at a construction site not long ago. The guy's body had been embalmed with copper sulfate. Preserved him perfectly. He only had one problem."

"Yeah," said Sims, his mouth arced in a crooked grin. "When the air hit him, he turned royal blue. Looked just like a smurff."

"Look at that spot that's not quite so green, O'Riley," Webster said. "Right in the area that's a little lighter. What do you see?"

O'Riley dropped to his knees and stared down. His eyes widened. "It's a goddam flower! Let me take a look."

"Whoa," Webster said. "That'll have to come later when we bag up the evidence. We have to follow procedure. We haven't even uncovered the skull yet."

"C'mon, guys," O'Riley begged. "How much longer is this gonna take?" He glanced at his watch. Just after 3 P.M.

"Most likely another two hours," Webster replied.

"At least," Sims added.

O'Riley got up and paced around for a few minutes. A stiff wind blew dirt and grit against his face, stinging like tiny pin pricks as he headed for Perry's car.

"If it's any consolation," Sims yelled, grinning wide, "we should be getting to the good part soon. The head area of every dig is usually pretty interesting. After all, every body has a good head on their shoulders or, at least, near their shoulders."

The excavation took less time than expected. Within an hour and a half, the bones were fully uncovered and pedestaled. Artifacts had been found but were yet to be closely examined. Then, with Webster at the foot of the pit and Sims at the head, they went to work with small paint brushes, each deftly flicking loose dirt to the edge of the pit floor.

After about fifteen minutes, Sims climbed out of the pit, picked up two six-inch wooden objects, and handed them down to Webster. The first, a scale to reference lengths, was placed at the base of the pedestaled femur. The other piece, painted black with an arrow at one end, was aligned on the pit floor pointing north. Webster climbed out, wrote *FA-142* on a small chalk-board, and placed it on the ground at the north end of the pit.

"Are we taking enough time with this, guys?" O'Riley asked. "It'd be nice to get a closer look at those trinkets you uncovered at some point in this lifetime."

Trevor Mills walked over to O'Riley and peered into the pit, fingering the knot of his tie.

"You're Irish, aren't you, O'Riley?" Sims asked, positioning his camera to photograph the pit's interior.

O'Riley rolled his eyes. "You're still up there with Einstein, Sims. How you figured that one out, I'll never know."

"My point is this. There's an old Irish proverb: 'Buried embers may turn into flames.' Let us do our job and you just may find what you're looking for." He snapped his pictures as Webster picked up a clipboard and began drawing on a piece of graph paper.

O'Riley turned to Mills. "Incredible. I got a blood-sucking zombie quoting me Irish proverbs."

Mills squinted. "What's the FA-142 mean? And what's with the graph paper?"

"Forensic Anthropology, case 142 this year," Webster replied. "That's how we'll file everything involving this case. As for the graph paper, I'm triangulating the grave site to the immediate surrounding surface area. That goes on one piece of paper. On another sheet I'm sketching the triangulation of the remains in the grave according to the bones we've found. Any other questions?"

"Yeah," O'Riley replied. "What is this, art class? First, paint brushes, then drawing pictures. I'm too old for this waitin' around."

Webster frowned. "Have a little patience. I'll be through in about ten minutes and we'll start examining the evidence."

O'Riley rubbed his sore shoulders. "I tell you what. Call me when you're ready." He ambled over to the chief's burgundy Buick and got in, leaning back on the car's headrest.

No sooner had he shut his eyes when Perry's car phone rang. O'Riley placed the receiver to his ear. "Hello?"

"Dug up any ghosts yet, Joe?"

"That you, Tasker?"

"None other than," replied the FBI agent. "We've found your girl."

O'Riley's mouth stretched into a wide grin. "What's she doing? Eating beignets at Cafe du Monde?"

"She's on her way to Vegas."

O'Riley's smile faltered. "Vegas?"

"You don't know the half of it," Tasker said.

O'Riley was disgusted with himself as he remembered Jean's note. "I shoulda figured that out right off the bat. She left me a note saying she'd *take a wager* that I'd *come up a winner* and find 'em. I think I better plead temporary insanity. Tunica came to mind but I blew it off. Too close to home. Was it tough tracking her down?"

"No, not at all," the agent replied. "We just followed the trail of blood."

O'Riley's chest tightened. "What are you talking about?"

"Well, not exactly a trail. We found a body in her train compartment. I checked it out while two of my guys followed her to the airport. Seems she whacked a New York hit man, Carmine Deloso. One shot. Right through the heart."

"His heart?"

"Dead center," Tasker said, admiration in his voice. "Used a Walther. She dumped it in a trash can at the train station."

"That was *my* gun."

"You want it back?"

"Hell, yes. What happened on the train?"

"Deloso disguised himself as a conductor," Tasker replied. "She must've let him in and then shot him when she figured out he wasn't on the level."

"What does the New Orleans P.D. think?"

"They were swearing it was a Mafia retaliation-type hit after I got finished with them. They looked up the alias she used when she paid for her compartment, and Jennifer Adair didn't register on the police wire. I'll keep you posted from Vegas."

"Thanks, Jerry. I owe you one. There is one thing that's worrying me, though."

"What's that?"

O'Riley was a bundle of nerves. "If it was so easy for you guys to keep up with her, it'll be just as easy for other people to do the same."

"We'll just have to play the cards we're dealt, Joe. Don't worry, it'll work out. She makes a connection in Minneapolis. I got two guys on the plane as we speak. I'm headed straight to Vegas on a charter so I can watch over her personally."

O'Riley's face hardened. "Let me know as soon as you hear anything, Jerry. Those two are real special to me."

"You got it. By the way, go easy on the Irish whiskey from now on, especially at bedtime."

O'Riley laughed. "You guys don't miss a beat, do you?"

"If we did, we'd never admit it. Talk to you soon."

O'Riley drew a deep breath and headed back to the pit, again pacing around the gaping cavity as Webster was finishing his sketches. O'Riley looked at his watch. 4:55. He stuck a piece of Doublemint in his mouth.

"Gentlemen," Webster announced, "the moment you have all been waiting for has arrived. After you," he said, motioning Sims into the pit.

"My pleasure," Sims replied, as Webster followed suit.

"Before moving anything, I want you to be aware of our initial observations," Webster said. Everyone lined up around the two. "There are an undetermined number of coins, including some pennies, concealed by the remnants of a pocket on the victim's dress at the greater trochanter of the right femur. The bones of the left hand seem to have been clutched around a gold pendant or locket of some type at the time of the interment and are still partially concealing the object. There is a gold necklace below the skull, resting on the sternum, which appears to be in the form of a script-lettered name. And finally—"

"Finally," Sims began, "in observing the skull, even an idiot could see this fracture. See it, O'Riley?"

"Funny, Sims, funny," O'Riley said, his mouth feigning a smile.

"Right temporal," Davenport said, blue eyes gleaming.

Sims picked up the skull and closely studied the crack in its right side. "Perimortem," he said.

Webster nodded. "Yeah, green bone."

O'Riley cocked his head. "Translation?"

"The skull fracture was perimortem, that is, at or near the time of death," Webster replied. "Green bone means the same thing. The fracture occurred while the person was still alive, not as a result of any incident after death."

Sims wrapped the skull in a piece of newspaper and handed it up to Davenport, who placed it in a cardboard box at the rim of the pit. "We normally start at the feet end," Sims said, "and save the head for last. But since you guys are in such a hurry for the juicy stuff, we thought we'd hit the skull first, no pun intended, and work our way down."

Webster reached for the dirt-encrusted gold necklace resting on the sternum and gently picked it up. "Sims, I can't make this out. My glasses are too dusty. What does it say?" He handed the mass of gold and dirt to Sims, took off his glasses, and rubbed the lenses on his blue shirt.

Sims knocked off bits of soil, smiled, and looked up at O'Riley. "It says Allison."

O'Riley remembered the last time he had seen the necklace. The last night he had seen Allison. A wave of sadness washed over him, but this was quickly replaced by elation at having solved a disappearance that had vexed him for what seemed like his whole life. "Allison Tucker," he said. "This proves it."

"Not so fast," Webster said. "We like to say *indications are*. In this case, I'd have to say indications are the victim was named Allison."

"Congratulations, Joe," Perry said, shaking O'Riley's hand and slapping his shoulder. "You've done a damn good job of detective work for a retiree."

O'Riley's grin spread from ear to ear. "We ain't home yet, but we're coming down the stretch. C'mon guys, let's get a look at the other stuff."

"Anything more we can I.D. on this babe?" Mills asked as Sims and Webster gently moved the bones of the girl's right hand.

"I'll be damned," Webster said, lifting a shiny gold pendant from the finger bones. "Looks like a Saint Christopher with a little latch on the side. Never seen one like this before." He examined the bell-shaped piece of metal more carefully. "It looks like a miniature stage with curtains on each side. Looks like Saint Christopher with the Baby Jesus on his shoulder." He flipped the locket over. "To Adam Hart Baldwin. I will always be with you. Lovingly, Grampa," he read out loud.

"See if that latch will open!" O'Riley barked.

Webster pushed the latch and inserted his left thumbnail into a tiny slit along the locket's rim. It popped open. "I'll be damned again," he said, pushing the locket into his partner's face. "What are the odds against these being intact, Sims?"

"The adhesive must have preserved them. Better leave it open to air out," Sims replied.

O'Riley dropped on all fours like a starving dog going after a steak. "Let me see."

"Isn't that old Mayor Hart in the photo on the left?" Webster asked, holding the locket up to O'Riley.

"And young Adam Baldwin on the right," O'Riley bellowed. "That son-of-a-bitch is *mine!*"

35

It was 7 P.M. and Jim was famished. He hadn't left his room in the Roman Tower at Caesar's Palace since the night before.

He fell back on the black-striped bedspread, gazing up at his image reflected in the ceiling mirror as he waited for room service. Had Jean and O'Riley figured out where he was? he thought to himself.

He let out a deep breath, sinking further into the fluffy bedspread as relief from danger washed over him like a waterfall. But the feeling quickly vanished, replaced by a piercing loneliness.

Suddenly there was a loud knock on the door.

Jim jumped up and peered through the peephole. "Who is it?"

"Room service." Outside was a short, dark man, maybe twenty-two, with lively brown eyes and a flashing smile.

"Just a second," Jim said, removing the door chain.

"Where would you like this, Mr. Harrison?" the waiter asked as he pushed the table through the doorway.

"Over by the bed, Carlos," Jim replied, having noticed the name embossed on the waiter's identification tag. "I'll watch television while I eat."

Carlos deftly lifted the silver covers from the plates and announced the various dishes with a slight Hispanic accent. "Sirloin strip, medium rare. Sauteed mushrooms in burgundy. Steamed broccoli with a side of margarine. Baked potato with chives. Shall I keep the apple pie in the warmer for you?"

"Yes, thanks," Jim said. "They don't scrimp on portions, do they?"

Carlos shook his head, smiling. "You pay for it in the casino. If you should need anything else, sir, please let us know."

"Thanks very much," Jim said as he slipped Carlos a crisp, folded ten-dollar bill that instantly disappeared into the waiter's pocket.

An hour and a half later, he pushed the table aside, feeling uncomfortable and overstuffed.

He toyed with the idea of going downstairs. He had been in Las Vegas almost a whole day, and nothing suspicious had happened. Hazarding a trip to The Forum Shops couldn't be too dangerous. Besides, he needed to walk off the meal. He pulled a black sport coat over his broad shoulders and flicked a brush twice through his thick, straw-colored hair.

Jim stood outside his door for a moment, glancing both ways. Then he turned right, toward the elevator bank for the Olympic Tower.

A group of laughing couples suddenly poured into the hallway. "Hey, follow that guy," shouted one of the men, pointing at Jim. "Looks like he knows the short-cut to the Olympic Casino."

Three couples and a blond in a pink-sequined dress with plunging neckline crowded into the elevator. The blond smiled at Jim as the doors closed, staring at him with large green eyes.

When the doors opened to the lobby, the sound of slot machines chiming and coins hitting trays filled the air. Jim headed for The Forum Shops.

After browsing through several stores, he spotted Field of Dreams, with its plaques of sports autographs lining the walls, and Antiquities, specializing in memorabilia from the early to mid-1900s. "Right up my alley," he murmured as he walked in.

*

Jean rushed over to the Caesar's Palace reservations desk as the automatic doors whooshed shut behind her. "I need some help finding a friend of

mine who is registered here," she said anxiously. "His name is Will Harrison."
Her temples throbbed, as if someone was lightly tapping them with a finger.

The grey-suited clerk looked down at her computer screen through over-sized bifocals. "We have two people by that name registered," she said, her large gold-hoop earrings dangling as she turned back to Jean. "Do you have an address?"

She thought for a moment, remembering that Joe said Jenny and Will lived on the next street east of North Avalon when the three of them were growing up. "It would be Angelus. In Memphis, Tennessee."

"Mr. Will Harrison, 229 North Angelus in Memphis. I can ring his room for you if you'll step over to the house phones."

"All right," Jean replied, nodding. "Thank you."

She held the white receiver to her ear, filled with excitement. So much had happened. So much to tell. Yet only a day had passed since they last spoke.

The phone rang as she nervously adjusted the collar of her blouse. No answer. A recorded voice came on the line for her to leave a message.

"I'm here. I'll call again later after I find my way around. I'm leaving my bag at the bell desk under your name. I love you, now and always."

Wiping tears from her eyes, she set out to find him.

After fifteen minutes, frustrated and almost overwhelmed by the size of the complex, she stopped at the Emperor's Club booth in the Olympic Casino for information.

"What can I do for you?" a tall young man behind the counter asked.

"I have a question about the shopping mall," Jean said. "Are there any memorabilia shops?"

"Two come to mind," the man replied, brushing red hair from his forehead with a flick of his wrist. "There's Field of Dreams for sports autographs. I don't know many females who get into that. You have to like sports an awful lot."

"And the other place?"

"It's across the hall from the sports shop—Antiquities. It's not really a memorabilia store. They sell reconditioned items and gadgets from the 1920s through the 60s. Old toys, movie posters, gas pumps, popcorn machines, bicycles. Kinda like an expensive flea market where everything looks brand-new."

Jean's eyes brightened. "Thanks," she said, quickly heading for the mall.

She had a feeling she would find Jim there. Lost among memories of not one life but two. Together they could make memories all their own.

*

As Jim entered, he felt as if he had been magically transported into the past. Lit up in neon on the back wall of the colorful, cramped store were names and images he had stored in the darkest recesses of his memory. A red Mobil Oil flying Pegasus from the 1950s. A 1940s blue neon Chrysler Plymouth Sales-Service sign. A three-foot bottle of Hires Root Beer in orange neon from the late 40s. Pontiac's red Mohawk Indian emblem from the 50s.

Other pieces caught his attention. They seemed familiar, too.

A Nickelodeon player piano in rich, dark walnut. A white, three-door ice box with brass trim from the 1930s. A National cash register tagged circa 1936. A yellow and red Shell gas pump from the early 1940s. A 1938 bright red Dodgem bumper car. A 1939 Zenith floor console radio.

Finally, he ended up near the cash register where he carefully examined trays of antique watches and jewelry. His gaze settled on a collection of wedding bands.

"Would you like a closer look at anything?" an attractive brunette clerk asked from behind the counter.

"If you don't mind," Jim replied, "I'd like to see that tray of rings." He carefully picked up a small gold band, admiring its smooth surface.

"Sure would make a nice diamond engagement setting," the clerk said.

250

"It really is pretty. When's it from?"

"1949."

"How can you be so sure?"

"Easy," the woman replied, grinning. "It's engraved inside. You could have it buffed off."

"How much?"

"Three hundred dollars."

Jim winced. "What if I'm *seriously* considering it?"

"How seriously?" the woman asked, dark eyebrows raised.

"This seriously," he replied, holding up his brown alligator wallet. "Cash."

"You picked the right person to wait on you. I'm the owner. How does one-ninety-five sound?"

"Sold!" Jim pulled the money from his billfold.

"I'll even throw this in," the woman said, placing the ring snugly in a grey velvet box and snapping the lid shut. "Come back and see us. And thank you."

Jim shoved the box into his pocket and paused for a moment outside the store's large show window, drawn to autographs of Clark Gable and Vivian Leigh dated December 15, 1939, from the *Gone With The Wind* movie premiere.

"Bet those cost a pretty penny," the blond in the revealing pink dress said. "I'm window shopping. About to meet my husband by the fountain." She pointed to a large statue of the seated Bacchus and other ancient gods towering behind them. "If he doesn't get here soon, he won't be able to find me. That group of statues comes to life like something at Disney World. They're automated. They start moving around with laser lights flashing and thunder booming. It's a real scream. People pack this area like sardines, the lights dim, and the show starts. Somebody could get shot and nobody'd even hear." She reached in her matching pink purse.

"I just might have to stay for that," Jim said, slightly nervous. "See that Schwinn bicycle back there?" He pointed to a baby blue girl's bicycle from the 1960s. "I gave one just like that to my little girl, Sarah, over thirty years ago."

At that moment, a jabbing pain in his side banished his nostalgia. Startled, he whirled around, glaring at the woman.

"Don't even scratch," she said, poking a Sig Sauer automatic against his ribs, in a pleasant tone that wasn't very pleasant at all. "Just shut up and act normal. You cause me any problems and they'll be stuffing you at the taxidermist and sticking your ass in the window with the bike."

"So you don't have a husband, I guess," he said, face pinched.

"Right you are. Since we're telling life stories, should I call you Mr. Hale?"

"How'd you find me?"

"Hey, I'm not the only one out looking. I just got lucky. You got a big bounty on your head. You know, you look just like your picture. When I collect that money, I can take my share and lay off turning tricks for a month."

"What's the bounty?"

"Word is, a lot more than it was a couple of days ago. Whoever you pissed off must be feeling some heat from somewhere. It's seven hundred fifty thousand bucks."

"Dead or alive?"

"Just dead," the woman replied as a crowd began to gather for the show.

"What's to keep me from just hiking right now?"

The blond's smooth skin wrinkled at the corners of her eyes. "You don't *look* stupid. There's an automatic pistol in your side. By the time you were two feet away, I'd have three, maybe four, bullets in you. So, let's turn *real* slowly and head down the mall toward Caesar's."

"Drop it, lady. Las Vegas Police! Drop it. Now!" bellowed a policeman in firing stance as the mall lights dimmed.

The woman whirled around, pointing her gun. They fired simultaneously, their weapons sparking orange-white flashes in the shadowy light. Jim slammed to the floor.

A nine-millimeter slug ripped into the woman's forehead above her left eye. She bolted upright, killed instantly. The officer crumpled to the floor, his left shoulder shattered by a bullet meant for his chest. Jim stayed on the ground, eyes shut tight. A spray of bloody mist spritzed his sweater as the woman's head hit the marble floor with a dull thud.

Shoppers screamed as they rushed through the mall toward Caesar's, storming down the narrow streets that resembled a small Italian town, a frenzied chaos like the running of the bulls in Pamplona.

Jim slowly got to his feet just as Jean threw her arms around him in a tight bear hug. Startled, he said, "What are you doing here?"

"Saving your life, what do you think?" she replied. They quickly moved down a ramp into the mall corridor. "Who do you think alerted that policeman?"

They were soon engulfed in a sea of screaming bodies. The surrealistic mall sky changed in seconds from a bright, daytime blue into the darkened, orange-purple tones of dusk.

Jean gripped Jim's hand tightly as they cleared the entry into the casino and threaded through the maze of gamblers clustering around the table games and dinging slots.

Suddenly, Jim spotted four men, two heavy-set and two medium-build, hurrying across the crowded floor behind them. All wore sunglasses, navy blazers, and carried two-way radios. They formed a semi-circle, closing in like jackals.

Near the escalator leading to the Omnimax Theater, two more men in navy jackets were waiting. One placed a radio to his mouth.

"Jean, this way!" Jim said, spotting a seldom-used secondary entrance to Caesar's on his left.

They burst through the brass-framed glass doors just as a Checker Cab pulled up.

Jim shoved Jean into the back seat of the still-moving car. "Step on it!" he yelled.

"It's your dime," replied the burly driver, flooring the gas pedal. With long, flowing, brown hair and an unkempt white beard, he looked like a Hell's Angel who had traded in his Harley for a taxi. Screeching tires left a cloud of white smoke that engulfed the navy-jacketed men bolting from the casino.

The cab raced toward Las Vegas Boulevard, zooming past rows of white columns topped with gold trumpeteers that lined the long drive leading to Caesar's.

"Look at that," the driver said as screaming sirens and flashing lights swarmed into Caesar's from all directions. "You two ain't robbed this place, have you?"

"There's a policeman down inside," Jim replied. "Somebody shot him in the mall."

The taxi raced past the Flamingo Hilton and the Barbary Coast, heading south through a green light at Flamingo Avenue, slowing slightly for traffic in front of Bellagio.

"Where to?" the driver asked.

"Keep on down the Strip," Jim replied, as they passed the gold lion in front of the MGM Grand Hotel. "I'm not sure yet."

They whizzed under the pedestrian overpass linking the Tropicana, with its cascading blue neon waterfall, to Excalibur, which lit up the night with its red, blue, and gold towers. On the right stood the Luxor, a giant black pyramid rising from the Nevada desert, complete with its own Sphinx at its base.

"Reminds me of home," Jim said, thinking of the Pyramid Arena in Memphis. He squeezed Jean's hand.

Jean nodded. "If only we were there now."

"Nick, we got trouble. A big Lincoln limo's dogging us. Make that two Lincolns," the driver shouted, squinting at the bright headlights in his rear-view mirror.

"Who's Nick?" Jim asked, eyes wide, as he put his arms around Jean.

"I'm Nick, my friend," a balding man with a scar running down his left cheek replied, unveiling a .357 Magnum as he slid up from the front passenger seat.

The driver shrugged. "Sorry, boys and girls, you picked us, remember?"

Jim pulled Jean close and glanced out the rear window at the blazing headlights in pursuit.

"See this?" the man said, pointing the Magnum at the couple. "It ain't one of those pray and spray semiautomatics. You try anything, mister, and your girlfriend's gonna have a hole in her chest the size of a dinner plate." He flashed a cold smile, then turned to the driver. "Hit the pedal, goddammit. We got to lose those S.O.B.'s and take care of business." He flicked his hook nose three times with the tip of the gun barrel as if scratching an itch.

The cab instantly swerved, making a squealing U-turn around the median at Sunset Park. Jim clutched Jean tighter and braced himself against the door.

The two black limousines followed suit, tires screeching west down Sunset.

At Eastern Avenue, the stocky gunman rolled down his window as the taxi made a hard right and fired off three booming left-handed shots.

"*Nobody* screws with Nick Verasco," he said, gritting his teeth. The bullets hit their mark, cracking the limousine's windshield.

The cab's speedometer hit ninety.

"Those bastards are in some kinda special limos," Verasco shouted. "The bullets didn't shatter shit."

A Delta Airlines 747 screamed overhead, its landing gear about to make contact with the runway.

"Jesus!" Verasco screamed, ducking as the car's back window blasted inward, covering Jim and Jean with fragments of safety glass. "One of those sons-of-bitches is firing a goddam M-16 assault rifle!"

The cab clipped the fender of a pink Corvette and barreled through a red light at Patrick Lane, zipping by cars as if they were standing still. Verasco fired four more shots, popping up from behind the front seat to shoot through the rear window. "Run it. Left," he ordered at the next red light. The cab swerved, skidding tires whining in a sweeping arc.

The lead limousine missed the quick turn and careened into a Mini-Market's parking lot, knocking two gas pumps into the air like tinker toys. The driver quickly regained control and raced after the other limousine as the gasoline island exploded, rocketing two massive orange-white fireballs into the dark sky.

"I can lose these guys if I make it back to the Strip," the driver said. "On the week-end, we wouldn't have a chance." He floored the gas pedal.

Jim hovered low over Jean like an umbrella. She pressed her face against his chest.

The cab was forced to slow down at the ninety-degree curve from Russell onto Paradise Road. Verasco peeked above the seat, looking for a clear shot.

Verasco made a gurgling sound as a bullet from a Glock automatic ripped into his throat. A split-second later another shot plowed into the middle of his forehead. He slumped against the door, blood spattering the windshield.

"Holy shit!" the driver yelled, crouching down. He reached under the seat and yanked out a .38-caliber revolver. With the Lincolns closing in, he aimed it directly at Jim. "One thing's for sure," he said. "If I gotta go, I'm taking you two with—"

Suddenly the back of his head exploded. Blood and bits of bone splattered across the dashboard. The car veered to the right as Jim frantically scrambled for the front seat. It hopped the curb at the entrance to the Las Vegas Mobile Park, leveling two cedar trees and a row of hedges.

Jim lunged for the steering wheel. The car headed across the open courtyard toward the mobile park's swimming pool. Jim pulled himself over the seat, slamming his left foot on the brake pedal. The battered white taxi skidded to a halt, its bumper pressing against the pool's fence, a cloud of dust swirling behind it.

Hands shaking, Jim opened the door and shoved the driver's body onto the ground. He eased himself out and opened the back door. Jean lunged into his arms.

The two limousines roared to a stop in the grassy area behind them. Five men, all dressed in navy suits and sporting clean-cut hair styles, slowly got out, placing their Glocks into shoulder holsters.

A tall, square-shouldered agent held out his hand. "Mr. Hale, I'm Jerry Tasker."

Relief swept over Jim. He gripped the man's hand firmly.

"Sorry about putting you two in that kind of situation, especially there at the end, but we had no choice. We could see he was about to fire his weapon. Our marksman over there said he could nail the driver, even moving." He pointed to a red-haired agent on his left.

Jim nodded. "I'd say he did a damn good job of it. Kind of spooked me when he shot out the rear window, though."

"He aimed at the top of the cab's glass for that one. We needed a clear sight line. Normally we don't like to bring in an M-16 for a mobile situation but—"

"You had no choice," Jim said, smiling.

Tasker motioned the other agents back into the limousines. "We need to get out of here pronto, before the place is crawling with police. Let's get you two to the airport and back home to Memphis. There's a chartered plane waiting."

As they drove off, a crowd streamed toward the blood-stained taxi, gawking at the dead as if eyeing animals in a zoo.

Tasker grinned at Jim. "That was a pretty fancy bit of brake work on your part."

"I didn't have much choice. Like you and the M-16."

"And Ms. King," the agent added, "your ability with a Walther is quite impressive."

Jean frowned. "How did you know about that?"

"We've been on your trail ever since you got off the train in New Orleans."

Jim looked around. "New Orleans?"

"We knew you'd been followed when that body turned up on the train," the agent continued. "We led the New Orleans P.D. to believe it was a mob hit."

Jim threw his hands in the air. "Body? What's going on? I thought I was the one they were after."

"You were," replied Tasker. "But when you ditched your pursuers, they tried to find you by going after the next best thing. Your girlfriend."

Jean sighed. "It's been a tough two days."

"One thing's for sure," Tasker said. "Joe O'Riley's gonna be glad to know you're both in good shape."

"So he was behind this," Jim said.

"He's pretty sharp," Tasker said, as the cars eased through the airport special-vehicle access gate. "He alerted us right before you high-tailed it from Memphis. We would have taken out that gun-toting call girl at the antique shop but, thanks to your own personal guardian angel here," he said, nodding at Jean, "we had to back off when the Vegas cop stepped in. The L.V.P.D. doesn't know a thing about this. We want to keep it that way. The crime scene back there looks like a mob skirmish. More so now with Nick Verasco one of the stiffs."

"You've seen him before?" Jim asked.

"In pictures," Tasker replied. "Heard about him. Always fired that cannon of his left-handed. Like tonight. His main gigs are, or were, mob-related up east in New York City. No more Yankees games for him—he's been sent down to the minors. Maybe a lot farther."

"I take it you guys are with one of the law enforcement agencies," Jim said.

"F.B.I.," Tasker replied. "Normally we handle problem cases in the witness-protection program. Ones where new identities have been uncovered."

"Is that where we're headed?"

"Well," the agent said, "if things work out according to O'Riley's plan, nobody else is coming after you. In fact, nobody's gonna give a damn who you are."

Jean rubbed her temples. "How on earth is he going to manage that?"

Tasker pulled his lower lip through pearly white teeth. "He's a smart old bird. The case he's got built against Adam Baldwin doesn't involve you two at all. Baldwin just might be trading in his political cleats for a new uniform—one with horizontal stripes, if O'Riley has his way. I'll fill you in on what I know while we wait for take-off." He looked at Jim's blood-stained clothes. "You can clean up on board. I've got a change of clothes that'll fit you just about perfect."

Jim nodded. "That's mighty nice. But I got one request."

"Which is?"

"You keep the gun."

36

"I can't believe this nightmare is over," Jim said as Jean buckled her seat belt.

Minutes later the Super King Air 350 raced down the runway and lifted into the Las Vegas darkness. As they relaxed into the soft leather cabin seats, Jean and Jim locked hands, looking out the round windows as the neon oasis in the Nevada desert slowly faded into a speck of light.

The agents seated behind prepared a game of backgammon on a board that pulled out from the wall.

Jean focused on the reflection of the red light repeatedly flashing off the vertical winglets that jutted from the tips of the wings.

"Coming close to death makes you think about what you have. And what you can lose," Jim said.

She turned and smiled at him.

"I don't ever want to lose you," he whispered.

She squeezed his hand and gently kissed him on the cheek before settling back into her seat and closing her eyes.

In an instant she was in the back seat of an old Model A, her head resting on the worn, brown mohair upholstery. Someone's hand lightly touched the side of her face, a fingertip tracing her lips.

"I love you," Will said, "more than you'll ever know. I want you to be with me always."

"Jean?" Jim whispered.

"Sorry," she replied. "Lost in a dream."

As she turned, their mouths were only inches apart. "I said, I love you," he repeated, "more than you'll ever know. I want you to be with me always."

Jean eased toward him, gazing into his vibrant blue eyes. In his face she could sense a reflection of her own life, a life stored in her mind as well as her heart. He was the one. For the rest of her life.

Jim reached into his pocket. "There's something I've needed to do for a long time now." He flipped open the grey velvet case and pulled the gold ring from its white silk holder, gently slipping the band onto Jean's finger. "Will you marry me?"

Her eyes filled with tears, moistening her long eyelashes. "I would like that more than anything else in the world." Their lips met in a deep kiss.

The F.B.I. agents clapped.

"What's going on back there?" the pilot called out from the cockpit.

"We have an engagement at 33,000 feet," Tasker yelled back.

"That's a first for me," the pilot said, signaling thumbs-up.

"A first for all of us," Tasker said, shaking Jim's hand.

"It's from 1949," Jim said as he ran his finger over the ring. "I thought that made it pretty special."

"Where'd you get it?" she asked.

"At that Antiquities store in the mall. Only I didn't think I'd be giving it to you this quickly," he replied, grinning. "We'll pick out a nice diamond to set right in the middle of it."

"I don't need a diamond. I've got you," she said, smiling into his eyes.

*

Joe O'Riley was waiting in his black Lincoln parked on the apron as the plane touched down at Memphis International Airport and taxied to the general aviation terminal. He got out as the air-stair door descended, shivering slightly in the cool morning air.

"You scared the bejeezus out of me, you know that, don't you?" O'Riley said, as Jean ran up and kissed him on the cheek. "I guess this is the man I need to thank for bringing you home safe and sound." He shook Tasker's hand. "I owe you and all your men some ribs at the Rendezvous." He grinned. "Tell Mr. Vergos to put it on my tab."

"You're on," Tasker said. "Dinner tonight. After we get some sleep. I don't deserve all the credit, though. You better watch out for that one." The agent pointed at Jean. "She's a real firecracker."

Jean, Jim, and O'Riley piled into the Continental's front seat and drove off. A nearly full moon rode a bank of clouds to the west.

"You want to drive, Jean?" O'Riley asked. "This is about the same time of morning you were catting around in it last night."

Jean winced and gave him a quick poke in the ribs.

"Just kidding," O'Riley added. "Hell, I didn't pick it up until eight tonight anyway. Charlie Perry drove me around all day. Tasker tell you the good news?"

"Sure did," Jim replied. "But I guess you want to tell us yourself, right?" He smiled.

"You're damn right. The best thing is, you two are clear from here on out. And, take my word for it, it's gonna be one helluva show. In the meantime," O'Riley continued, "I want you two to stay at my house for a few days so I can keep an eye on you. And please," he said, glancing over at Jean, "if you want to leave, taking my car and gun, let me know first so I can join you, okay? I can use the excitement."

"I have one question," Jean said, a grin spreading across her face. "Do you have a honeymoon suite?"

O'Riley's eyes widened. "You didn't!"

"Not yet but we're going to!" she replied, flashing the gold band.

"I was hoping I could count on you to be best man," Jim said.

"Hell, yes, I will. If there was still a Davis White Spot, we could celebrate."

"I think a nice, quiet evening at your place will do just fine after all we've been through," Jean said, smiling over at him.

O'Riley reached for a small bottle of Dasani water and hoisted it into the air. "I hereby give a toast from the past, for the future. To happiness in marriage for two of the best friends a guy could ever have."

"And to our special friendship, our special tie that binds," Jim said. "May we feel it not only now but in the decades to come."

37

"This is more like it," O'Riley said, taking a deep breath of the slightly muggy air as he sat on his front porch with Jean and Jim. "I fancy eighty-one degrees a lot more than that cool weather we had last week. Indian summer's the best time of year."

"Not in my book," Jim said. "Give me the cold any day."

"I'm just happy to be alive," Jean said, squeezing her fiancé's hand.

"What happens next?" Jim asked.

"For our friend, Adam Baldwin? The proverbial shit has hit the fan." He glanced at his watch. 5:25 P.M. "I talked to the D.A. at noon. The grand jury returned a sealed indictment against the S.O.B. and it was gonna be served the minute he stepped off his jet at the airport this afternoon. I hope nobody was standing under the ramp 'cause he sure as hell dropped a load when they took him to the Criminal Justice Center for booking instead of The Pyramid for his speech and rally. Now that it's in the hands of the national media, they'll chew him up and spit him out like a piece of rotten meat." He stood up and headed for the front door. "C'mon, let's see what the news has to say."

They gathered around the RCA console in the den, O'Riley in his green tweed recliner, Jean and Jim on the small couch. Bullet curled up at his master's feet.

"Our top story tonight—the American political scene is thrown into chaotic disarray by the stunning arrest of Democratic Presidential nominee, Senator Adam Baldwin," the newscaster said over the opening theme music of the NBC Nightly News, as taped footage showed Baldwin being served an arrest warrant as he stepped from the ramp of his jetliner at Memphis International Airport.

The announcer's image filled the screen.

"Good evening. In one of the most bizarre scenes ever to be played out on the stage of American politics, Democratic presidential candidate Adam Baldwin was indicted today by a grand jury in Memphis, Tennessee, on charges of second-degree murder. Baldwin was greeted on the runway at the Memphis airport by two Tennessee Bureau of Investigation agents sent by the District Attorney of Shelby County. They whisked the astounded senator to the Criminal Justice Complex in downtown Memphis as aides and the media staged an impromptu motorcade in wild pursuit. Baldwin was . . ."

O'Riley changed channels with a quick punch of his remote control.

". . . booked and processed on the building's tenth floor and was then brought before Criminal Court Judge Ronald Hoffman for the purpose of making his $100,000 bond," reported the CBS Evening News. "The Senator wrote a personal check and was released with his arraignment scheduled for one week from today, on the ninth of October.

"Meanwhile, a wave of stunned disbelief surged through the crowd of twenty-five thousand Baldwin supporters who waited most of the afternoon at The Pyramid arena in Memphis. Baldwin never showed up for his scheduled speech.

"Not only Baldwin's nomination but his very freedom hangs in the balance as details of the case against him become public. What we know so far is this. In late December, 1949, a young woman was reported missing in Memphis. The District Attorney of Shelby County, John Paratti, who is a Republican, stated in a press conference after the arrest that eyewitness testimony implicates Baldwin in the death of the woman. According to Paratti . . ."

O'Riley clicked the remote again.

". . . second-degree murder has been charged rather than murder in the first degree due to the testimony of the eyewitness," said the newscaster on ABC's World News Tonight. "The unidentified eyewitness has stated that the death appeared to be accidental, not premeditated. Premeditation would have warranted the more serious charge.

"Informed sources tell us that Baldwin will announce his withdrawal from the presidential race 'in the best interests of the Democratic Party' as he fights what he has already termed 'this heinous slander upon my good name.' A nationally televised statement by the Senator will be carried live tonight at nine o'clock, Eastern Daylight Time."

"I've seen happier men hanging from the end of a rope," O'Riley said as he flicked the television off and stood up to stretch. "What say we go for a little walk? Work up our appetite for those steaks while the charcoal heats up on the grill."

Within minutes they were on the sidewalk, majestic trees, their branches full of leaves changing color, swaying above them.

Jim put his arm around Jean's shoulder. "What do *we* do now?" he said to O'Riley.

"If it was me, I'd sit back and have a nice long rest. The case is pretty much open and shut. The district attorney has all he needs. Whether or not he can get a conviction is up to the lawyers and the jury. E. Crowder's testimony and Baldwin's St. Christopher locket found in the girl's hand will be hard to discount. Whatever happens, I'd say the Senator's political career, not to mention his freedom, is about over." O'Riley smiled. "What do *you* want to do now?"

"I'd like Jim and I to buy some land and a house. Maybe even move someplace away from all these memories. But then . . ."

". . . we wouldn't know if anybody was taking care of you," Jim interrupted.

"Nancy'll be back from France in six weeks. She'll watch out for me." He patted his perspiring forehead with a white cotton handkerchief. "I sure wouldn't mind some extra company, though."

"Got any ideas where we might find a nice little house we could call our own?" Jean asked, winking at Jim as they passed some empty lots.

"Sure," O'Riley replied, jingling the keys in his pocket. "We got loads of 'em right here on North Avalon. Over there on the left," he said, pointing to two new houses directly behind an old brick building at the end of the street. "Those two beauties are next to where Green's Drug Store used to be. Remember?" O'Riley shook his head. "What am I saying? You two weren't even born. You couldn't remember it if you tried."

"Don't be so sure, Joe," Jim said, eyes gleaming as he stared at the building. "I remember tricycles rolling down the sidewalk. Three of them. Two boys with a little girl." He smiled first at O'Riley and then at Jean.

"And I remember two Black Cows and a strawberry soda, for three children sitting at the fountain," Jean said, a faraway look in her eyes. "The strawberry soda was for the little boy wearing a miniature policeman's cap . . ."